Jim Nash read order

Jim Nash The Beginning
Pirate Cay
Thrill Kill Jill
Greetings From Key West
Lost Paradise
No Angels
Mexico Gamble
No Picnic
Fallen Angels
Vendetta
A Girl's Best Friend
Dead End
No Harbor
Dog Days
Startup Blues
Last Stop To Nowhere / The Last Goodbye
Revenge Is Justice
Escape
Wedding Bell Blues
Snap Brim Fedora Caper
Breakdown
Little Girl Lost
Forget Me Not
All The Glitter
Mexico Time
Partners In Crime
Shop Till You Drop
Lobo
No Free Ride
Gone
Stealing America
Blame It on Djibouti
Trouble in Paradise

SEASONAL
Trick or Treat
Helping Santa

JIM NASH INVESTIGATES
The Snap Brim Fedora Caper
The Lady in White
The Lady in Yellow

Print Books

Jim Nash

Jim Nash The Beginning
Gun Crazy
Gun Crazy 2
Gun Crazy 3
Fallen Angels
Last Stop to Nowhere
Revenge is Justice
Escape / Forget Me Not
Wedding Bell Blues / Breakdown
Mexico Time
LOBO
No Free Ride / Gone
Stealing America
No Escape

Harry Delaney Adventures

Dead Reckoning
Lie Cheat Steal
Uncharted
Go-Around
Sand Storm

Frank Ross Biker Tales

No Way Out
Bad Girls
Bank Robber Dames

Other

The Last President

LAST STOP TO NOWHERE

ISBN 978-1-928161-58-5

Last Stop to Nowhere and *The Last Goodbye* are works of fiction. Any resemblance to persons living or dead is purely coincidental. Places mentioned by name are entirely fictitious and purely products of the author's imagination, and are not meant to bear resemblance to actual places or locations.

Publisher: P X Duke
E-mail: peterxduke@gmail.com
Web site: pxduke.com

9 8 7 6 5 4 3

Printed in the United States of America

LAST STOP TO NOWHERE

PX DUKE

For family, friends, and other miscreants.

CHAPTER 1

Bobbie Dawson stretched beneath the sweaty sheet. Sat up. Listened.

The dead air below deck lay thick with too much humid, fetid air.

Her legs flailed, fighting the sticky sheet.

Finally won when the sheet ended up at the foot of the bunk. It was a small pleasure with not much result.

Water slap-slapped the side of the sloop.

No sound of sails flapping.

No engine sounds, either.

Only gentle rocking.

She groaned and forced her exhausted body out of the rack.

She pulled on socks and pushed feet into well-worn, low-cut boots before sliding the hatch back and climbing on deck.

Relief from the humidity was immediate.

"Where are we?"

Rising sun reflected off the water.

She brought up a hand to shield her eyes.

Low dark clouds in the distance told her rain

would come sooner rather than later.

A yacht-club flag flapped crisply in the wind. The rope slapped the pole, forcing it to sing.

"We're in a marina. Put some clothes on."

"In a marina where?" She wasn't moving until she had an answer.

"Diamondhead."

The man stood up from tying off.

Kennedy.

We'd been together for a week. Or maybe it was ten days. She had lost count.

That's how unbearable the job was.

She crewed on his yacht into so many ports she lost track of them, too.

"Diamond Head? What the hell? Did someone drug me? Why am I in Hawaii?" she asked.

Kennedy's eyes roamed over her naked body.

She didn't care. For spite, she arched her back and raised her arms while pretending to stretch.

His eyes found mine, finally.

"Mississippi. You're in Mississippi."

She laughed, relieved, and ran fingers through long, tangled hair. It was a futile motion to rid herself of the bedhead that followed her topside.

"Go below and put some clothes on."

She dropped her arms, stepped down into the cabin, and disappeared.

She splashed water on her face before pulling on cargo shorts and an old, ratty tee.

Added a woolen shirt to ward off the damp, chilly, early morning Gulf air.

Soft-soled ankle boots and rolled-down socks covered the rest.

Topside, she searched pockets for the pair of cheap sunglasses.

"What's the plan?" She looked at the man.

He stared back, a hard look.

She didn't care what he saw this time, either.

"You packed?" he asked.

She dropped the duffel at her feet and gave it a desultory kick as a clue.

"Got the phone?"

She nodded, and he stepped aboard. The weight rocked the sailboat.

She picked up the duffel and made to climb onto the wharf.

Kennedy stepped back, making room for her to pass.

She didn't see the fist pulling back. It smashed against her face.

She tumbled back against the rigging.

Her sunglasses flew into the water.

"Bastard. What was that for?"

She didn't bother hiding the hateful expression.

He had made so many unsuccessful passes at her, he took it for granted by now.

"There'll be more if you screw up, Bobbie. A lot more. And because you're a bitch."

Kennedy's upper body shifted, telegraphing the second swing.

She dodged and leaned.

He missed, and the fist thumped hard against her chest.

The force of the blow launched her backwards a second time. It left her breathless and in pain.

It was the jackline's turn to save her. She grabbed

it for support.

Brought up a boot.

Kicked.

Connected. Hard.

Kennedy doubled over and collapsed.

"Screw you, Kennedy." Still gasping for air, she spit out the weak exclamation.

Kennedy stayed on his side, unmoving but for knees coming up. Hands moved to grip his balls.

Bullseye.

"That was because you're an asshole."

Bobbie went through the man's pockets to find the wallet she knew was always there.

She pulled out the wad of cash. Stuffed it into a shirt pocket. Tossed the empty wallet on the deck.

Climbed onto the wharf.

She turned in time to see him grab for the rigging. Still doubled over and struggling, he pulled himself up.

For good measure, she gave him the finger.

He was still struggling to get enough wind to yell.

"That's it, girl. Feisty and looking for trouble." Huffing and puffing. "Don't screw up or you're dead. Remember that. And not only you. Your family, too. All of them."

Pretending to act braver than she felt, she kicked up her heels and danced in a circle while making for shore.

Too scared to look back.

She hitched the duffel over a shoulder before throwing up double fingers and then straightened and hurried past the gate at the end of he wharf.

How stupid was her brother, though?

Thanks to him, the gravity of the situation hadn't sunk in. How was she responsible for him? It was all too much. She had places she wanted to be, but now she was forced to find him and help him.

Would Kennedy be crazy enough to kill her entire family?

She'd heard about that happening on news reports about the drug situation in Mexico.

Did they do that in America, too?

She couldn't remember anything about it on the news channels. Surely it would have made endless TV headlines, over and over.

She counted out five hundred and change from Kennedy's wallet.

Not so bad. It was in her pocket now.

She changed her mind and stuffed it into the duffel.

The truck stop was due north, if she remembered the map.

The weather wasn't about to do any favors. The storm looked to be more than local, and it was moving in fast, brought on by the wind.

She made it past the yacht club gate in time for the black sky to open up.

Wind-driven rain poured down.

In minutes, she was looking and feeling like a drowned rat.

Bobbie hauled out a waterlogged thumb just in time for a redneck half-ton to brake.

She knew it was redneck by the painted flames coming out of the wheel wells. That it was jacked-up on tractor-sized tires only served to prove her right.

The wheels locked, and the truck slid sideways on the wet road. It halted in front of her. The door opened. She tossed the rain-soaked bag onto the bed.

It took effort and a handrail to step up.

She wheezed, thanks to Kennedy's beating.

She wondered how many prom dates in heels and gowns the driver might have hauled around in a truck outfitted the way it was.

She made it plain where I needed to be, and in that instant, knew for sure he didn't have a girlfriend. Or a prom date.

Ten-day stubble, a wife-beater, and bib overalls spoke to that.

That, and the redneck, jacked-up truck.

CHAPTER 2

Jim Nash finished packing his go-bag with the automatic and two oversize mags.

Allie chose that moment to walk into the trailer. Her eyes flicked from the table with the open bag to Jim.

"You're going."

"I have to. I'll not have any peace until I end it. Once and for all." There was nothing more he could say that would be capable of convincing Allie of anything.

"That won't bring Pilar back," she said.

He stopped what he was doing and looked at Allie. "No. I know that. It's going to bring me back.

He hoped. The downward spiral since losing his wife, Pilar, had been endless.

"Or you'll die trying," Allie said.

"Something like that."

Allie leaned against the counter. Her gaze remained fixed on him.

He looked away and carried on, pretending to be busy.

"You're not fooling me, Jim. After I leave, it's

going to be Erica's turn, so don't think you're getting off Scott-free."

"I wouldn't have it any other way," he said. "Erica must have mellowed, though, if she's planning on talking me out of leaving."

"If you bothered to pay attention, you'd have seen it. She forgave you a long time ago. You just don't realize it."

He found that hard to believe. Erica hated him from the moment he got involved with her sister, Kara. That he ended up married to her had sent Erica over the deep end for a while. It was as though she knew he wouldn't be any good for her sister.

And he wasn't.

Kara was dead, killed in an explosion.

He wanted to see the body, for without that, who the hell knew anything for sure? The thing is, there was no body. None that he could find, at least.

"Well, if you insist. But I'll have to hear her tell me to believe it."

Allie wrapped her arms around him and hugged, hard. "Be careful. Please."

He hugged her back, just as hard. "I will."

"There's a place for you here. No matter what," she said.

"I know."

But did he?

He had to be the stupidest son of a bitch in the world every time he walked away from Allie and everything she offered. He'd done it more than once, too. In fact, he wore holes in his shoes walking away.

"The keys are in the car if anyone wants to use it," he said. "I'll be cabbing it to a beater I picked up."

"Then you're driving?"

"Yes," he admitted. "But you don't know that. No one does."

"All right. Here comes Erica with the whole family. Be nice."

"You know I will, Allie."

"Remember. Everything is here. When you decide what you want."

Lily and James and Zelda and Zoe bounded through the trailer's narrow door, laughing and talking a mile a minute.

Erica brought up the rear as though she was the one shepherding them in his direction.

"You guys are like a pack of wild animals." He laughed. "Take it easy. You're like tornado and you know how long trailers last in one of those."

Lily said, "I heard you're going away again, Uncle Jim. I wanted to come and say goodbye. So did James and Zelda and Zoe. We're all going to miss you until you come back."

Even the dogs had long faces. He couldn't get away from it. "That's nice of you to say. It means a lot to me."

Erica rested her hand on her daughter's shoulder. Her other went to James, as though protecting both.

Just as Kara, his mother, had done on the resort's wharf the first time he saw the two of them together.

"James, what do you say to taking care of Zoe for me? Do you think you could do that until I come back?" he asked.

The boy looked up at him, shy, awkward, still not sure where he stood in the grand scheme of his life.

"I'd like that," he said, as a huge smile grew.

It pleased Jim to hear him say it.

"Zelda a good dog. She listens. She comes when she's called. But you know that, right? She likes you, too. That's important. And you like her."

"I'll take good care of her. I promise. Lily will help, won't you, Lily?"

The pair of them were almost inseparable too, like the dogs.

"Thank you, James. Maybe Zelda can help if you need it. Right, Lily?"

Lily nodded furiously.

Zelda woofed. She was convinced, too.

The kids, followed by the dogs, scrambled out of the trailer.

Only Erica remained.

Allie had warned him. Still, it surprised him when Erica went to the door and closed it.

"So, you're going through with it."

"News travels fast in this part of the marina, doesn't it?" He smiled at her.

"You must know by now you don't have to do it on my account. I forgave you a long time ago."

She might have, but he hadn't forgiven himself. Not yet, at least. He still had demons that needed chasing down. He was prepared for it to take a long time.

"The car is there. I left the keys in case you want to give Lily driving lessons."

"She gets those at school. I suppose a few lessons in someone else's beater would be a good thing."

"It's no beater—"

Erica grinned and held up her hands. "I know, Jim. I'm just trying to keep it light."

"Like your sister. In more ways than one."

"I can't talk you into changing your mind—" Erica halted.

"If Allie couldn't, you can't. I need to do this, Erica. I'll find out who the boy's father is, too, if I can."

"That doesn't matter," she said.

"It might not now, but one day, he'll be wondering. And asking. What will you tell him?"

"You're right. I know that. But—" She halted.

"Let's agree to disagree for now. We'll talk about it when I get back."

"We're all counting on you getting back. No matter what. Have you got everything you need?" Erica asked.

"I think so. If not, well, I'll make do."

Erica hugged him too tight, and he figured out all by himself that she had finally forgiven him.

Even so, a job needed to be done. He wouldn't rest until he ended it.

"Take care of James."

"I will. And thank you," she said.

He didn't ask her for what.

He already knew.

CHAPTER 3

It was wasn't yet first light. The cloudy sky kept it even darker.

Jim threw his bag into the taxi and directed the driver in the general direction of the abandoned lot and his stashed beater. He got out two blocks distant and made his way on foot. Better safe than sorry. Even though he'd never be sorry until this was over with.

If he had time, even then.

The wind was picking up fast, whipping dust and debris and anything else it could throw in its frenzy. The storm was looking to be a doozie and he was glad to be underway. He faced sixty miles of slow going until he hit the 10 and turned west.

His automatic was stashed, along with the special mags. They'd turn up if the car was dismantled for a drug search. He hoped a drug-sniffing dog would show up before that happened.

He had two knives with sheaths. He came up with a strap and figured he could make his way with both attached to his lower legs. The break-apart sheaths would provide an edge. If worse came to worse. Even though he knew he'd never be as proficient as Kara.

He'd make do in close quarters.

Finally, at the on-ramp for the 10, he turned west.

Only a thousand miles to go.

He set the cruise and readied for the long, solitary haul across the interstate.

He wasn't at the first gas stop and already he realized he should have flown.

The storm blowing in off the gulf wasn't a local event. There would be no driving past it. Wind-driven rain streaked across the flooded highway in waves. Come daylight, the cloud base darkened and descended with a vengeance.

Cars swerved.

Semis pulled off at exits, leaving the road to fools like him.

He turned on the radio, looking for a weather report. Unintelligible voices broken only by static came at him. Smashing a fist against the dash in frustration did nothing to improve his disposition.

He gave up with the radio and instead and fiddled with the weak stream emanating from the AC. It wasn't doing him any favors, either.

Before long, windows began to fog. He reached across and cranked down the window on the opposite side. Water soaked the seat, but the windows kept clear.

If the wipers held, he'd pull off at the next turnout to wait out the storm.

But for one woman only, Jim wouldn't be making this trip. His wife. Pilar. It turned out the plane crash that killed her wasn't caused by mechanical failure.

By the time the Feds tied up the loose ends in their investigation, a small amount of explosive residue had been discovered in Pilar's luggage.

That was news. And that was why he wasn't able to put his hands on her luggage once the investigation concluded. He wondered about that, but figured it was just a standard part of an aircraft accident investigation.

Like the third degree he was subjected to regarding his wife and her ties to violent extremism.

He was pretty much fed up with bureaucracy. TSA. NSA. FBI. Homeland Security.

Screw them. They were all show and no go.

Pilar was no terrorist. Dead and buried, she was branded as one.

The investigations halted when they figured out they could use her as a scapegoat. No going deep into backgrounds. No wondering why the residue had been placed in her luggage. It was straight out dereliction of duty by everyone.

He wasn't surprised. In fact, by the end, he had become accustomed to it. Disgusted by the stonewalling and finally by the outright denial of any further need to investigate, his wife Pilar was tried and convicted in absentia.

He was blindsided. Fed up with the incompetence, he decided on the spot he'd be the one to do the investigating.

He was intent on making the score even. One way or the other. It was looking like it would be the other, ending up on the receiving end of his lot in life as it had.

He settled back in the seat.

Even with the window part-way down in the rain, he wished he hadn't cheaped out on the rental. Air that worked would be nice. And a radio. On the other hand, his growing mean streak would only get worse the hotter it got.

And in nine hundred miles, his mean streak would have plenty of time to fester.

The problem would be losing control. He had to stay calm. Think things through. If one course of action didn't work, he'd be forced to stop, hold up, and try another.

Piece of cake.

The fierce wind driving the deluge turned the water laying on the interstate into a wind-swept river. Water was piling up in the ditches. Tired windshield wipers were barely performing.

The green and white sign hanging over the interstate said Diamondhead.

The break in the weather heralded by a patch of blue most likely wouldn't last long.

He passed the massive truck lot populated by idling semis.

Two waterlogged women walked the line. Lot lizards, most likely, struggling to make their way in the wind down the long line of parked and idling semis. They'd be climbing up on the driver side and knocking on windows, looking for work.

Driven by the wind, diesel perfume floated into the car's open windows.

Huge banners planted in cement-filled tires

flapped something about a sale. Of course. Everything was on sale.

Gas and go. And maybe a burrito.

He eased up to the building in the shelter of the downwind side. The wind died immediately.

A lone woman leaned against the building, obviously using the same shelter.

He pulled up to the pumps and got out.

Opened the flap. Hung the cap on it.

Stuck the nozzle into the tank.

Pulled and locked the lever in place.

He took another look at the woman. She didn't look anything like a lot lizard in her loose jeans and a jacket over a t-shirt.

More like a drifter.

And like him, the drifter didn't look happy to be here, either.

More likely a hitchhiker taking shelter from the storm. Her relief would be short-lived. Still, she looked like a drowned rat—or whatever a drowned rat looked like.

He felt sorry for her until she turned and gave him a better look at part of a face turning from deep purple to almost black.

He felt even sorrier.

"Quite an eye you have there."

She tossed a sullen look in his direction and placed a foot on a duffel bag.

Maybe she thought he'd make a try to take it from her.

"You should see the other person."

Jim threw a grin her way. "Yeah, I've said that a time or two myself. I never for a minute believed my own bullshit, though.”

He pulled open the door into the stop'n'go, on the prowl for coffee and a burrito.

Music blared from overhead speakers.

First things first.

He headed past the shower rooms, on the lookout for the restroom.

Found it and took a bathroom stop before standing over a sink.

He splashed cold water on his face.

Washed away sticky perspiration.

Cleaned up as best he could before he returned to the store.

He navigated past racks of CD movies and gift cards and candy bars and bags of potato chips.

He overheard someone say the food was fresh-made.

A burrito called his name. He added a coffee to go.

On the spur of the moment, he doubled the order and threw extra sugar and creamers into the bag.

For luck, he picked out a pair of trendy-looking, huge-lensed sunglasses, paid for everything, and headed for the exit.

CHAPTER 4

Jim walked out of the store in time to see a black, jacked-up half-ton with shiny, thousand-dollar rims wearing oversize tires rumble past.

He halted and it disappeared around the side of the building.

Tires whined on wet pavement.

A door opened and slammed so loud he could have heard it from inside the stop'n'go.

The woman's redneck boyfriend, no doubt.

In a redneck town filled with redneck women pretending to be the town toughies.

Probably with more than a few tattoos to convince the locals it was true.

The scream wasn't quite blood-curdling, but it was loud enough to cause him to retreat into the store until he knew more.

There was no sense letting the burritos go cold, either.

"Put these in the warmer, please. I'll be right back."

He ventured forth for a look-see and a second scream said go faster.

The black-eyed girl was competing in a wrestling match with a fat man who must have gotten out of the truck.

She wasn't in his weight-class, either.

She swung a roundhouse.

Missed.

Kicked and missed.

Couples therapy. It had to be how she got the black eye.

The fight looked to be over until fat man got his arms around her.

She stomped him a good one on the instep with her heel.

He yelled and cursed, and she shimmied and ducked and almost slipped out of his grip.

Fat man number two behind the wheel got out to help his friend.

He circled behind the pair, took over, and got his arms around the woman.

He squeezed. Hard.

The yelling halted.

The air blasted out of townie's lungs so loud and fast he could hear her wheeze.

Fatty number two lifted her off the ground.

Her feet began to dance and he carried her to the truck.

There was a last bit of struggle left in the woman, but it was only her feet kicking feebly at empty air.

Townie was done for.

The look he got before she was forced to surrender said help.

He would have moved in sooner, but she was doing such a good job until she was outmatched.

That wasn't right.

Two men against a lone girl.

He kept eyes on stranger number two and sidled over to the fat one with his arms full of woman too limp to struggle.

Maybe he could even the odds if the odds needed evening.

"What's going on here, woman? You know these rednecks?"

Townie's eyes shifted. The look of panic behind them said no.

"One of them your boyfriend?"

As if he needed more convincing, townie shook her head from side to side even faster.

Jim shifted his attention to the man with his arms full of woman.

"Let her go."

He turned to look at him, still dragging the girl.

That was number two's clue. He advanced, thinking he wasn't paying attention.

He waited for him to get close.

Kicked out with a roundhouse foot, wanting to connect with the outside of his knee.

Missed.

Caught the kneecap instead.

Made a second attempt and connected with the side of his knee.

Fatty dropped like a stone. He almost took the girl and his friend with him as he tumbled against the pair on the way down.

He owned him.

For good measure, he gave him a foot in the gut. That was fat-man's cue to toss the girl and make good on his friendship with number two.

He wanted to take care of him, and he wasn't having any of it.

Jim said, "You can turn tail and walk or you can get on the ground with your friend. Your choice."

Fat man stayed.

His mistake.

Face to face, he kicked upward, looking to meet kneecap with the toe of boot.

It connected.

A shocked look crossed his face.

He doubled over in agony and dropped. The damaged knee landed on asphalt. He wailed like a baby.

He pulled back a fist and drove it into fatty's side. It sunk in like it was quicksand.

He let him have one to the side of the head and fatty hit the rain-soaked ground like a sack of flour minus the dust.

Game over.

Jim looked over at the girl. She was shaken and pale as a sheet. It forced the black eye to stand out even more. She looked to be okay otherwise.

He remembered to shake his hand and flex his fingers. It felt like he broke it.

"Thank you," she said. "I don't know what I would have done—"

She reached to take his hand like a mother comforting a child.

He let her touch it before pulling away.

"It's fine. Don't go away."

He used the break in the action to search through pockets.

Found what he was looking for.

Moved to the truck and found the truck keys still in the ignition. He pulled them out and tossed them.

He went back into the store and retrieved the bag of goodies and sat down at the picnic table.

He waved for the traveler to sit with him.

He took the sunglasses out of the bag and handed them across the heavy wooden picnic table.

She hesitated, using the opportunity for a studied stare into his eyes.

She grabbed for the glasses, yanked off the tag, and propped them on her nose.

"Good choice. They suit you. Even better, they conceal the damages. Most of it, anyway. So far."

More would be showing up.

He grinned, and the light rain and the wind chose that moment to declare another truce.

Blue sky broke through, followed by sunshine. It wouldn't last long. Low dark overcast was blowing in as a reminder that the storm would only get worse.

"You might want some of this, too."

He passed the bag across the table.

She settled in and waited until I withdrew his hand before making a grab.

Wary.

She looked inside.

Hauled out the burrito.

Unwrapped it faster than a raccoon and devoured it in three bites.

Jim said, "I'm always on the lookout for a good story. You got one about that eye?"

She stopped chewing long enough to swallow.

She opened the bag and looked in a second time.

It was obvious idle conversation wasn't the first thing on her mind.

She said, "You gonna eat the other one or what?"

It looked like she wanted to devour the bag. He didn't want to get in the way.

"It's yours."

"Thanks. The manager threw me out when he figured I was a storm refugee with no money to buy anything."

She looked up from the empty bag.

"There's plenty more where that came from. What do you take in your coffee?"

She looked at him through the dark glasses. "My eye's not so bad."

From what he could see, it was only getting blacker.

He wanted to know if she often deluded herself.

"If you believe that, you might get a second opinion by looking in a mirror. I could give you an unbiased opinion. If you want one, that is."

She didn't even crack a bit of a smile.

I grinned anyway, just because. Breaking the ice with this one would be a challenge.

He wondered if he'd get the chance.

"Cream and sugar, please and thanks. Maybe you could pick out a cap for me, too."

He returned with the goodies.

She dumped it all in her cup and replaced the lid.

While she busied herself doing that, he spied a black and white on the other side of the building, driving the line of semis in the enormous lot.

From where she sat, she couldn't see it.

Yet.

"I crewed a sloop into this dump. Nothing but old people, tennis tournaments and dog shows. When I didn't get paid, I clipped the owner and rummaged his pockets for my money."

The half-ton and its occupants were out of sight. The black and white started to make its way toward the store.

He caught the girl glancing at the reflection. She rummaged through her open bag in a hurry.

She found what she was looking for, tugged off her top, and groaned.

She struggled to get her arms through before pulling it down. The second groan was a lot shorter, but it was a lot louder.

"It's time to go. I'll bring the car around."

"That would be all right."

She pulled on the ball cap.

He felt eyes burn into his back as he made for the car.

No doubt she was wondering if she'd need to tackle him at some point if she accepted his offer.

That was all right. He'd wonder, too, if he was her.

He reached across the seat and opened the door.

"Thanks."

He must have passed the test.

She tossed her water-logged bag into the back and hurried to slide in.

"I'm Jim Nash."

He didn't bother holding out his hand.

Neither did she.

He figured she'd talk when she wanted to.

Instead, he went with flattery.

"Those wraparounds do a good job."

She reached across for the mirror, adjusted it, and took off the glasses.

She leaned in for a better look, brushed her fingertips across the bruise, and winced.

He took a good look, too.

Black eye and all, she looked pretty good.

Green eyes.

Long, black hair.

Her skin seemed too pale to have crewed on a boat.

He'd ask about that later.

She dipped a finger against a tube of lip gloss and smoothed it on. She must have decided I'd be all right for a couple of hundred miles of silence, at least.

Women.

She had an eye blacker than midnight and she chose lip gloss.

She pushed the seat back, put her feet up on the dash, and closed her eyes. Long, dark hair fluttered out the window. Inside, it flowed over her shoulder and down in front.

He took a better look.

Well-worn clothes, but clean.

Low-cut boots on the floor were not too new.

Cared for, though.

What looked to be a nice-sized pair hid behind a thick wool shirt and a torn tee. That was all right, too.

And she was soaking wet.

He cranked up the heat.

He readjusted the mirror and went back to driving.

Out of the corner of his eye, he caught her

checking him out.

He ignored her and hoped she felt safe, at least for now.

He'd take his time and wait for the story he hoped would come in due time.

After a dozen miles of silence, she stopped shivering, came around, and fiddled with the radio.

He guessed listening was a better choice than talking.

She couldn't get it to work, either. In frustration, she thumped the dash.

"Yeah. No. That didn't work for me when I tried it more than once. There's no air, either," he said.

She flipped billowing hair over her shoulder and looked across the distance between them.

"I noticed. Traveling on a budget, are you?"

She cracked.

Finally.

He smiled and went on staring out the window and down the rain-swept highway.

CHAPTER 5

Bobbie Dawson had turned them all down. All the offers for a ride, that is. Rain-soaked and cold, she still had a bit of pride remaining that hadn't completely washed away.

This one humped a beater over the flooded rain gutter.

Splashed through the puddles collecting on the asphalt parking lot.

Slowed to a stop at the side of the building.

A rental, maybe. You could never tell for sure these days unless you walked around the back of the car and checked for stickers.

The door squeaked open.

The driver got out and she gave him driver a good, hard look.

Male. All by himself.

Wrinkled clothes, but they looked clean.

Sweaty-looking, but the windows were down.

Probably no air.

He looked her way.

She looked away.

He caught her out and made a smartass comment

about the black eye.

Typical.

He had a nice enough smile, though.

This was the one. Had to be the one. She was sick of being cold and wet. Even sicker of going nowhere when she needed to be on her brother's trail.

The storm wouldn't be breaking any time soon, even with the blue sky overhead. The wind was too strong and everything around was low black cloud.

Bobbie made a show of putting a foot on her duffel bag. She wanted him to know she was traveling.

It was obvious he didn't believe her when she said she gave as good as she got with the black eye.

He carried on into the store.

She stole a quick look at her reflection in the window. A one-eyed, waterlogged raccoon reflected back.

Her eye was even blacker than when she checked it out in the restroom. She tried to make up for it by rubbing on some lip gloss and hoped a nice, sweet smile would do for the rest.

The jacked black half-ton circled the store. She recognized the driver as the same one who had dropped her off.

It braked hard. Rubber squealed on wet pavement. The truck wheeled into the parking lot and screeched to a halt, even on the wet pavement.

He had a partner in the passenger seat.

The friend got out and grabbed for her.

She reacted by ducking out of the way.

Too late.

He connected and a powerful grip tightened over

her arms. It forced them to down to her sides.

He shoved and she was forced toward the truck's open door.

The movement forced her off balance. She tried a kick.

Then a fist.

Both connected with empty air.

By then, he had his arms all the way around her.

He lifted her off the ground in less time than a heartbeat.

She continued to flail and kick and make feeble attempts to smash the back of her head into the mugger's face.

She screamed and screamed again.

Meaty arms tightened around her chest, forcing out what little air she had left.

Bobbie looked after the man she thought was so shit-hot in the beater with no air.

He was running back into the store.

Chickenshit.

And then, in what seemed like far too long, he was back.

She forgave him just as slowly.

"Friends of yours?" he asked.

Her captor squeezed harder.

Out of breath and unable to talk, she shook her head. It was all she could do.

"Would you like some help with that?"

She didn't think she had to, but she nodded anyway.

"All righty then."

And that was that.

Chickenshit went to work.

It was like a fight scene out of a movie.

A single kick put one on the ground.

It happened that fast.

She couldn't figure how he did it.

He went for number two and it was over in a heartbeat.

At least, it was for her.

She was free.

She got off a kick to a fat man's gut and then chickenshit lifted her up and carried her off with flailing feet against empty air.

"That's only fair if you put him there. Next time, okay?"

He went for the truck keys in the ignition. He pulled them out and heaved them across the lot.

"They never take their keys," he said. "You want something to eat?"

She looked across at the bodies on the ground.

He followed her gaze.

"Don't concern yourself with them. They're good where they are. They'll come around by the time we're ready to go."

Chickenshit must have known she doubted him.

"You didn't think I was coming back. That's all right. I didn't want my food to get cold. Then I figured you probably hadn't eaten for a while, so I ordered for two."

He smiled a lopsided grin. His eyes crinkled.

"Are we good now?"

Yeah, we're good now.

But she didn't tell him that.

He handed over the paper bag and that was when she realized she was starving.

She sighed, and he passed a pair of sunglasses her way, too.

She picked up her duffel bag and followed the man like a found puppy to the picnic table at the side of the building.

She still needed to know if he'd be the one.

She dropped the rain-soaked duffel and threw a leg over the bench.

Her chest was killing her, thanks to the man who'd squeezed the crap out of it.

She eased down slowly and groaned. She tried not to. She couldn't help it.

She tried inhaling slowly, too.

Her chest was beyond aching. Hidden by her shirt, she had to be black and blue to match the damned eye. So much for the breasts covered by the camouflage.

He asked about the eye. She knew he would. He wanted to start a conversation. She gave up just enough to let him know she had crewed into town on a schooner.

"So you're a sailor. Got any tattoos?"

He grinned.

She tried to ignore the crack. She couldn't. The severe look she was dishing out relaxed. She couldn't prevent the corners of her mouth from curling into a tiny smile.

"For me to know." She hesitated. "And you to find out."

And you to find out? Where did that come from?

She tried to cover it, though. "Thanks for the food," she added in a hurry.

"Yeah. I could tell by the way you chewed up the

tinfoil. Remind me not to get between you and the kitchen if I ever get you into an actual restaurant."

She caught the black and white reflecting in the windows. It turned into the parking lot and slowly walked down the lines of semis on the opposite side of the building. She pretended she hadn't seen it.

She rummaged in her bag and came up with a fresh shirt. The groans surprised her as she rushed arms through openings and tugged the shirt over her head.

"Time to go, is it?"

That was it.

She heaved her duffel into the back of the man's beater through another groan and climbed in.

She kicked off her boots and propped her feet against the dash. She only wanted to close her eyes, but not before she got a good look at the man.

He reached for the mirror and tilted it. "Take a look. It's not so bad. Yet."

She leaned into it and caught him checking out her chest. She was accustomed to it, but it wasn't like he was being as obvious as most. She let it go. Besides, he was good-looking in a rough and tough kind of way. Something about him. Rugged good looks. Besides, he just kicked the shit out of two men. That was nothing to sneeze at—not that she wanted to sneeze with the way she felt.

"I'm Jim Nash. Pleased to meet you."

He needed a shave.

She wondered how much she should tell him about the black eye.

She was a good liar, but there was something about this one.

She stopped worrying and pretended to sleep. Eventually, it became the real thing.

It sounded like a gunshot and Bobbie knew she wasn't dreaming. She made a grab for the door and the dashboard just as the radio blared.

The car swerved into the second lane.

Jim wrestled with the steering wheel. Worked it back and forth until he got the skid under control.

He never touched the brakes.

The car slowed on its own enough to pull onto the shoulder.

"It's a flat tire," he announced. "I hope this wreck has a spare."

Oh great. She was just starting her journey and now she was going to be held up until they get a tow. "Want me to check the trunk?"

"It's all right. I'll do it."

He was right to hope. There was a spare. Minus a jack stand. Frustrated, he rubbed the back of his neck.

"Come in out of the rain, at least. In this fog, a car might not see us."

She might have known when one halted in front of them.

She was worried it could be highway grifters.

She needn't have.

It was another kind of grifter.

Kennedy.

And she wasn't happy in the slightest to see him.

Jim noticed, too.

"You all right?" he asked. "You look like it's a

zombie horde coming to help. I'm hoping the horde has a jack."

If he only knew.

Her friend from the sailboat in Diamondhead walked up to the driver's side and lowered his head. He ignored her but for a quick flick of his eyes.

She couldn't ignore him. Her face had to go from pale to picket-fence white.

"We're missing a tire jack. Any chance we could borrow yours?" Jim asked.

Kennedy popped his trunk and handed over the jack stand.

Jim went to work on the rear tire.

Reluctantly, she joined Kennedy at the back of his car. "You're following me."

It wasn't a question. It was obvious.

"I'm only looking out for my interests. Now get your ass back there. I don't want him getting suspicious. And remember what I told you."

Not soon enough they were good to go with the repair.

Jim slammed the trunk closed and climbed in.

Cold and wet from the rain, nervous, shaking, Bobbie's heart went into pounding overdrive.

Even away from the boat, Kennedy was intent on monitoring things.

"You two were gossiping like old friends. What were you talking about?" he asked.

Kennedy was right.

She tried to cover it off. "Just the usual travel stuff. Weather. Restaurants. Motels."

She was sure Jim wouldn't want to hear how she'd been threatened with death if she didn't come up with her brother and the missing drugs he was supposed to have stolen. She'd more likely get left on the side of the road if she offered a half-assed explanation.

Any explanation, most likely.

She was being chased. Followed. Whatever.

How else would Kennedy have been so close?

Kennedy didn't trust her. And it was even more obvious that no matter what happened, she'd be watched until she found her brother or came up with the drugs.

She wondered if her wanted poster had dead or alive scrawled across the bottom.

CHAPTER 6

Jim Nash pulled his beater rental off the 10 into a gas'n'go and halted at the pumps.

He took a good look at the woman through the open window. Her head tilted against the seat back. The long dark hair that kept it covered up to now spilled over her shoulders. She looked at peace but for the huge purple welt and the growing bruise surrounding her eye. It was beginning to creep down her face.

"You want anything?" he asked.

Not a sound.

He walked around and opened the door and gave her shoulder a shake.

He should have known better.

She closed a hand on his thumb and twisted. It was just hard enough to let him know he shouldn't be doing that and then she released it.

"Point made. Sorry. Do you want anything?"

He exaggerated his glance at the camera and touched his ball cap.

She fished an elastic out of a pocket and tied her hair back in a sloppy ponytail before putting on her own cap. She pulled it low over her eyes.

"Whatever you had last time works for me," she said. "Thanks."

He returned to the car with coffee and a bag.

"There's a rest stop down the road. We'll stop there. I could use the break."

The storm broke, and they shared the solitary table in sunshine and measured silence.

She wolfed down the food again.

She finished and stood up off to the side, on the grass, and began working her way through a tai chi routine beside the table.

Smooth. Measured. Proficient. She was all of those.

He pretended not to notice.

He hurried to stand up and found himself confronted by a woman in a half crouch. Hands were fists at the ready.

"Take it easy, cowgirl. I'm only stretching."

She relaxed her wide eyes, and they shifted to the bit of a paunch growing over the belt thanks to the soft living over the past year.

Allie's cooking hadn't hurt, either.

"Looks like you could use a little exercise to go with that stretch before you stood up. It works wonders for muffin tops."

She grinned.

He shook his head. He guessed it made them even, given his tattoo remark earlier. "You want to walk? I'll toss your bag out at the crossroads."

Her smile froze.

Maybe the comment was a bit much. "No need. I'm Bobbie. With an i and an e."

It didn't look like a fake smile. Something had changed.

Bobbie offered her hand, and they shook.

"Jim. Pleased to meet you, Roberta."

Her eyes flickered for a split second.

He knew then he had her first name nailed, at least.

"Come on. Let's get this shit-show on the road before la migra shows up. In a couple hundred or so I'll be getting a room. I'll try for twins at a minimum. You okay with that?"

Bobbie didn't say word one.

"Traveling on a budget, remember?" he reminded her.

"So I heard. Too bad."

Light rain accompanied by more thick gulf fog took over once more. The fog meant the wind quieted. There was no more steering-wheel wrestling to keep the car on the road. Surrounded by interminable gray fog and the constant squinting into it, the long, tired miles piled up.

The neon said motel.

Jim pulled into the lot, relishing the break in what was turning out to be an endless highway. He was thinking driving might not have been such a smart move—but only for the last hundreds of miles.

Bobbie had the bags out of the car and was waiting when he returned from the office.

He slipped the key in the door. "All they had was a single."

She shrugged and followed him into the room.

He offered up the bed.

"No. But thanks. I'll take the floor," Bobbie insisted.

She headed off to shower, and made sure the water was on full hot. It only helped with the bruising a little.

Jim used the opportunity to look through Bobbie's bag.

Clothes rolled to take up a minimum of space.

A couple of skirts.

Cargo shorts.

Shirts.

An old flip phone.

Nothing of significance showed up other than a passport in her name. At least, in Roberta's first name. Her last was simple enough, too.

Dawson.

By the time the water stopped running, he had everything back the way he found it.

"Your turn," she announced.

Somehow, he knew she'd be wanting to give his bag the same once-over.

She was too cautious not to.

He didn't have time to conceal the knives before she returned wearing a towel and a very swollen black eye.

Legs. She had great legs.

She caught him looking.

How could he not?

She seemed to know, too, but she didn't look upset about it. In fact, she didn't look upset at all.

When it came to his turn, he let her have plenty of warning. Even so, he was surprised to catch her still bent over his go-bag.

He looked long and hard.

She knew that, too.

"Nice outfit."

Panties revealed themselves beneath a thin shirt that was just long enough until she bent over.

She was bent over.

She straightened slowly and turned to meet his gaze.

He kept looking. Hell, he was a man.

She was a woman.

He knew for sure because he already noticed more than once.

"Are you done yet?" he asked. He shifted his eyes to look into hers, straight on.

"No."

"Fair enough."

Bobbie turned back to searching through his bag.

He said nothing. He waited her out and used the opportunity to look some more.

"Tanto. Good knives. You have two. Should I be concerned?"

"I think if you were, you'd have grabbed your bag and hightailed it out the door and down the corridor, all the while trying to dance your clothes on without falling on your ass."

She ignored him. When it came to the women in his life, he was accustomed to that.

"You can have the bed for now," Bobbie announced. "You might wake up with me beside you. Don't take it personal."

She made a show of taking a knife and putting it in her own bag.

He didn't doubt for a minute it would end up on the floor with her.

"If anything's going to happen, I'll let you know in plenty of time. Okay?"

Jim shifted on the bed in the dingy room. An elbow brushed against something soft and warm. Wide awake now, he listened.

Bobbie tossed and groaned.

He disentangled from a stray leg and climbed out of bed.

He walked to the window and checked the lot for the car. It was beneath the light where he left it, undisturbed.

Headlights turned into the lot and traveled back and forth along the line of parked cars. The car slowed and hesitated beneath the light over his car. It was just long enough to tell him someone was checking. He took another look and allowed the curtain to fall back.

Was that for him, or Bobbie?

All at once he realized he didn't know a thing about the woman.

She'd taken a couple of phone calls after he picked her up. Most of her words had been monotone single syllables. Guarded.

He pulled the curtain wide before heading back to bed.

Light streamed into the room, illuminating Bobbie's form stretched across the bed.

He was trying to figure out how to climb in without disturbing her when she rolled onto her side.

She faced him and propped her head on her hand. "Are you done yet? Men. Can't live with 'em and a woman can't live without them. Now get back in bed. You've had your notice."

She sat up and stripped off her shirt.

He saw why she was groaning. Even in the dim light, the huge black bruise on her breast stood out.

He didn't waste any time looking.

Her breathing labored.

He stepped into his pants and pulled on a shirt.

"What does a girl have to do to get your attention?"

A smartass, too.

He found the key on the dresser and rushed out the door.

"Are you going to pay the bill at least?"

He left the door open, and she mumbled something about never hitchhiking again.

Bobbie was relieved when he came back.

Then she saw what he had in his hand.

"You're more beat up than you know. Believe me when I say that because I'd never turn you down otherwise—even if you are a bit young for my liking. Now lie back and enjoy it."

He grinned.

She gave him a look that said she didn't know what to think.

That was fine by him.

Bobbie seemed like the type that needed to be kept wondering.

Jim woke up in the morning in a bed soaked with ice water and a body snuggled against him and shivering something fierce. Goosebumps covered the body.

He knew, because he took a quick look before pulling the wet sheet up.

"It's all right. I'm awake too. I won't mind you looking any more if it'll get you to go for more ice."

"Yeah. No. No problem on the ice, but first you're going to lie back and take it."

She gave him a look like she wanted to kill.

He eased the sheet down.

His hand went in the general direction of her swollen breast.

She moved to brush it away.

"All right. You can pull the sheet up. I've had my look. You're going to have to suffer through my hand, though. I'm going to check you for broken bones."

She didn't replace the sheet.

Her breast was almost black.

Her injury was so bad he didn't want to touch her.

"You need to see a doctor."

"Not unless I need reconstructive surgery," she insisted.

"Well, in that case, at least you've got a spare. It's still in pretty good shape, too."

Bobbie pulled the sheet up and smiled.

CHAPTER 7

Bobbie Dawson had to go through this Nash guy's bag. If she didn't, she'd worry the entire time. He appeared kind.

He'd rescued her, after she first thought he was a chickenshit. That idea got shot to hell in a hurry.

The knives bothered her, and she almost regretted finding them.

He hadn't made a pass.

She wondered about that.

Whatever.

Then the water stopped running, and she was caught.

"Are you planning on putting everything back where you found it?"

She turned back to the bag. She didn't bother pulling down the back of her tee. For some inexplicable reason, she wanted him to know her ass was first-rate to go along with the long legs she knew he was staring at.

"Tanto. Good knives. Why two?"

"Why not? One gets dull, the other isn't."

"I guess."

He never bothered to ask how she knew about Tanto.

"So. Are you staying? Or going?" he asked.

She pretended to consider and hoped she wasn't too obvious. "I'll start out on the floor. If you wake up with me in bed beside you, don't take it personal. If something is going to happen, it's going to be up to me. Understood?"

He nodded, and she took a measure of comfort in knowing he'd at least heard her.

The floor was too uncomfortable. She knew it would be, but she wanted to make her point. She was stubborn that way.

Her bruised chest ached. Her eye ached. Every part of her body ached on the hard floor that soaked through the cheap, thin carpet. Enough was enough. She was tough, but not stupid. Besides, she liked the guy.

So far.

Maybe she could talk him into taking her where she needed to be. Maybe she'd convince him to sign on to her agenda.

She opened her eyes and caught him looking.

"I see you changed your mind. Probably a good thing, considering the shape you're in."

Why did he have to be so good-looking? He was a smartass, too.

Still, she felt safe. It was a feeling she'd rarely had about a man.

She moved to pull the t-shirt above her breasts and gave up when she could only get it as far as her neck.

He gasped.

He danced into his pants in a hurry and left the room. A man on a mission. She'd never had that effect on one before now.

He was back with ice in plastic bags. By then she had the shirt off. She covered her unbruised breast with it and struggled to lean back against the headboard.

"Give me that shirt."

"You're the charmer, aren't you? No small talk with you, I'm guessing."

Bobbie lowered her forearm.

"Just as I thought. You're banged up pretty bad."

He sat down on the edge of the bed.

She leaned back and pulled down the sheet, exposing both breasts. She couldn't believe she didn't blush. "That's the way the bad one should look."

He looked and grinned a silly, lopsided grin.

Sweet. He was sweet, too.

"Well, it would, but in most cases, and in my experience, one is usually larger than the other."

"You're evil," she said, and broke into a smile. She couldn't help it.

"And you're not?"

The ice was a treat.

She couldn't ignore him after that.

And she didn't.

He was careful not to hurt her too much when he insisted on checking for broken ribs.

If she wasn't so beat up and in so much pain, she'd have allowed him to bed her.

Later, when the ice kicked in, she reached for him beneath the sheet. She let her hand linger, and when he laughed, she did too.

He said, "You're shaking. I don't think it's with desire."

"It's the damned ice that's coming between us. We're both freezing our asses off."

After they stopped laughing, she checked again. "Oh."

Her hand lingered.

He didn't complain.

Neither did she.

She decided she couldn't do it. She was too banged up from the beating.

She withdrew her hand. "I'm sorry for leading you on—"

He didn't let her finish.

"It's all right."

Bobbie woke with a start.

Jim was standing at the window looking out over the parking lot.

"What is it? Who's there?"

He let the curtain fall back. "Nobody. I thought I heard someone at the car. Go back to sleep."

She wanted to believe him. She stopped worrying about it after he climbed into their shared bed.

She felt safe again.

She forgot about Kennedy and the boat, too.

Jim figured they looked like a couple on vacation, despite her being a little on the young side. He hoped she'd stay with him for a while, maybe all the way to Brownsville. He didn't let on, though. She'd have to guess. He'd be able to spend the time trying to figure out what her deal was.

"You want out in Houston? I'll be passing through on my way," he said.

"Which side?"

"Sugar Land." A vision of an old movie played as he considered.

"Where to from there?" she asked.

He let Bobbie's question slide. He covered by trying the radio again. Music decided to blare right along with the wind whipping at her hair.

It was so damned warm and humid he couldn't catch a breath of fresh air.

Last night didn't help.

He hated to admit it, but he was looking forward to having Bobbie along for the duration. She was turning out to be good company, even with the smart mouth.

What sealed the deal occurred in the room.

She had braided her hair while he was in the shower. She asked him to fasten the bottom. Hair so dark it was black flowed uninterrupted in the back-and-forth pattern down to her waist.

"Brownsville. You interested?"

She didn't answer right away, either. She could play the game too. She was so much like someone else he once knew, it was scary.

If he was lucky, maybe this woman would help with his cover. Perhaps he could talk her into helping him get across the line. Once across, he couldn't risk her becoming tangled up in his deal. He'd have to ditch her.

"Yes. Although—" She hesitated. "There won't be a repeat of last night. Just so you know."

He waited, surprised there had been anything last night.

"I could go along as far as Brownsville. If that's all right. As long as you don't want gas and expenses. I'm busted, in case you didn't notice when you went through my gear."

He could have been mean. He could have told her last night was payment enough. It crossed his mind. A comment like that would make sure they didn't become more involved on a physical level than they were.

And then that damned woman crawled over the seat.

He tried to keep an eye on her in the mirror, to no avail. He heard a rustling, and then she crawled back. Wearing a skirt. A light, filmy, summer fling thing.

Damn.

And perfume. Just a hint.

What the hell?

If he was smart, he'd dump her by the side of the road. She'd be lucky if he left her bags behind.

Except, he wasn't ever known for smarts when it came to women.

CHAPTER 8

Bobbie lay in bed, tangled in the man's arms and legs in sweaty, messy abandon, shivering from what was left of the ice. Wet, cold sheets lay scattered beneath her. She tried to pull them away and gave up. The motion made them feel even colder.

She sighed and stretched against him and then groaned as the pain returned instantly. Damn but he was so nice and warm. So why was he shivering?

He asked if she was okay to get out of bed and she almost broke out in tears at his concern.

She had to turn away and then sobbed with pain and couldn't talk.

He wanted to go to the front desk to ask for painkillers but she talked him out of it.

"We'll get something on the road. If that's okay."

Still, she wondered how far down the road she'd be able to get with this one. She'd have to find out where he was headed. How long he'd be staying. Could she keep him with her? She groaned. Forced herself to sit up. Threw her legs over the edge of the bed. Tried to stand up.

"Tramp stamp."

He noticed. Finally.

"You weren't complaining last night."

"I couldn't see it last night," he said.

In her nakedness, she took a step, meaning to distance herself. Wanting to escape.

"Wait."

She stopped and sighed and backed up. Still shy about turning to face him. Even after sharing a bed, naked. In a lot of pain. She knew she was showing off, probably. Wanting him to see all of her.

Christ, was she showing off her body for this one, battered as it was?

The bed squeaked, and he was sitting up on the edge. His feet swung to the floor and found their way to either side of her own.

Warm hands roamed.

Touched the tattoo.

Goosebumps rose beneath his fingertips.

There was nothing she could do.

She tried to move away.

Couldn't.

Gave up.

Another word came to mind.

Surrender.

"It looks recent. Does it commemorate something?" he asked.

"It does." She kept her voice flat, unlike the goosebumps he was encouraging.

He didn't ask.

Good thing.

She didn't know what she would have told him. If she wanted to tell him. She changed the subject. "That feels nice."

His breath was too warm against the back of her thigh. It moved up and his lips kissed her in a random dimple. Soft. Gentle.

His mouth opened and teeth bit.

"Ouch. What was that for?"

She tried to pull away.

He wouldn't let her.

"Just marking my spot. You know, in case you want to remember."

She didn't want to step away from him now. The goosebumps traveled up to her good breast and back down to other places.

Was he kissing her?

Damn him. He was.

She turned and cradled his head in her hands. "I'm a mess. Thanks to you. Do you want to share the shower?"

"No."

"Oh." She was disappointed now. Wondering.

"Come back to bed. Take the top. I don't want to hurt you."

He didn't seem to notice the smile that hung on her face for what seemed like forever.

He was a man.

He had to be vulnerable.

She finished with him and laid back and lounged longer than she wanted to.

"Where are you headed, Bobbie?"

She wasn't sure she wanted to answer. She wondered if he had told her his own truth earlier. "South. You?"

"The same. We better get that shower you promised and get back out on the highway."

The passenger seat was a soggy mess, soaked through with rain. She didn't remember leaving the window down.

She slipped over the bench seat to occupy the semi-dry middle. After last night, she didn't mind. She was sure they must look like a couple, romantic, joined, happy.

She turned to look and caught him smiling.

Don't even, she'd said. But she smiled back.

She couldn't help it.

Didn't want to.

They barely made it out of the parking lot and five hundred feet down the road when the black and white cruised past going in the opposite direction.

She looked over the seatback to follow it. Her voice turned panicky. "It's turning into the motel. Do you think—"

"I'm wondering. Is it because of me or you?"

She jumped into the back, rummaged through her bag, and came up with a dress. She figured she might as well treat the man who would end up taking her to Brownsville.

Just for spite, she dabbed a dash of perfume between her breasts and grimaced at the movement.

The pain was so bad she almost didn't make the return trip over the seat to the front. She settled in and kept an eye on the side mirror.

The cop car didn't reappear.

CHAPTER 9

The storm had broken overnight, leaving behind a dying wind. Bits of blue broke out of the heavy overcast and the sun came through. The air turned cool and fresh.

They rolled down the windows and fresh air circulated in the damp, humid car.

Perhaps the sunshine was the reason he was unconcerned about the car. It had followed them when they pulled out of the motel. It could have been normal traffic. Hell, the road was a busy one.

Why wouldn't it be there?

He kept an eye on the vehicle in the side mirror as it pulled into the outside lane and moved up beside them.

It wasn't the black half-ton from the gas and go.

It remained only for a moment before moving behind to stay in the number one lane.

Pacing, he'd call it.

But why?

They were on a long straight stretch. Perhaps whoever it was wanted a better look. He wanted the truck to go by. When it didn't, he worried. Concern got the better of him.

"Roberta. Can you climb into the back seat for me?"

"What? Why?"

"Just do it, okay? When you get there, pull the seatback forward and fish between the back and the seat. There's something I might need."

She did as she was told, but she was still hurting. He knew by the heavy breathing and the groans she didn't try to hide.

"There's nothing there." Rustling as she tried the other side. "Got it."

She held up the box.

"Stay back there and pass it over."

She ignored him. He knew she would. She dropped it on the seat beside him before struggling to climb over the seat.

"Is there something you should tell me? Is someone following you? Anything? I need to know right now, Bobbie."

He ticked a couple of miles off the cruise and slowed.

The chase truck passed.

It drifted across into their lane and pulled ahead.

"No one. Why?"

"Are you sure? I need to know. Please."

"Nobody. I'm not an escaped felon. Don't worry."

But he was worried. If he believed her, he had just drawn her into his life. Sharing a bed could do that. It occurred to him they might be using each other.

"You know anything about firearms?" he asked.

"A little. Why?"

"I need you to do something. The sooner the better. I need you to load a magazine. Can you do that?"

Bobbie fumbled with the steel case. Undid the latch. Flipped it open.

Removed the automatic.

She looked at him, at it, and back at him.

"What's with this? Who are you? A cop? A crook?"

Funny she went with the cop first.

There were so many reasons to have a concealed firearm.

"No. Not any more."

She didn't ask whether cop or crook any more.

She looked at him again for an instant too long before she opened the box of cartridges. She slid them into the magazine one at a time.

"A crooked cop? Or was the yes for an even worse crook? Were you sent for me?"

A strange question, that. Why would she ask?

"Not that I know of."

"Well, that's reassuring. This isn't a legal magazine, is it?"

This while she kept loading the oversize mag and doing a good job, from what he could see.

She finished and banged the mag into the grip with the heel of her hand. She placed the pistol between his legs.

"If I'd known last night what I know now—"

"You'd still be here. I can tell that about you."

The vehicle in front chose that instant to hit the brakes.

He stomped on his.

Thanks to no seatbelt and her injuries, Bobbie slid forward and slammed against the dash.

She screamed in agony.

Jim steered around the brake-check in a cloud of dust and ended up on the gravel-covered shoulder. Sand and rocks spit up and rattled against the undercarriage.

The car drifted sideways in the dirt. He counter-steered, bleeding off speed until they came to a stop, low in the grass-covered ditch, facing straight ahead.

"Get in the back seat and get down. Now. Do it now," he ordered.

Bobbie struggled over the seat, groaning the entire time. He had no sympathy for her.

"Didn't I tell you to stay there? You don't listen, do you?"

He knew the lecture was useless.

He fished on the floor for the automatic. It wasn't there.

Bobbie passed it over. "It must have slipped beneath the seat," she said.

He jacked one into the chamber and dialed in full auto.

"How long are we going to wait?" she asked.

"Until we don't have to wait any more. Get comfortable. It could be a while."

"In that case, why don't you join me?"

He shook his head, and they laughed uncontrollably.

CHAPTER 10

Bobbie Dawson forgot to roll up the passenger window. Consequently, she had plopped herself down in the soggy seat. She cursed and scrambled over the wet spot.

She found herself hip-to-hip against Jim. For an instant she pictured them a couple of teenagers running off on a joyride. Except it was too early in the day. And they were too old.

Their eyes met, and they grinned.

Damn but he was one good-looking man.

He still needed a shave. She'd take care of that the next time they overnighted. If there was a next time.

"Maybe we could do that again sometime," she said.

She was testing.

He ignored her. As usual.

There had to be something in his past.

Hell, she didn't know.

So she ignored him, too—until the vehicle overtook them and took up a spot beside the car.

At first, she thought it might be the truck from the parking lot, but it wasn't.

Jim didn't recognize it either.

The truck stayed behind, in the second lane. Pacing. Or whatever it was doing.

Challenging?

A teenager bent on racing?

A redneck maybe, who'd seen them in the motel parking lot.

Jealous.

Whatever rednecks do.

Wanting to be sure, she checked again.

It wasn't the redneck truck from the gas station.

Then Jim asked if she'd climb in the back.

He wanted a box. It seemed a strange request, and it wasn't what she wanted to do, considering the pain she was experiencing.

She climbed over the still-wet seat anyway.

Why was she so eager to please him?

"There's no box. What are you talking about?" she asked.

"Look behind the seat," he said.

So I looked behind the seat.

She fumbled through the exercise and came up empty-handed.

Frustrated, she kicked the seat-back and groaned.

It dropped and the heavy box fell out.

He wanted her to stay in the back, but she refused. He might as well know how stubborn she could be.

She regretted it the instant she moved to climb over. The pain went through her body like lightning.

The request wasn't such a strange one when she finally opened the box.

A handgun and two magazines stared back.

The magazines had to be something special, because they were really long.

"You know how to load?" he asked.

She nodded.

Kept silent.

Spilled the box into the bag and began slipping shells into the long magazines.

It took forever.

When she slipped the magazine into the grip it stuck out a long way past the end.

It felt heavy and unbalanced.

She placed the pistol between his legs.

Hesitated before removing her hand.

The truck overtook them and accelerated away.

"What's going on?" she asked.

"I have no idea. Don't you?"

He checked the mirror and fumbled with the radio.

She figured he was trying to mask his concern. He wasn't very good at it. His eyes narrowed as he looked across at her.

She looked away.

"Is there something you haven't told me, Bobbie? Is someone after you? Something you should be telling me?"

Where to start?

Bobbie didn't want to tell him a single thing. She couldn't. Not now, at least. She avoided the questions and ignored the badgering by not looking at him.

Maybe she thought he'd go away. Not likely, considering they were trapped in a car speeding down a highway.

"Not that I know of."

As punishment for the lie, the car chose that instant to veer to the side.

A wheel went off the road into the soft gravel shoulder.

It caught and Jim scrambled to keep control.

She screamed.

He ordered her into the back.

"And stay down."

Despite the pain and her ignorance, she scrambled over in a hurry and slipped to the floor.

Trying to make a joke of it, she invited him to join her, and that's when they erupted in uncontrollable laughter.

Funny girl. At least it broke the tension.

The laughter died, and Jim stuck his head up.

He looked right, past the deep ditch they narrowly missed.

He craned his neck to see down the road, flicking his eyes from one side to the other.

Nothing.

He checked the back seat.

Bobbie was out of sight and on the floor as if she had bothered to listen to him.

The chase vehicle had disappeared.

Or so he thought until something plunked against the hood.

It was a familiar sound.

Light caliber.

He kept searching.

Then another weak plunk, and he glimpsed

someone he took to be the shooter.

He slipped back in the seat.

Crouched behind the door. Not that it would do any good to stop a bullet.

He aimed out the window.

The third round hit the tin.

He was ready.

He gripped with both hands and prepared to brace.

His finger found the trigger and went to work.

He pulled once and full auto took over.

Shell casings ricocheted off the windshield, danced off the roof, and landed in back.

More brass than a rifle association meeting came to mind.

Shell casings scattered and bounced.

Bobbie screamed.

"Holy shit. Jim? What the hell? What are you doing? Who are you shooting at? Why are they shooting at us? They're shooting at us, right? Tell me you're not a crazy battling a good Samaritan stopped to help us get back on the road."

It was too late for explanations.

Whoever it was had turned tail and was scattering in the wind.

It wouldn't be the first time a shooter did that when his answerback was his pistol in full auto, spitting lead and brass.

"Thanks for loading that magazine. You might have saved both our lives."

Bobbie crawled over the seat. Her skirt came up a little too high, revealing more than a bit of firm thigh. She huffed and the groan she wanted to silence went audible.

"You're welcome. I think. Now are you going to tell me what the hell you're running from? Or to?"

"Can it wait? I need you to drive. Just in case."

He gave her credit. She didn't ask just in case of what.

Bobbie straddled him and crawled over his lap.

Her breasts pressed against his face.

He caught the painful grimace as she settled in behind the wheel.

Without a word she drove out of the ditch and back onto the 10 like nothing happened.

Well, except for the white knuckles and shaking hands.

The death grip on the wheel was no use in quieting them.

Her elbows joined her hands, and not long after her shoulders and the rest of her body went along for the ride.

"You need to pull over," he told her.

She did, and he held the woman in his arms until the shaking quieted.

He stroked her hair.

It felt good. He buried his face in it. Any excuse. She smelled too good.

"Are you all right now? What's the name of that perfume? I want to buy you a barrel."

"Oh god. I'm so sore. Not too tight, okay?" she pleaded.

He relaxed his grip, but he didn't let go. He was enjoying it.

Probably too much.

CHAPTER 11

Bobbie Dawson wasn't sure if Jim noticed the truck overtaking them. She was concerned it could be the same one from the battle in the gas'n'go's parking lot. Tinted windows didn't allow her to see in until it pulled up beside them.

She was sure she recognized the driver through the open passenger window.

It wasn't the same truck, and it sure wasn't the same driver. This one lived across the street from her.

It was her neighbor, Terry. Or his twin, maybe.

Except, Terry didn't have a twin. And he was friends with her brother.

Then the truck passed and she did a double take. If it was Terry, what was the deal with her brother?

Was neighbor Terry a part of it?

Did he have a grudge with her brother about something? Was he in it with her brother? Had they stolen the drugs together?

She debated telling Jim. In fact, it tore her up not to. She couldn't. That was before they drove off the road and someone took potshots while they were stalled in a ditch.

The rat-a-tat-tat explosions followed by empty casings raining down inside the car wasn't good.

She bit her tongue and stayed silent for the rest of the day. Her chest ached so bad she couldn't think straight, anyway. She wanted to get out of the heat and humidity and slather herself in ice.

What had she gotten herself into with this man?

She was a nervous wreck.

If she could just get some sleep—

Then she remembered.

Neither of them got any sleep.

A huge faded sign on the side of the highway announced a motel coming up.

Jim caught Bobbie looking wistful out the side window as it went by. Letting her drive might not have been the best idea.

"Maybe we could stop for the night," she said.

"I don't think that's a good idea. You saw what happened. We need to put some distance between us and them."

Whoever they were. He still didn't know what was going on. And Bobbie sure as hell wasn't talking.

"Yeah. I was there too, remember? I think I peed my pants just a little."

He wanted to cheer her up. If anyone deserved it, Bobbie did for being such a cool cucumber under fire—literally.

A little lie couldn't hurt.

"That happened to me the first time, too. You get used to it—not peeing your pants, I mean."

And then he said out loud, "We need to ditch the car."

"In that case, we're stopping at that motel. You can do the ditching. Got any cash?" Bobbie asked.

"Yeah. It's in the back, too."

Bobbie slowed and pulled off the road. Still behind the wheel, she hiked up her skirt before crawling over the seat one more time. She dug around and came up with her stash.

First things first.

"You know, you could have opened the door and leaned in," he said.

She looked at him like he was a nutcase. "What, you don't want to look at my legs any more? Or anything else? How am I supposed to keep you coming back if I don't use womanly wiles?"

He went on ignore. "If you've got any dope, I recommend you smoke it now or toss it. Just in case."

"All right. I can do that." She fished around in her bag and tossed a small plastic baggie out the window.

Jim pretended not to notice, but he'd seen the baggie when he went through Bobbie's bag in the room that first night.

"Let's go while the getting is good. And if you're sleeping in my bed tonight, you better talk or I'm out first thing in the morning.

He looked across the seat at her and grinned.

"Your bed? I guess that means you're buying."

We were gaining on the outskirts of Harlingen. He didn't want her to skip on him. Not now.

"I know a place," she said. "Take the Sunset exit." She pointed. "That's it on the left."

It was perfect. It was the place you picked when

you were down and out and had nowhere else to go. Or maybe one where you holed up and hoped for the best when life was throwing shit in your direction and you were on the run from it.

Withered hedges and brown flower beds made a desultory try at greeting visitors to the sloping flat-top, single-story motel of the no-tell variety. Stunted weeds grew up in places through what remained of the asphalt.

"Is this part of the budget experience?" she asked.

He looked across at her and wondered if she'd ever gone broke traveling.

"Smartass. Do you want to pay?"

She didn't say no, so he grinned and she got the message.

They'd be invisible and unknown. Two desperadoes, running for all they were worth.

She slowed to turn.

"Don't turn. Keep going," he said.

"I thought we were going to get a room."

"I need to know if we're being followed."

Bobbie did as she was told, managing to look at him and shake her head at the same time. "Followed? You are a wanted man, aren't you?"

Yeah, and maybe she was a woman on the run. If that was true, they were a good match.

They were getting more comfortable with one another.

"Don't be so quick to put the blame on me, woman. You're the one I rescued from the hillbilly half-ton."

She cruised past the motel.

Like the perfect professional.

He had questions that needed asking, but now wasn't the time.

"I have to clean up my brass in this wreck. How many did you load?"

"Full. I think."

Bobbie pressed the back of her hand against a breast. She reached into her top and came up with shiny brass in her palm.

"Damn. That's what was making me itch."

He grinned and held out his hand and palmed the warm brass. "And I thought it was because of me."

She grinned right back. "Well—"

When she wasn't looking, he slipped the casing into his pocket. Whatever was going on between them, it was working its magic. Or something.

"You can turn around and make for the motel now," he said. "We should be good."

The motel wasn't the finest. Too many coats of paint peeling from the heat. It was out of the way on the north end of the city.

He got out and took a room in back, just as out of the way.

Bobbie parked and we unloaded.

The motel door creaked open on its hinges.

A wall of hot, humid, fetid air slapped them in the face.

A low, dirty window overlooked the lot.

He found the light switch and flipped it.

A stained dresser with cigarette-burned edges and a small table stared back.

He already knew by the box that the bed was going to be a treat.

Bobbie discarded most of her clothes. "I don't

mean to be presumptuous, but it's just too hot in here."

His eyes followed her every move on the way to the shower.

Another casing fell out of her bra at the bathroom door. She knelt to pick it up and tossed it in his direction. "Have a souvenir."

Too busy rewarding his eyes with a good look, he missed the catch, but it confirmed what he already knew to be true. This one was better looking than any woman he ever wanted in his life.

"Aren't you tired of looking yet?" she wanted to know.

"Fat chance. Am I the only man you ever had in your life? We never stop looking."

"I'll think about it. Right now, I'm too sore and tired to care."

The water in the shower was loud against the cheap wall.

He locked the door behind him and backtracked to a chicken place for biscuits and naked. He picked up ice, too.

There was no sense changing his modus now that Bobbie was settling in.

In fact, he was liking it, much as he hated to admit it.

CHAPTER 12

Bobbie's hands shook. Her swollen, black and blue breast ached like the devil. Her elbows joined in with the rest of her arms and then her entire body gave it up and trembled uncontrollably.

Scared shitless.

A delayed reaction, she guessed.

Jim didn't get upset. He talked her into pulling over, which was all right with her. He put his arms around her and held her until she settled down. Dammit but he felt good. Even on the side of the road in the middle of nowhere. "Not too hard. My breast is killing me."

He stopped squeezing. She was still happy.

"You good now?" he asked.

"I'd feel a lot better if you could hold me like this for a long time." Why had she said that? She was betting he'd be more than happy to be rid of her when it came time. Like a lot of the men in her life.

She eased out of his arms.

"It's only driving. I can do it."

He made her drive past the old, single-story motel while he checked for a tail.

Her own tail was exhausted. Her breast was aching ever more like the devil. She couldn't wait to get in the shower and let the cold water run.

The tiny room was empty by the time she dragged her sorry, swollen, black and blue body out of the shower.

Jim was gone.

She pulled on a pair of panties and a shirt before parting the curtain. The car was gone, too. Shit. He wouldn't dare leave her alone after what happened.

Would he? That son of a bitch. He would.

She was about to start cursing him out. Then the key rattled and the door creaked and he appeared with a grin and a bag of chicken and biscuits. Even better, he had more ice tucked under his arm.

"You're a mind reader."

She stripped off the shirt without a modicum of embarrassment. It was long past time for that. She was comfortable with him now—naked or clothed. She plopped onto the bed without bothering to cover up.

"Lie down," he said.

She gave him a look she didn't mean.

He ignored it.

She stretched out and tried to get comfortable while he dumped ice into a plastic bag and placed it on her breast. She winced and he took her hand and placed it on the bag.

"Your turn." He grinned the whole time until it turned into a fading smile.

"I'm sorry someone kicked the shit out of you. I'm sorry your eye is black and your breast is blue. It's a nice blue, though." He smiled again, and she surrendered one more time. Giving in was starting to annoy her.

"It's a nice breast, too. Not as nice as the other one, but it will be. Given enough time. If you let me take care of it for you."

She giggled and blushed and burst into laughter and blushed even more. "Ouch. No more. Please."

He pulled the covers over her nakedness and settled in beside her.

"Let me know when you get tired of holding it."

She couldn't help it. She giggled again. "You are a bad, bad man."

Son of a gun but he was becoming irresistible. Suddenly she had to have the last word. She gave him the look while she brushed his cheek with the back of a hand.

"Not until you shave."

Bobbie wasn't sure what she meant by not until.

They holed up in the no-tell motel looking too much like a pair of hard-boiled criminals on the run. It wasn't difficult to look sweaty and dangerous. The car had no air outside of open windows. The motel room's desultory window-shaker was incapable of keeping anything cool.

Heat and humidity forced them to strip down to sweaty underwear.

Perspiration pooled in places he didn't know existed.

Bobbie encouraged his tongue to bathe in her salty skin. Encouragement wasn't something he needed much of when it came to this one.

They ended up wanting more.

She obliged him by leading the way. The bra came off.

Two pairs of underwear followed and joined the damp pile of clothes already discarded on the floor.

At the end of it they collapsed in a pile of sweaty sheets and even sweatier bodies. The air conditioner gave up and chugged to a loud-pitched, grinding halt.

"I think I saw something like this in a movie. Refresh my memory, would you?"

Jim forgot the pain she was in and pulled her on top.

She groaned in agony. Perspiration flowed between her breasts and trickled down her stomach onto his.

"I'm sorry. I forgot for a minute. It won't happen again."

"It's all right. Just this once I'll make an exception," she said.

"If you insist."

"I do insist. Now get busy."

CHAPTER 13

Jim woke to Bobbie's frantic shaking. Or maybe it was the thumping his chest was taking from her fist.

Damn but that woman could punch.

He jerked up and brushed against a firm and shapely undamaged breast. "What? What is it?"

"Someone is checking out the car. Did you get it cleaned up?"

"As best I could. I counted twenty-nine, plus two in your cleavage. That's a full mag—in more ways than one."

Bobbie frowned. She didn't appreciate his humor.

It wasn't difficult to desert the damp, sticky sheets and the lumpy mattress.

He cast his gaze through filthy glass past a broken screen into a dark parking lot. A door slammed and the car's interior light went out. He let the curtain fall.

Already Bobbie was tossing clothes and boots and sandals into her bag.

"What the hell are you doing?"

"We have to get out of here. Someone made us."

"Relax. No one made us. Someone got curious is all. That's why I left it unlocked. Now get back in bed and I'll help you relax."

She wasn't having it. "Screw this. It's time to go. Now."

With her own bag packed, she started on his. She made an even bigger mess of it, if that was possible. She didn't appear to notice a key missing element.

"Very nice. Are you going to put something on? Or are you planning on dragging a sweaty sheet along for the ride?"

She looked down and laughed uncontrollably.

He recognized a sob somewhere in there, too.

"Jesus. I'm sorry. I'm on edge. I can't seem to calm down."

He searched his pockets and came up with a handful of change.

"Tell me you're not going to flip a coin to help you make the decision to keep me."

"Something like that." He dropped a quarter into the slot on the box attached to the head of the bed.

She stretched out as and it began to shake, rattle, and roll.

"What the hell?"

She sat up looking confused.

He couldn't stop grinning.

She pulled him down beside her and they lay there, laughing and giggling in a vibrating bed like it was the first experience for two runaway teenagers.

"Feel any better?"

"Only when I stop laughing. I wondered what that thing was for. This isn't your first hideout, is it?" she asked.

"Yeah. No. Consider it my gift to you. A trip to the spa in the no-tell motel part of town."

The ride finished, and the bed quieted.

He picked up what she left on the floor when she was in a hurry to share her nakedness with him and handed it over.

"Finish getting dressed. I'll bring the car around."

He searched the floor for his jeans and a still-damp shirt.

He tossed underwear her way.

She tossed it into her bag.

"Planning on going commando, are you?"

"You're the one said I should leave the bra behind."

He didn't mind. He kind of liked the idea, and he grinned like a guilty teenager.

They pulled out of the motel and managed about half a mile down the road toward Harlingen before the black and white passed them heading in the opposite direction. He checked the rear-view and saw brake lights before it turned into the motel.

"You were right."

"Told ya."

Shit. How did they know? Who went through the car looking for—what? Roberta?

If people were on the lookout for her, he needed to know.

While all of this was running through his head, she slipped across the seat. She tipped her head and rested it on his shoulder. It seemed like an awful fast reaction—unless she turned out to be a mind reader.

"Is there something you're not telling me? If there is, I need to know. The sooner the better."

How many times had he asked?

"Well—"

She halted.

If she wasn't going to level with him, he'd have to get off the well-traveled roads. He needed to be invisible.

Without a word, he followed the 77 south to the 510. He headed toward the gulf before reconsidering.

"Don't lie or in a New York minute you'll be standing by the side of the road with your thumb hanging out. Your bag will be in the ditch with you."

"I'm sorry. I should have told you." she said.

His mind was made up. He prepared for the worst. He couldn't hold it against the woman. He had his own problems, and they didn't include hers.

Before she could start, he pulled into the shade at a gas'n'go. Not wanting to leave anything to chance, he took the keys before departing for the store. He wasn't convinced Bobbie wouldn't run off, and he didn't want to end up stranded in some Texas shithole with no money, no clothes, and no gun.

He picked up a road map and headed back to the car.

The woman was going through his bag again as if the first time wasn't enough. "Did you not find out what you needed to know on your first pass? You're not giving me a show of your ass this time."

She turned to face him. A tear rolled out of an eye. It reached her upper lip and her tongue flicked, making it disappear.

By now, he knew her well enough.

"That won't cut it. Why don't you make some shit up and tell me about it? You've had enough time."

"Well, you're just harsh, aren't you?"

"Remember what I told you down the road? Talk or walk."

Or else.

CHAPTER 14

Damn that man to hell.

Bobbie couldn't lie to him. He would see right through her. Of that, she had no doubt.

She couldn't even take off her clothes. She already did that with abandon and loved every look the man gave her.

Dammit.

She couldn't be falling for him. She couldn't. They had only just met. He was supposed to be her ticket out of town. Well, he was. But now look at her. She allowed him into her bed and loved every minute.

Loved? Did she just think that? Crap.

"Jim?"

"What's it going to be?" he asked.

In that moment, she surrendered. She had to. She became incapable of doing anything else. She didn't want to do it. At least, not at first. Would he believe her? Could she go on using him to get where she needed to be?

"It's my brother. He got himself in a situation with one of the cartels. He didn't know what he was doing. He couldn't help it. I can't get in touch with him. I don't know where he is. I think he's gone on the run."

The words tumbled out. She couldn't stop if she wanted to.

"How old is he?"

How old is he? There was something about the tone of his voice. Skeptical, maybe. Or maybe he thought she was out-and-out lying. Could she blame him?

"Thirty."

"And he didn't know what he was doing? Don't fling your shit onto me hoping it will stick because you swallowed your brother's bullshit. At thirty, he knows exactly what he's doing. So what's your plan?"

Bobbie had to have Jim on her side. Especially now that she was falling for the man. She had nothing else. Dammit to hell. She had to make him believe her. She needed him to believe.

She needed to start at the beginning.

She was desperate for Jim's help to find her brother. She'd get it any way she could.

This was getting better and better.

He'd be able to head across the line with Bobbie in tow. She would think he was doing it to help her. While he didn't discount that he'd be willing to help if he could, he had his own priorities. They were first and foremost.

Green. Her eyes were green. All this time spent looking at her in and out of bed and he just noticed. Shit. She was getting to him. He'd have to be careful with this one. Everything about her was tempting, not the least of which was her personality. Long legs to go along with everything else didn't hurt, either.

Some personality.

"Goosebumps."

Did he say that out loud?

"What the hell are you talking about?" Bobbie asked.

Dammit but he did. "Your ass turned into goosebumps the other night."

"Along with everything else. What did you expect? I wasn't exactly shy about what you were doing with me," she admitted. "I'll let you do it again as soon as I can."

Christ. He was falling for her. In a big way. He knew it now. He wondered if she could tell. Thankfully, she changed the subject.

"About my brother—" Bobbie hesitated.

He only wanted to know what was coming next.

"He ran off with a couple of hundred thousand of cartel money."

Finally. There it was.

He had to know how dumb the brother was. "Money or drugs?"

"Drugs. Why? Does it matter?" she asked.

Shit. The woman had no idea.

He sat her down and took the chair opposite the bed. That they were both naked made it surreal, but he had to get her to pay attention any way he could.

"They'll kill him. They'll kill you. They'll kill your mother and your father. They'll shoot your dogs and set fire to your cats. They'll burn down your house and everything in it."

First-hand experience told him that, and he

learned from it. It was no exaggeration. "Now then, what was it you wanted again?" Did he even get through to her?

"I need your help."

Well, there went that idea.

"In that case, have I got a deal for you. But first you're going to have to tell me a story." And it had better be a good one, or he'd be sneaking out of here like a dog first thing in the morning.

If he waited even that long.

Feelings be damned.

CHAPTER 15

Bobbie was afraid. Scared. She didn't know where to start. Or how to start. Once she had it all out in the open, would Jim still want to help her find her brother, Ray?

She hesitated for longer than she knew she should. Finally, she gave in. Resigned, she sighed and took a deep breath, certain she'd lose the man once he learned the truth.

"We grew up in Brownsville. Browntown, the locals call it. I left in my teens. I wandered around like a gypsy before I got smart. I went back to complete and graduate high school. Ray, my brother, stayed. He was typical of the guys in a border town. He flipped back and forth across the line with his friends to sample the clubs and the women and the drugs."

Jim waited, not saying a word.

He must have meant it when he said he wanted her story. She couldn't look at him. She drew another breath.

"Ray was never hard-core, as far as I could tell. He sampled, like his buddies. But they seemed to help each other stay on the right side of the law, mostly.

He lived at home. In the basement. Then, one December when I was back home for a month, he told me he was hauling drugs across the river."

"What? Living in the basement?"

"I don't know. Maybe Ray thought it would be a measure of safety if he got caught."

It had to sound like her brother wasn't playing with a full deck. And for all she knew, maybe he wasn't.

"For crying out loud, Bobbie. Your folks would lose everything if he got caught. The government would seize everything as drug proceeds. Your parents would have to go through a lengthy and costly court process to prove otherwise. If they ever could."

For sure Ray hadn't been born with all the smarts in the family, but Jim would change his mind about him once they met. She was certain.

"Yeah, well, explaining that to him didn't go so well, either. When I heard he went missing, I figured he'd been arrested. At first, I had no idea he disappeared, all right? Missing with drug cartel money. Only it was product, not money."

It seemed like he was considering. She halted. She hoped for a look that announced he'd want to help.

"The man stole from a cartel. He's nuts. He has to be. That, or he was stoned out of his gourd and nuts to boot."

"He's no user," she insisted. "He wanted to pay off mom and dad's mortgage."

Maybe she made that part up about the mortgage on the spur of the moment. She didn't want Jim to think Ray, was a complete dud—even if he was. But she didn't think that about him, either. He was her older brother, after all. She had looked up to him when she was a kid.

Why would Jim believe anything she said? Should she go with the truth about the yacht? That she allowed the owner to pound the shit out of her on purpose? It was time to dive in. She had to put the feelings she was developing for this man on the back burner. She had to dedicate herself to finding her brother.

No matter what.

Jim said, "Stealing cartel product isn't the way to go. It's a death sentence. For your entire family. Just so you understand, that includes the pets. Do they have any pets?"

That was the second time. So maybe he knew more than she did. She had to tell him about her black eye. She couldn't hold back any longer. Not after revealing everything else.

"About the bruises. My body—"

"They'll heal. You'll be pink-skinned and back to normal in a week. Ten days, max. Guys will be beating a path to your door again."

The trouble was, this man was the only one she wanted beating a path anywhere. For an instant she questioned her decision to let him know. She knew he'd think she was attempting to use him.

"Yeah. About that." She drew a breath. "The bruises and the beating were self-inflicted."

Jim's head snapped up.

Dark eyes bored into hers.

That Bobbie finally opened up came as a complete surprise. He never thought she'd ever spill her guts. She must have thought letting him share her bed allowed some leeway.

As he saw it, the problem was with the brother. He was looking and sounding more and more like a dumbass, and he hadn't even met the man. Obviously, he hadn't been born with the smarts in the family. He hoped his sister might have been.

As much as he hated doing it, he'd have to put the feelings starting to develop for this woman on the back burner. She was turning out to be pure trouble, even from the outset. Perhaps a liability, too. He hadn't realized it until her confession.

While their end games were different, they were linked by drugs. He could probably use that to his advantage. That they were going to end up in Brownsville by choice made things much simpler. She knew the city. She had to know something about the drug trade because of her brother's shenanigans.

That her battle scars were more or less self-inflicted concerned him. Who had she allowed to do it, and why? Why did she feel a need to present the abused-woman front just to hitch a ride? She didn't. There was more going on with this one than she was letting on.

That Bobbie had let him into her bed a little too soon either said needy, or she was hunting. He'd go with hunting, and he was finally finding out for what. She had to think he'd be the man to help find her brother. That he'd showed a bit of ingenuity with a handgun and a stash of cash probably didn't hurt.

But damn, whoever laid that beating on her did a

job. She was black, blue, and hurting. While he might not trust her, he felt sorry for her. He believed she didn't know what she was letting herself in for when she took the beating.

And then it occurred to him, all of a sudden. What if it wasn't her brother that was the apple of her eye? What if it was the drugs she was focused on retrieving?

"Roberta, I'm going to help you. But first, we need to make a deal. You might think you're about to make it with the devil. You might be right. But if you refuse, I'm done. Right now."

He halted to let her consider.

She paced. She worried. She opened her mouth to speak and closed it too many times.

"If we find my brother, I'll help you with your deal. But I'm not sleeping with you until we do. No matter how much ice and tenderness you bring me."

He'd just been told.

"We need a car. A beater. And whoever it is you're texting, stop. Give me that phone."

He didn't wait for her to hand it over. He grabbed it out of her hand.

She moved to take it back.

He turned away, and while she struggled to reach around, he pulled the battery and the SIM, and tossed the phone.

She looked a little too concerned.

"No need to panic." He went positive on her. "We'll pick up a couple of burn phones when we get to town."

He slipped the SIM into a pocket.

He'd check it out later.

CHAPTER 16

Bobbie would have jumped for joy if she could. And damn Jim Nash to hell. He accepted without blinking an eye. It was like he was waiting for her to step in it and ask. As though he already agreed, but was only waiting for the inevitable invitation. Well, he had it.

Now she would own the man's ass.

All she had to do was keep her goosebump-coved ass out of his hands.

As simple as that.

They both knew where that would lead.

She had it bad enough for this one. She didn't need any more heartache than she could handle at one time. What she couldn't understand was why on earth she was falling for him. That wasn't a part of any plan.

Hell, she didn't even have one.

She told him she wouldn't be sleeping with him again until they found her brother.

Okay, so if she had a plan, that was it. Simple, wasn't it?

Those words coming out of her mouth were a

complete surprise. Would it work? She didn't know, but she had to try. What else did she have to hold over him? He seemed rather comfortable with her in bed.

It was almost like they were lovers and partners. They were already the first. Now they'd be the second, but not in the sense of lovers.

Or so she thought she understood—until she made the mistake of standing by the side of the bed while she searched for the clothes she'd flung onto the floor in the lead-up to their fevered love-making.

Before she knew what was happening, what he was doing, she literally melted beneath his hands. Putty. And more goosebumps. They were everywhere in an instant, not like the last time.

Goddammit but would it never end with this one?

She wanted to kick herself.

Instead, she sat back down on the edge of the bed.

Wanted to turn around.

Wanted to give herself over to him.

Wanted to offer herself up like a virgin on her wedding night.

Did anyone even do that any more?

Shit. She was completely lost.

She tried to stand up.

She couldn't.

Her legs wouldn't allow it.

Instead, she sat, trembling. Unable to move.

"Would you like more ice?" he asked.

More ice?

Damn you to hell, Jim Nash.

No.

She wanted to be in bed with him.

She wanted to feel warm and safe and happy and secure.

She couldn't say it.

No matter how much she wanted to.

Reluctantly, she forced herself to push off the edge of the bed. Through watery eyes she found her clothes, and without turning, made her way to the bathroom.

She made sure to close and lock the door.

Bobbie exited the bathroom. She was dressed and sporting puffy red eyes. Either the woman had just smoked a joint or she had been crying.

Jim went with the dope, probably because he was one.

Women.

He never could understand them.

Even the ones he cared about.

Or loved.

Same difference.

He said, "I need a Brownsville map. And you need to get me up to speed on the lay of the land. Any ideas where we should start?"

Bobbie stormed out of the room, slamming the door behind her for effect.

It was as though he didn't exist. He took it in stride and turned on the television. An all-day news channel with a blond-haired, blue-eyed reporter was in the process of wrapping up her report on the latest cartel killings across the river.

It wasn't news to him.

Bobbie returned with a map and coffee for one.

Her expectation was that it wasn't for him. He belabored the point anyway.

"Why didn't you get one for yourself?"

She ignored his lame attempt at humor and busied herself clearing off the table before laying out the map.

A couple of the locations were burned into his memory. They were the sites he had staked out during his search for Kara. Maybe they'd be a place to start for his part of the job. He didn't let on. He wanted Bobbie to think he was all hers for the duration of the hunt for the woman's brother.

And then a nagging thought crossed his mind. It had been bubbling beneath the surface for a day. At least. Maybe more now that he realized he was going to have to commit to helping Bobbie.

She barely got the map spread out.

That was when he didn't want her to think she was going to be in charge.

"Grab your bag. We're going. Now."

The woman didn't have time to object.

He tossed everything into the car and slammed the door. By the time he made it to the driver's seat, Bobbie was up front.

"We're about a half-hour out. Pick up 14th and I'll show you where to go from there," she said.

He didn't let on. Where she was leading them was close to one of the safe houses he'd scouted so many years ago.

Didn't tell her that he had been searching for a pretend wife.

Thinking that he had rescued that one from whatever demons had taken over.

He didn't tell Bobbie because he refused to admit he had been an abject failure in the rescue department.

He'd taken a pretty good beating at the time, too.

If he admitted the failure, how could Bobbie possibly keep believing he'd be able to help find her brother?

Which raised another question.

Would he be able to help her?

He let it go.

The woman was getting antsy.

"We're getting close. Slow down. Slow down. Keep right. We want to be on 14th East."

She was panicked and glanced from the street in front of them across to him again and again.

"Take it easy, woman. If we go past, we'll turn around."

"There it is. Stop. Stop here," she ordered.

"Christ, woman. We're supposed to be on the lookout. If we stop in the middle of the road, we'll be giving ourselves away."

He accelerated past the dive bar and pulled into a parking lot.

"What are you doing? Turn around. Go back."

He made sure to take the keys before leaning across to open the door. "Get out."

"Jim—" she began.

"Get out. Please. And put your jacket on. We're going for a walk."

He hurried off toward the bar.

She rushed to catch up. "Where are you going? What are we doing? Aren't we going to the bar? I thought—"

She really was annoying. And that was only part of her problem. Too much thinking was the rest of it.

"Don't think. Follow my lead. Don't open your mouth. Nod. Say yes if it calls for it. Never say no. Understand?"

Her head moved beneath the hoodie.

He couldn't tell if she was sulking or nodding a response.

He pulled open the door and walked into the dingy, low-ceilinged bar.

It had no windows.

Weak lights.

A filthy, streaked mirror.

The floor was uneven.

There was shabby, mismatched furniture everywhere.

It was his kind of place years ago when he was solo in Mexico.

He held open the door and ignored the commands to close it until his eyes adjusted.

"I'm going to check for an exit out back. Don't leave."

He didn't hold the door for her. He allowed it to slam shut behind him.

Bobbie took a good one in the chest thanks to the door and gasped.

If they were going to play true to form, he'd be no gentleman.

"You bastard."

"That's it. You're doing good. Keep it up and they'll believe us."

He wanted to grin. He couldn't. At least, not right away.

Instead, he hesitated. Scowled at her.

Made his way past the bar.

He checked out a reflection in the dirty mirror and almost didn't recognize the familiar face looking back.

And then the realization struck him.

It wasn't about Kara any longer.

It was about Bobbie.

And more importantly, when was done with Bobbie Dawson, he knew it had to be about Pilar. His real wife.

With a vengeance.

CHAPTER 17

Maybe she shouldn't have told Jim. She agonized to where she thought it had to be only fair, considering how he treated her.

So yes, she was feeling a little guilty about the lies. But did he need to know all of it? Once her lips began moving, she couldn't shut up.

It couldn't be helped. Sort of how she'd fallen into bed with this one, and then not been able to say no ever after.

Dammit to hell.

So she told him about when she was a kid. About being raised on a farm. About strict parents who went to church regularly but weren't overly religious. How her dad taught brother and sister about handling guns and how to shoot.

About how she was a bit of a wild child, not to mention a tomboy. That she didn't fit in at school and had few friends. Unlike her older brother, who had a lot of them. Maybe even too many.

Then the farm got sold, and they moved into the big city where dad took a job and mom babysat for working parents. That her parents still wanted to keep her down on the farm even though they were living in the city.

So she had packed clothes in a bag and ran off.

By then she had discovered short-shorts and a tube top got her pretty much anything she wanted. How anything she wanted included a ride out of town, fast. How having a body tucked into a tight top and shorts made it easy.

She ended up on the northern Gulf coast and took a liking to the marina bars for the rich boat owners.

Her wardrobe improved.

She learned to sail.

Eventually, she gained enough confidence to begin crewing on yachts. After a few years of experience, she taught rich owners how to sail their boats.

So what did it all teach her? That a little makeup, nice clothes, and a pair of high-heeled sandals could get her pretty much what she wanted, until one day it didn't.

That day occurred when she learned her brother had gone on the run with stolen cartel drugs.

What it didn't teach her was that she would become a pawn in the search for brother Ray.

She halted, finally. She didn't want Jim to know about how she led him on from the first moment she saw him and his junker rattle over the curb into the gas station.

Maybe she'd tell him later.

Or maybe not at all.

Jim didn't know the name of the man sitting at the bar. They'd never been formally introduced beyond a black hood and a couple of roundhouse punches once he and his partner had dragged him inside the safe house and removed the hood. Were it not for Kara coming to his rescue, he was certain they'd have had even more fun.

Consumed by memories, he slipped up. He blanched. Before he could turn around to leave, Bobbie caught him out.

"What is it? What did you see? Was it someone you know?"

He made a show of rough-housing the woman toward the door.

"Do you have to follow me everywhere, bitch? Go home and make dinner. Pick up some beer on the way. I'll be home later."

No one batted an eye.

Outside, he grabbed her arm hard and dragged her to the car.

"What's going on? What are you doing?"

She shook free of his grip.

"Can I get an answer out of you for a change?"

Jim was completely blindsided by the man in the bar. He had to buy time.

"Get in and I'll tell you."

But he didn't. Instead, he U-turned and backed into the alley across from the bar.

"I'm sorry about the door. I wanted to set us up as an unhappy couple fighting."

He kept an eye on the bar, using it as an excuse not to look at Bobbie. He already knew she was angry.

"And that's how you chose to do it? You might

have told me. I could have faked it, you know."

He didn't know.

Maybe next time.

"You recognized someone, didn't you? Are you going to tell me? Or do I have to wait a day for you to wake up?"

The woman could be brutal when she wanted to be. He ignored her and let her think she was winning. Winning what, he didn't know. He put her problem on the back burner for now—at least until he figured out where Kara's contact would lead him when the man decided he had enough to drink.

His mind was wandering again, thanks to the self-imposed stakeout.

He had already made up his mind to forget about Kara.

So what the hell was he doing? Did he really believe the man who hijacked hm into the safe house would have anything to do with Bobbie's brother?

It was a tense twenty minutes with Bobbie in the car.

She refused to stop haranguing him about what he'd seen.

Jim caught a break when the man walked out the door and headed up 14th.

He waited before following in the car. Traffic jammed up until he turned off, traveled another couple of blocks, and walked into the same safe house Jim was in so many years ago.

It looked like these people were in snooze mode, too.

Now that he knew what he would be doing later, Jim turned his attention to Bobbie.

"All right. We're good to go. Back to the bar."

Bobbie said, "Do I need to dodge the door this time?"

"Probably. And no backtalk, woman."

This time, he grinned. She didn't take it well. By the look of it, Bobbie wasn't accustomed to being on the receiving end of backtalk from her men. All the better to play-act. If he could keep her uneven, it would make them look more realistic as a fighting couple.

The exercise was a time-waster.

The man behind the bar didn't seem to mind that he ignored the woman he was with. He made a play, and it looked like he'd be going home without her. Except, he didn't have a home. They hadn't checked into a motel.

"We'll be staying with my parents," Bobbie finally said. "I haven't seen them in years."

Maybe she felt guilty about flirting.

"So the bartender is out of the picture?"

She gave him the look. By now, he was accustomed to it. "How are you going to explain me to dear old mom and dad?"

It was her turn to grin. "I'll figure something out."

"When you do, it would be nice if you'd let me know."

She ignored him. Nothing new there.

"Let's get out of this shithole, Nash. And welcome to Browntown. Home of impromptu car shows in closed mall parking lots, dog shows, and shady bars."

CHAPTER 18

Bobbie Dawson had no idea how she'd introduce Jim to her parents. He was older. Probably by ten years, at least.

She knew they wouldn't care for that. She'd dated an older man before she had moved out. When he showed up to take her on a date, he got dirty looks, and when she got home, she was on the receiving end of a stern lecture every time.

By the end of that relationship, they mellowed, but by then she had moved on and moved out, fast. She made no mention of the men in her life ever again. There was no use. None had been any good anyway.

And then this one showed up in a gas bar.

She had glommed onto him like a lot lizard looking for a ride to the next truck stop. She got the free ride, all right. In more ways than one.

"You're going to be my partner. All things considered, it shouldn't be that difficult. They'll cluck and you'll get side-eye from my mother checking you out, but you'll pass. Mom always had a soft spot for the good men in my life." She aimed a grin at Jim. She couldn't help it.

"So then, I'm the good one?"

"Don't push it, okay? There's a walk-up over the garage. They'll put you up there. It has an outside staircase."

Jim didn't seem to mind. It was all good. She hoped she'd be able to find something, anything, in Ray's room. She needed to get the show on the road. Without a clue, she'd be lost. If she had nothing, there was no telling how long Jim would hang around.

They drew up on the house and she pointed. "That's the place. You can park in the driveway."

Dad must have just cut the lawn. It looked a perfect green.

Jim said, "Should I collect the bags and follow you in?"

He didn't want to admit it, but he was nervous as hell.

"You can do that later. I want to get introductions over. They'll have way too many questions."

What she wasn't prepared for was the neighbor. Terry.

They had no sooner pulled into the driveway than the man rushed across the street, almost running. He asked too many questions, and they came rapid-fire and non-stop.

Was Terry driving the vehicle that overtook them? He was right in front of her, and she couldn't be certain.

Jim seemed to take it in stride, though. That is, until he pulled her aside. He didn't mince his words, either.

"You need to shut up about us to Terry."

That only confirmed her suspicions.

"He's looking like a puppy happy to see anyone home and he's asking too many questions. Was he always like this?"

Bobbie had to tell him no.

"Then just shut up. He's fishing. Someone has him on watch. It's why he couldn't wait to get across the street. He wants to collect the bounty. I'll handle him. Just be ready."

She nodded, uncomprehending, yet wanting to please him.

"No way do you let on your neighbor's cover is blown, Bobbie."

There was something wrong, and it was too obvious. The instant we pulled into Bobbie's driveway, the house across the street came alive. The door slammed open and a man rushed out. The door swung shut behind him with a harsh crack.

He slithered across the street with a too-big, too-friendly smile. He ended up hugging Bobbie after looking her over with an appraising glance. The questions came too fast. Who, why, what, when, where, in a blurred rush of words and sentences as though he had to have the information all at once.

Or it was a checklist the guy had memorized.

It was coming too fast as far as he was concerned. It was too pat. And he was too friendly. Not to Bobbie. To him, when he finally noticed him.

Bobbie was glad to see the guy, though.

He stood back and took it all in.

The whole thing set the alarm bells ringing. Not too loud, but they were beginning to tingle. It was the smile. Too much. The neighbor wanted to know things. Way too many things. That, and the fawning.

Bobbie didn't seem to notice, but then, why would she? She'd just arrived and the guy probably wanted an update on where she'd been and why she was home.

Neighbors were like that. Especially the ones that stayed behind, too scared to make a move and take a chance.

That. And former boyfriends.

"Did you two ever date?" he asked.

He got it out of the way first thing. He already guessed the answer was no. It was all happening too fast. And there was no way he could separate the two of them to warn her. She gave him the look over his shoulder when they hugged.

Terry. That was his name.

It was her father who introduced him. Like it was nothing. Of course it was nothing—to him.

Terry chased them into the house and he knew for sure there was something else going on.

Jim followed Bobbie's lead. He shook hands and smiled and nodded and smiled some more.

Her mother didn't seem to be as bad as Bobbie made her out to be. She welcomed him with a warm smile. But then it was still early in the grand scheme of introducing a strange man her daughter was supposedly dating. And sleeping with.

And then the sleeping arrangements came up. Her mother seemed pleased when Bobbie's father led him toward the walk-up suite over the garage. He used the time and the conversation to do some sizing up.

He must have passed, because he ended up getting invited to the patio for a beer after getting settled in.

"Terry will be there," dad said. "He comes over quite often asking about Roberta. It'll be his chance to get it straight from her."

"That's nice."

For Terry.

For Jim, it was concern enough to raise the hair on the back of his neck.

"Yes. Terry used to be a pretty good friend of Ray, her brother," dad admitted.

It was starting to come together. Why Terry had been watching for something—anything—going on across the street.

He figured Terry for a paid watchman. Or maybe someone who owed. Keeping watch was the man's way of making good on a debt.

He couldn't know for certain, of course. But if he was, he knew who'd be doing the paying.

This deal he had willingly entered into with Roberta wasn't looking so simple now. He suspected it would be taking over more and more of his time.

By the time Jim picked up his bag from the back of the car and hauled it upstairs, Terry was waiting for him.

He was already at the table, smiling and looking like an old friend. He appeared to be waiting for the coffee he thought he might make and a story about missed adventures and whatever else he could get him talking about.

Jim regarded the pasted smile, appraising. It was crooked. Insincere. Shady. Nervous. All of those and more.

Yes, Terry.

He already knows things about you.

Jim pretended to look over the kitchen.

Unzipped his bag.

Came up with a roll of tape.

He went to work with a vengeance, giving neighbor Terry no time to react. He forced his arms behind and taped his wrists.

When he finished, Terry's shoes were off and his ankles were secured to a kitchen chair.

For good measure, he wrapped his torso and the chair-back in tape.

Terry had to have it figured out by now, given the frantic squirming and the whining.

Jim ignored him before pulling the black bag out. He held it up in front of him.

Wide eyes and a head shaking no wasn't able to overcome the panic descending.

He yanked the bag down to cover Terry's head.

If Terry didn't know before, he knew for sure now. It took a few desultory shakes of his head before he seemed resigned that something bad was about to happen.

Jim went for a towel and wrestled with the chair to place it under the back legs. He pulled both chair and attached man across the floor into the bathroom.

He left Terry alone in the bathroom to

contemplate life and went to check the small kitchen for evidence left behind.

There was one text on a phone that wasn't his.

they're here

There was no reply.

CHAPTER 19

Bobbie couldn't find Jim. Knowing him as she did, she figured he skipped out on the family stuff with Terry's help and headed to his room over the garage.

She walked in through the upstairs door. The place was empty but for water running in the bathroom. She knocked, hard, and called out, already anticipating the answer.

"You want some company in there? I could use a shower, too."

Jim called through the door. "You told me you were holding out, remember?"

"Funny man," she said.

Was he trying to get rid of her? She grinned like the devil and twisted the doorknob. For only a split second, she thought she might be pushing it with the friendly banter.

Then the door opened. Her smile froze. Her eyes went wide as saucers. She leaned back against the door. It closed, and instantly she became trapped in the tiny room.

"What the hell are you doing?" She almost screamed.

Terry struggled against the tape holding him in the chair, twisting and turning, fingers wriggling. A wet black hood covered his head. His head tossed from side to side. He struggled to breathe. Gasped. Panted. Every hungry breath sucked the bag into his wide open, greedy mouth. Every desperate exhale forced the bag off his face until the next panicked breath.

She was just as panicked.

Who in his right mind travels with a black hood? That's the first thing that occurred to her. She didn't think it safe to ask out loud. Jim was too busy.

He checked the drawstring and tipped the chair back. He released it to balance perfectly against the edge of the tub.

Terry's hood-covered head flopped backwards under the shower's running water. He struggled, shaking his head from side to side, desperate to take in air. Water soaked past the hood.

"What the hell? Jim?" She couldn't believe what she was seeing.

"He's tattling on us. Look at the phone in the kitchen. Turn it off when you're done."

She returned with the flip-phone in hand.

"There's no way to tell who he's calling, but I've got a pretty good idea," Jim said.

She flipped it open. She didn't say anything. How could she?

"Stop. You'll kill him."

Terry recognized her voice. He shook his head in a useless attempt to escape the water. His feet twitched. He strained to sit up in the chair.

All this while Jim shook his head and mouthed

one word.

No.

The chair tipped forward and thumped onto all four legs.

Terry sputtered and sobbed. His relief was short lived. Uncontrollable tremors took over his body.

She could sympathize. Hers had done the same thing when she took over driving duties to allow Jim to ride shotgun. At the time she wasn't being waterboarded.

"Are you going to get anything useful? Or are you only making him pay for some unconfessed sin?"

She remembered reading somewhere that torture rarely, if ever, worked. She decided not to press it with Jim. Now didn't seem like the right time.

"He's an amateur. He'll talk. He already believes he's going to drown." Jim tipped the chair back.

Terry's hood-covered head tipped beneath the running water. He sputtered and strained against his bindings.

"You didn't ask him anything," she said.

He looked at her like she was crazy, yet he was the one waterboarding her neighbor with the hood over his head.

"Of course not. I'm only making sure he's warmed up first. You should get back downstairs before someone comes looking."

Horrified, Bobbie opened the door in the cramped bathroom. She backed out and slammed the door.

She stopped to inhale half a dozen times. It was a challenge to work up enough nerve to pretend to chat amiably with mom and dad while a man upstairs tortured her neighbor.

Maybe Jim was right. Maybe he would learn something they could use to find her brother. And then there was that phone number.

She recognized it, all right.

It belonged to the man on the yacht. Kennedy. The man who blackened her eye. He had programmed the same number into the burn phone she had carried until Jim tossed it. Would she be forced to come clean with Jim?

Or was it already too late?

It took more time than Jim wanted, but Bobbie finally calmed down to where he could talk to her.

She listened as he tried to convince her to hustle Terry across the street. He gave her instructions to talk him into leaving town. The faster, the better.

"It'll give me some alone time with your folks, too."

A panicked look appeared on her face.

It confused him. He couldn't tell if it was because of what he'd done to Terry, or because he'd be spending alone time with mom and dad.

"It'll give me a chance to convince them I'm not too old for you," he added.

It would give Bobbie a reason to hurry back across the street after convincing Terry to hit the road if he didn't want more of the same.

Bobbie's folks looked to be in their early sixties—too old to be involved in the drug trade as far as

Jim was concerned. They knew nothing about their inadvertent involvement with their son. If Ray got caught, by the Feds or by the cartel, they'd be in deep shit. No amount of paddling would be capable of getting them ashore.

Bobbie returned from across the street and gave him the nod. It wasn't soon enough as far as he was concerned—and he wasn't talking about her nod.

She took one look at his situation with mom and dad, grinned, and knew right off he was a nervous wreck.

It didn't have anything to do with Terry. It was about dealing with her mother and father and fielding what seemed like a hundred questions launched at him in scattergun fashion.

He wasn't accustomed to family dynamics. In fact, he was a real dope as far as they went.

It was a welcome relief to have the woman back.

She drew him aside, and he lowered his voice. "Did you do what I asked? Did you dump him across the street? Can you get me out of here?"

He was exhausted from the grilling.

Bobbie only kept on grinning.

"As we speak, he's packing a bag. I suggested it might be a good idea if he left town for a while."

"Good. I wouldn't feel comfortable with him around here after we leave," he said.

"He'll be fine. I turned on his phone and parked it beneath the back seat of his car. He should have a nice trip."

And he would. Until the cartel got on his ass with tracking software and figured out he was on the run. Then? Who knows? Problem solved.

"All right. You did good."

Good? Hell, so far, she was spot on, and thorough, too. He wouldn't have known to do the phone thing even if he'd thought of it. Having our spy traveling on down the road and away from them was a bonus. He'd pat her on the back for it later.

Bobbie was good at explaining to her folks that she had to leave. She hugged and kissed and cried and generally made mom and dad feel as though she'd been there a week and didn't want to leave again.

Even he believed her.

She dragged herself out to the car.

He didn't ask. He had to admit, he was worried, too.

"That was tough."

"Yeah. I noticed. You did good with your neighbor. I half expected you to start screaming at me upstairs when we were in the bathroom." And he had, too.

"I know. I'm sorry. It took a while to process everything. When I finally realized we were into it, it helped a lot," she said. "I'm still processing, Jim. It's difficult. It's my brother."

He sent her back inside to be alone with her parents. She had some convincing to do if they could be talked into leaving town until they got Ray back. He figured she could handle it on her own without having him around to complicate the discussion.

He used the time to drive solo to the bar on 14th. On the lookout for the man he recognized earlier, he had plenty of questions for him. Who did he work for? Had Kara been his boss, or was she only a drone? And who gave the order for her to be killed?

So far, he hadn't gotten to the part where he'd be dealing with what happened to Pilar, his actual wife.

Christ but it would never end for him. He couldn't even keep thoughts of Kara out of it though he'd promised himself he'd forget about her.

Perhaps Bobbie's problem with her brother was a part of it. Just maybe, two sets of problems could become one. He wasn't holding his breath.

Bobbie proved herself more than capable of handling the details.

If he could accept the woman as being on his side, perhaps they'd be able to accomplish more together.

CHAPTER 20

Bobbie Dawson gave herself a pat on the back for thinking to conceal neighbor Terry's cellphone in his car. If anyone was searching—and after listening to Jim's explanation, they would be—cartel henchmen would be on him in no time.

That accounted for the huge farewell wave and the giant smile she gave the man as he pulled out of his driveway.

Convinced by Jim that Terry was with the bad guys, Bobbie was happy. He'd been chased away from the neighborhood and sent packing, far from her parents. Possibly he'd be seen by the cartel as a coward on the run.

She almost danced across the street, just as she had danced down the dock to the mainland only days earlier in Diamondhead.

Except now, she had to accept whatever she was into. What she and Jim were into. It couldn't be good.

It took Jim a while, but he admitted she had done all right. She didn't think he had a hard time admitting it. It appeared as though he realized he wasn't alone. Whether he liked to admit that—

She hoped this man knew she could help with his problem as he had helped with mine. Exactly what his problem was, she had yet to learn. As for circumstances concerning her brother, she was no farther ahead. She suspected that it more than likely wasn't going to be pretty.

She joined Jim at the car. "Where are we headed?"

"We're going back to the bar. I need to take another look. And the safe house where my ex was taken is just around the corner."

She opened the door to get in.

"You can't, Bobbie. You have to convince your folks to get out of town until we find Ray."

She wanted to ask Jim what happened to him that hurt so much it. Who was she? Ex-wife? Ex-girlfriend? Where was she?

She decided to wait him out. He was doing the same. Maybe they were in standoff territory. Maybe they weren't.

Just the same, she'd thank him when the time was right, even if she was no closer to finding Ray.

In record time she convinced her mother and father of the folly of staying home when Ray hadn't been found. Mom took it in stride when she explained about his drug dealings. She got it about having the house under threat.

Dad, not so much. He wanted to keep believing his son could do no wrong.

It finally took mom dragging him out of the house after she'd packed a couple of bags.

Even then, her dad was reluctant to leave.

Jim checked the text that pinged his phone. Bobbie was ready, having convinced her parents to get out of Dodge. He picked up sandwiches and coffee before doubling back. He guessed her folks hadn't been so difficult to convince after all.

"Are we going to be camping out?" she asked, after spying the sandwiches.

"It's a diet change with sandwiches. Prepare yourself for a day of boredom. There's two of us. We'll take turns sleeping and dozing and sweating and cursing each other after a couple of hours. If no nosy neighbors come out to ask questions, it will be a bonus."

"Whatever you say."

"It's a stakeout," he explained. "It is what it is."

He drove them to the first house and positioned the car with sightliness that would allow a clear view.

In half an hour, Bobbie's head was back against the seat and she was quietly snoring. He let her be. In another couple of hours, he'd be doing the same. The nice thing about having her along would be letting her take her turn to try and keep awake while he counted sheep.

Or maybe cartel coca.

Jim's head banged against the window. He came to with a start. His eyes opened on the empty seat beside him.

Shit.

Where had that woman gotten to? His hand was set to pull on the door handle when Bobbie showed up and climbed in.

He sent a fierce look her way.

She looked back entirely too pleased with herself.

He was so angry he was forced to wait before saying something he'd regret.

"Yeah. I know. I couldn't help it. I had to pee. I took a leisurely stroll and circled back along the alley behind the house. There's a garage. I looked through a window. It looks like my brother's beater is in it."

Jim's face softened listening to her explanation. Dismay at her disappearance turned to admiration for her initiative. "Are you sure?"

"Pretty much. The window doesn't let in much light, but it sure looks like it."

He started the car and drove down the street, searching for a new location for their stakeout. He pulled into a spot shaded by a tree. It would keep them out of the noonday sun.

"Did anyone go into the house?"

Bobbie shook her head.

"We should check it out," he said.

Jim walked around back and tried the door. It opened almost too easily. The entire scene was a puzzle. Something wasn't right. Why would a car belonging to a drug smuggler be stashed out back of a safe house? It made little sense. Unless—

The safe house was no longer so safe. More likely, it had been dropped from the list. It was used for something more sinister. Empty, it could be used for storing drugs. Or cash. Perhaps both.

He sniffed the air. There was no lingering smell

he could discern.

They made our way to the beat-up garage. He looked through the filthy window into the dark interior.

"Are you sure it's your brother's car?"

The light in the garage wasn't so good. It could be anybody's car, as far as he was concerned.

CHAPTER 21

"Yes. I'm sure. It's Ray's car. How many times do I have to tell you?"

Jim considered for a moment. "Come on. There's something we need to do."

He took them back to their car and positioned it in the alley next to the garage. He looked across at Bobbie. "Go get your brother's car."

She looked at him like he was crazy. "I don't have the keys."

"They're in the ignition. Do I have to do everything?"

It was a long shot. But if he guessed right, they'd be on easy street.

Bobbie punched him in the shoulder. Hard. "You've got a brother, all right. I'm thinking you gave as good as you got."

She grinned.

He rubbed his shoulder.

"Maybe I'll console you later if it hurt that much. With ice, even."

"Promises. And one more thing—"

Bobbie raised an eyebrow and waited.

"If the keys aren't in the ignition, check the sunshade. Don't forget the ashtray, either. Look beneath the floor mats on the driver's side."

"I thought you said—"

He got a dirty look for his trouble.

Bobbie jumped out of our car, scrambled for the garage door, slid it open, and climbed into Ray's car.

In less time than it took to unload their luggage, Bobbie started the engine and reversed out of the garage.

"Where did you find them?"

She ignored him.

He backfilled with their car and forced the door closed over the uneven ground.

She loaded the bags into the trunk of her brother's wreck and slammed it shut.

"Now what?"

"Our bags are packed. Let's make for Mexico," he said.

"What about—"

He already knew she wanted to ask about the handgun. He didn't give her the chance. "Did you bring your bikini?"

"As if." She handed him another dirty look.

He pulled Ray's car to the side of the road and popped the trunk. He put the pistol beneath the spare tire while Bobbie rummaged through her bag.

She got back in the front with her top and some concealer.

How could he not look? Hell, he stared, open-mouthed, as she pulled off her shirt and began spreading concealer over her bruised breast. She made it even more difficult when she arched her back to don the bikini top. She caught him out in the mirror. "You want to pull over and help? You know you do."

Jim grinned evilly. "Why would I? I've seen it all before."

He should have known better. He rubbed at his shoulder even longer this time. There'd be another bruise for his troubles. Damn but the woman could throw a punch.

"What are you doing? You're not really pulling over."

He was in the middle of a U-turn, heading back to the alley and the garage. "Did you look beneath those blue tarps? What's under them?"

"I didn't even think about it. I was in too much of a hurry," she said.

He stopped at the garage entrance. It was an older wooden building. The door swung open on rusty hinges. The floor was dirt. The tiny window hadn't been cleaned since it was built. The walls were bare. The dim light revealed nothing but their car.

He lifted the corner of a tarp for a quick look and hurried back to Bobbie. "Got a match?"

"Not since I met you," she joked. "Why?"

"Funny. Push the lighter in, would you?"

"The lighter? What are you talking about?"

"For crying out loud. How old are you again? Push in the thing sticking out from the power outlet. When it pops out, hand it to me. Carefully."

She sniffed. "You reek of gasoline. What did you do?"

"Wait and see, kiddo. Wait and see," he said.

"Don't call me kiddo."

He caught a whiff of more fumes. The tiny hole he managed to inflict on the rental's plastic gas tank was doing a yeoman's job of spilling fuel inside the small building.

The cigarette lighter clicked out of the holder. Bobbie handed it to him.

He tossed it beneath the car and separated himself from the conflagration as fast as he could. On the way he caught Bobbie's arm and dragged her out, too.

The garage went up with a loud whump and orange flames. The door flew open and then banged shut as air rushed in to feed the flames.

They watched from inside her brother's car until the heat became too much. Growing orange flames and screaming sirens finally chased them away.

He eased the car out of the alley and turned onto 14th.

Jim felt compelled to give Bobbie a pat on the back. Even if she broke the rules. "You did good when you abandoned the stakeout and took a walk. I would never have thought of doing that."

In fact, it was a no-no he learned the hard way a long time ago.

"Maybe, but I got lucky. Who would have known my brother's car would be there?"

The house didn't appear to be lived in. Bobbie was right. He would never have thought a car would be stored in a garage at a safe house. Someone must have figured it would be a good place for it.

"We need to take a better look at your brother's junker.

He parked by the side of the road and did a walk-around. The plates were Mexican. Tamaulipas State. Just across the border. "Any reason he'd put those plates on this thing?"

He popped the trunk and shifted their bags. He came up with Texas plates tucked under a rag. "Well, that explains things a bit more."

It couldn't be that simple. Surely the border checks would catch a car and driver swapping out plates. Unless.

Unless the fix was in.

That would mean crossing at times of the day when certain guards were on duty.

Shit.

"Roberta. Are any of your brother's friends border guards?"

"A couple. Why?"

He walked her through what he was thinking. The brother driving north, returning from a night of partying. A Mexican national to drive the car back with Mexican plates in place.

She refused to consider any of it.

"His friends were like brothers to mom and dad. To all of us. They came to our place to eat and sleep over and mom treated them like they were her own. There's no way. No way in hell."

"Are you sure? Remember what was going on with Terry. He was on the lookout, photographing everyone coming and going from across the street and sending the images to his cartel friends. He even sent a text when you arrived with me in tow."

Bobbie turned away to avoid his gaze.

Why was this woman still in denial? He made sure

to show her the text on Terry's phone right after he discovered it. How long would it take her to wake up?

What else was going on that he didn't know about?

He was starting to think Bobbie was working at cross-purposes with him. Sure, she said she'd come along for the ride once they located her brother. She was all smiles and yapping a mile a minute when things were going her way.

The instant he came up with something obvious, she shut him down and refused to believe him. The text had been obvious. She knew that number. He could tell by the way she avoided looking at him.

He needed to keep his eyes open with this one, or he might end up desaparecido in Mexico.

CHAPTER 22

Surely her own brother wouldn't be dumb enough to collude with friends to transport drugs across the river. It wasn't unheard of, of course. Were his friends in on the deal? And if it was true, no one had been caught. Wouldn't she have heard about it if they had? Jim had to be wrong. He had to be.

Except—

Somehow, the cartel found her. On pain of death, they forced her to find her brother, or else. So she went along. And ended up beaten and bruised for her trouble.

Sure, maybe she'd brought that on herself. She wasn't exactly enamored of Kennedy on the yacht. He was an asshole. And she wouldn't sleep with him.

And then she met Jim. He seemed to be a nice guy. One of the good ones. But there was something. She couldn't put a finger on it right this minute. Possibly he was on the lookout, too. For what, she didn't yet know. But she'd find out. If curiosity didn't kill the cat.

So she asked.

"Are you ever going to tell me what your deal is

down here? It can't be to help out a hitch-hiker because she invited you into her bed." It wasn't the first time he looked at her like she was nuts.

"Are you sure you want to know?"

Bobbie waited, afraid he might turn away from her yet again.

He pursed his lips and shook his head as though resolved and yet fearful.

"I'm an ex-cop. I picked up some contract government work to help pay the bills after I decided I didn't want to be a big-city cop."

He hesitated, probably wondering how much he should reveal. Maybe wondering if she could be trusted.

"I got tangled up in this one deal. Fell in love with the agent. Got tasked to do a couple more assignments with her, probably because I was led to believe she loved me."

A fairy tale love story. This was starting to get interesting. She waited for him to go on.

"We got married in Todos."

The way he said it sounded Mexican.

"Todos?" she asked.

"Todos Santos. On the Baja. She told me she was pregnant. Our boat exploded. She was killed. So was our baby."

Wait. What?

His pregnant wife was killed? He's a sailor? He owned a boat. That exploded?

Where the hell was he and what was he doing when that was going on?

She feared if she interrupted, he'd stop. She'd never get him to talk about it again.

"I went ashore offering a mordida—a bribe—to buy a berth in the harbor. I stopped to pick up food and was headed back when our boat disintegrated in front of me. Everything I thought I knew and believed in was taken away in an instant."

The man wouldn't stop. He just kept on going, like a windup toy that had been converted to batteries. Perhaps she should have stopped him. She couldn't.

"I stayed drunk for months. And searched. And went broke. I finally gave up. It took years to get over it. I remarried. To a wonderful woman. She was pregnant when the plane she was on exploded in mid-air."

Holy shit. And she thought she had problems.

"The federal investigators found explosive residue in Pilar's luggage. They were convinced she was a bomber on a mission. There was a problem with that. It was a small plane. A charter. Not an airliner."

Wide-eyed, she kept staring at him, wanting him to go on. Afraid that he would.

"The investigation ended with no resolution that would ever satisfy me. It only made me angrier."

She couldn't look at him any longer. Then, like passing a car wreck on the highway, she turned back. Not to look, but to listen.

"I'm going to find the sons of bitches and kill every last living one of them. Then I'm going to kill their families. And their dogs. And burn down their homes. I'll poison their cropland and kill their livestock, if they have any."

Bobbie's eyes filled with tears.

"All of them."

He halted, finally.

Sobs that wouldn't stop wracked her body. She swiped at her face with the back of a hand and sniffled like a kid.

"Maybe we can get going on finding my brother."

Had she just said that? It had to sound ridiculous. She had no experience with any of it. "The sooner we're done with that, the sooner we can get to tracking down the killers you're looking for."

She looked at him. Still not believing. Wondering if or how she could help. If he'd let her. Wanting to believe.

"You're sweet, Roberta. But I think what I have to do is beyond your pay grade. Do you have any sisters?"

What? Sisters?

"No. Why?"

What the hell?

"Just wondering. I'll let you know."

He'll let her know? He just spilled his guts. Two women he once loved were dead. Now he wants to know if she had a sister?

Damn but this man was frustrating to the nth degree.

Jim had no idea didn't know why he was in such a hurry to tell Bobbie about his predicament. Perhaps he thought it would scare her off. Finding her brother and discovering his links to the local cartel might speed up his quest. If he had to have her around, it would be because she could be a means to his own ends.

It occurred to him the delay her missing brother would cause could turn out to be a lot longer than he figured on. His was more than a simple missing person case. While he was parading back and forth across the border in a car set up to smuggle drugs, he was out looking for him.

Had Bobbie thought to stake out the border as a part of her own deal?

So be it.

He shut out his problems and began an attempt at looking at hers from a new angle. The trouble was, he liked her.

Perhaps a little too much.

"Have you got a plan?" He dropped the question on her like he knew what he was asking.

Hell, even he didn't have a plan.

"I was hoping you might have one."

Just as he thought.

"We've got a car all set up to smuggle. What do you say we do some smuggling?"

Bobbie grinned. She hitched her thumbs through her belt loops and flapped her elbows. "If I didn't know better, I'd say that kinda sounds like you want to do dirty things. With me, maybe?"

Hell, yeah.

What he wanted to do with her didn't involve smuggling.

He couldn't help smiling. "We don't have time. Maybe later."

Promises. He'd been good at making promises with Allie. Now he was unhappy to be on the other end.

"Come on, Roberta. It's time."

They climbed into the beater and headed toward the river.

"Wait a minute." He pulled the car over. "There's something I think we should try."

It was something simple. Something they should have tried when she told him who her brother's friends were.

"You want me to take my top off again?" she asked.

Jim ignored the woman's grin.

"What if we left this wreck near the border station parking lot? In plain sight where those two have to walk past to get to work. Or off shift."

Maybe they could scare up some action. Put the fear of being outed into them. Perhaps it would force them to make a mistake.

"What do we have to lose? Let's do it," she said.

The lot would be full of cameras. What border lot wasn't these days?

He stopped for ball caps and dark glasses and hoodies. Gangsta style. It might look suspicious, but if they got away with it, no one would find them through facial recognition.

"Check the parked cars. We need something to sit in while we keep an eye open."

He drove up and down row after row of cars baking in the heat.

Bobbie pointed out a space close to the walkway. Coming or going, they'd have to walk right past it.

"That was too easy. All we have to do is watch. And no sneaking off when I fall asleep."

"You keeping late hours I don't know about?" I asked.

"Not since you won't share a bed with me. I've taken to sleeping with you in public on our stakeouts."

She grinned and I smiled.

"I'll see what I can do," she said.

He left it alone. "Will you be able to recognize these guys? It's been a while."

"No problem. I'll wake you gently."

He parked Ray's car in plain view close to the lot entrance. They left it and strolled nonchalantly toward the watch car.

Waves of heat reflected off the dark asphalt.

Unable to power down the windows, they cracked the doors and left them open.

With nothing else to do, Jim slipped the seat back and settled in down low.

He dropped the sun visor and pulled the cap down over his eyes.

An over-excited elbow dug a fresh hole in his side. His head snapped up. So much for being gentle.

"Stay down, Jim. They're fifty or sixty feet away. Pretending to talk. But they've been giving Ray's car the stink-eye."

"You sure it's them?" he asked.

Being on the receiving end of a dirty look from Bobbie wasn't high on his list of favorites.

"Of course I'm sure. I've known those two all my life. Now what?"

"We wait. Just to see what they do. If they do anything. I don't think they'll do it here, but you never know."

The two friends continued standing around, hands in pockets. Heads turned nonchalantly, searching. They looked like a couple of guys just off shift trying to decide whether to stop on the way home for a beer.

They strolled closer to the car for a better look. One checked the plate and nodded. They weren't trying to hide their curiosity any longer.

What he didn't want was for them to call in reinforcements and seize the wreck. "They know it's the one."

They continued toward the lot, not looking back. "Now we know they're involved up to their eyeballs. We got lucky, Bobbie."

What do they do about it? They didn't have time to figure it out. They parted company suddenly. One headed in their direction, double-timing it all the way.

Bobbie jumped out of the car and ran toward him. Bobbie's shouting moved on to shoving. She yelled loud enough to wake the dead and he thought world war three was about to unfold.

Using the diversion, he crawled out of the car on hands and knees. He made his way back a couple of cars and sat on the curb while he waited for Bobbie to calm down.

She walked calmly past the drug car to meet up with him. "Well?"

"He denied everything. He's not happy about it, though. I'm pretty sure he wanted to take me in. The only thing stopping him was fear of being discovered if I talked. He'd better know that I'd talk."

"You did a job convincing him from what I could

see. What do you want to do now?"

"We'll wait. When has anyone with a job like his hesitated to get in touch with their guilty friends? Especially when they're all crooked."

Bobbie was right. Eventually, they moved off the lot like they owned the place.

He wanted a place to stay, to use as their base. He wanted to figure out which way they'd be headed. It didn't help that he had no clue. His problem would be on the back burner for now.

It was obvious Ray's two friends were involved up to their ears. Now that he had something to work with, he'd help Bobbie find her brother.

When she was satisfied, it would be his turn to make a move.

He'd solve the problem he'd set out to solve before he picked Bobbie up at the gas station.

Come hell or high water.

CHAPTER 23

Bobbie was clueless. She was feeling pretty good about it, though. Or maybe she was being delusional. Sure, she knew Jim had it all figured out. Maybe she'd been reluctant to disclose everything she knew. But the more time she spent with him, the more she believed in him. He was competent. He knew things. Sure, he was older. But that didn't detract from any of it.

And he still needed a shave. She'd forgotten about that.

She was a neophyte. At all of it. Except the falling in love part. How can someone end up with feelings so intense about someone after only a few days? What was going on in her life that she had allowed these feelings to develop virtually overnight?

And how was she going to tell Jim the truth about what was going on in her life?

"Jim?" She scraped her fingers along the line of his jaw. "You need a shave."

He gave her the look that said it wasn't the most important thing in his life.

She gave him one right back that said I love you

and left it unspoken.

He ignored her, as usual.

But that was all right.

She was getting accustomed to it.

But that would have to change—Jim's ignoring her, that is—or else.

Bobbie would not be satisfied until he put her hands on her brother, and he couldn't blame her. Just knowing two of his friends, both border guards, could be a part of the problem wouldn't help. She needed a lot more.

"We need to regroup."

He turned the car around and headed back to 14th. "We need a base. Know any decent motels?"

She ignored him. As usual.

"We have a perfectly good place to stay. I used to live there, remember? It's called home. Why do we need a seedy motel room? Are you still traveling on a budget?"

Bobbie wiggled a hand into a pocket and ended up fishing a handful of cash out of it. She counted up to five hundred and halted. She waved it at him. "It's courtesy of my yachting friend. Kennedy. The one who beat me up."

Jim didn't know if the woman was trying to convince him they were broke, or if she was going to volunteer to buy them a room for the night.

"Stop and think about it for just a minute, okay?"

But he didn't let her. "You want to take us back to your home. Where there was a lookout across the street. What if he's been replaced? What's the plan then?"

She tucked the wad of cash back in her pocket and grabbed at her flying hair.

"Christ. Can we get something with air next time? I don't know, Nash. I'm trying. I really am. I'm new to all of this. In case you haven't noticed."

Jim said, "Look. We need to stop and regroup. We're already steps ahead of where we were yesterday. That has to be obvious. We know Ray is hooked up with those two. The way they checked out the car made it plain."

"You're right. I know. But—"

"We need to catch our breath and work on a strategy to hook up with them. They have to know where Ray is. Otherwise, why the concern about the car?"

He passed a motel and turned around. "You want your own room?"

"I feel safe with you. Is that all right?"

Jim wondered how long it would take to change her mind?

He signed up for the room with the biggest bed.

Bobbie made for the shower.

He stripped the automatic and made sure the magazines were properly loaded. An obsession with things like that paid for itself more than a few times in his past.

He felt Bobbie's presence over his shoulder. Her warmth from the hot shower. The slight scent of perfume.

"I like that on you. It's nice. So is the perfume."

He turned.

Her robe opened. Inviting.

Her eyes sparkled.

Long, damp hair was combed close.

Lip gloss. She had put on lip gloss. Damned if she wasn't one of those women who only needed a bit of lip gloss to look like a million bucks.

A hand reached to caress his chin.

"About that shave—" She kissed him.

He kissed back.

He stood up.

She wrapped her legs around him.

He left her and headed for the shower.

She joined him and then hurried out before he had a chance to encourage more.

By the time he dried off, Bobbie had slipped into a brightly colored skirt and sandals.

Damn but the woman looked good with her clothes on, too.

"What are you looking at, mister?"

Bobbie did a twirl.

The loose, filmy skirt flared and exposed just enough thigh to get him interested all over again.

"Not a chance. I can tell by the look on your face. I didn't put this on just to take it off right away. We're going out. And you're buying."

"You're the one with all the cash in your pocket, woman."

"Maybe. But it's the reserve fund. I reserve it for the men I care about."

"So then—" he began.

"I'm not talking. Change the subject if you know

what's good for you," she said.

Bobbie led them up the street to a honky-tonk place she knew.

She led him through a parking lot populated by half-tons and into a place with too many long bars, plenty of men for too few women, and a huge dance floor filled with sweaty people in a row. They were all kicking up their feet.

More than a few seemed to know her.

She answered plenty of questions about her brother and his whereabouts.

She was careful to avoid the obvious and told everyone who asked he was off traveling.

Judging by the questions, she didn't need to explain that Ray was a popular one with the ladies.

Bobbie caught up on the local gossip and traded stories about some of her friends.

He went with it and let her have her evening.

Too many drinks turned into more of the same.

When they called it quits, they ended up strolling arm in arm back to the motel.

She rested her head on his shoulder the entire way.

His senses filled to overflowing with this woman.

The way her hair and other parts swayed when she walked.

The slightest wisp of perfume.

The way she held his hand and bumped against him, hip to hip.

The rhythm and flow of footsteps that matched his.

They stopped to kiss, and stopped again.

The motel loomed.

He picked her up and carried her to the door.

Bobbie fished for the key card in her bag.

"Be careful. This could turn into habit," he said.

He thought they were headed for bed. Big mistake.

Bobbie walked out of the bathroom and headed for the door.

He hesitated for a second before wising up.

He followed her into the motel parking lot.

CHAPTER 24

Bobbie convinced Jim to accompany her to a second road house a couple of blocks distant. He lagged behind and he knew what he was doing, because she'd stayed in the bathroom to dress, surprising him with the skirt and blouse.

She already knew she looked good. Maybe too good. She knew she was in trouble, too.

Did Jim know?

"Is there some reason you're bringing up the rear, mister? This is Texas. A girl expects her man to keep up, or else. In fact, I insist on it."

She twirled for him and kept going.

He gave her a smack that had her rubbing her rear all the way to the traffic light.

"You know you're not going to get to see that, right? You're cut off."

The hang-dog look didn't do any good, and she made sure he knew it. She smiled angelically all the way into the copy-cat bar, almost indistinguishable from the one they were in earlier.

Back when her friends all hung out, they would traipse back and forth. She expected it was no different now.

She drew the attention of a good number of singles and a few not so single.

Jim noticed, too.

She grabbed his hand and hung on.

"You must be used to it by now."

He didn't seem to be the jealous type.

"No. Not really. In a place like this, I want them to know I'm yours."

"So then, I'm not cut off?"

"We'll see." Which was as good an answer as he had forthcoming for the rest of the evening.

Keep 'em wondering, she always said, and not out loud.

Bobbie showed her heavy-footed, clumsy oaf of a boyfriend a Texas two-step and they laughed and hugged and slow danced and had a great time. She liked slow dancing best of all.

Jim said he was scared of hurting her if he hugged too close and tight.

She said she'd let him know.

He hugged some more, and she kept quiet. She permitted him to keep their sweaty bodies close. She figured he couldn't see her wincing with her head on his shoulder. It gave her a chance to wonder what she was up to with the boyfriend part of the night.

Browntown being what it was, she ran into more friends from the old days. They wondered, and she tried to explain over the music and the dancing. She ended up inviting them to join Jim at their stand-up table.

Conversation, dancing, and beer flowed into the wee hours as they caught up on old times. Jim left for a bathroom break.

The rest of them scurried outside to cool off and trade stories without a man around.

Jim was zipping up over the porcelain when a server banged on the door and barged in.

"Your women are being hassled out in the parking lot."

"My women? What?"

"The women you were with. You better get your ass out there in a hurry. It looks like some locals are taking exception to you having three all to yourself."

It couldn't be. We had walked from the hotel.

He left the washroom and made for the table. The top was covered with empty glasses. The women were nowhere in sight.

He took the server at her word and scrambled to dodge bodies on the crowded dance floor on the way to the door and the parking lot.

A jumble of jacked-up half-tons blocked his view. Howling pipes and clouds of rubber from burnouts made sure the women would never hear him. He couldn't figure where they could have gotten to in the huge lot.

Out of the corner of his eye ,he caught a flash of reflected light. He went to investigate.

A chrome short-barreled handgun accompanied one of the women at our table.

She had it aimed at the backs of two men.

They stood with arms outstretched and hands planted firmly against the wall.

The handgun turned into a chrome short-barreled .45 revolver. He recognized it when he got closer. It had to look even bigger than that to the two good old boys it was leveled at.

One of them moved an outstretched arm.

"Move again and it'll be your last, asshole."

The high-pitched voice from the short woman he had just met and knew as Sally drew about every eye within hearing range.

Sally's hand went over her head in the direction of the night sky. A thunderclap sounded as the .45 echoed off the stucco-covered wall.

Sally definitely had everyone's attention.

The two men were all about hugging a wall and they didn't seem so happy to be there. Worse, their friends were giving them more than a little grief in loud voices that spread over the lot.

Jim used the break in the action to try and smooth it over.

"All right, ladies. The getting looks to be good. What do you say we all high-tail it out of here before john law shows up?"

No bigger than a minute, tiny little Sally looked in his direction. He hoped she wasn't so drunk she didn't recognize him.

"You're right, Jim. My car is this way."

He thanked his lucky stars and grabbed Bobbie's hand.

Sally held out her own after tucking the pistol into her purse.

"You want to take mine too, Jim?" Sally asked.

Sally grabbed onto him and Bobbie gave him the look.

Together they stumbled their way to an

immaculately restored, bright-orange Judge.

He pulled at the seatback to let Bobbie into the back. Before the door closed, Sally stomped on the pedal and the car guzzled gas and laid rubber all the way out of the parking lot.

She spotted him looking over her prized possession's interior.

"You like it?"

"Nice car. Who did the work?"

"I did. All by my lonesome. If you weren't attached, I'd let you drive it sometimes."

He about had the hugest grin ever. For a minute, he thought he should open his mouth and firmly insert his foot.

Then Bobbie looked over and caught him out. From the back, seat she jabbed fingers into his ribs. Hard.

"Just like old times. He's taken, Sally. Take us back to the motel. By the look of it, he needs to know he's taken."

"Well, well, stranger. Your girl hasn't changed in the slightest."

Jim's grin went even bigger at the prospect.

Sally dropped them at the motel. Bobbie's grip on his hand wasn't about letting go until she dragged him into the room and far away from her friend.

"The couple that goes together, and leaves together, stays together. Is that what you're trying to tell me?" he asked.

"Something like that."

Bobbie shimmied out of the important stuff in plain view.

"Good to know."

144

CHAPTER 25

Jim Nash woke with a start and focused on the flashing digits in a dark room.

He reached behind and slipped a hand beneath the sheets, searching.

Bobbie's side of the bed was stone cold.

"Bobbie?"

No answer.

Where had that woman gotten to this time?

He gave up and dozed off, alone and warm beneath the sheets. Content knowing that she disappeared for more ice.

He didn't give it another thought.

Through the open window a blood-curdling scream assaulted his ears.

He sat bolt-upright.

He kicked off the sheets and scrambled to find his pants in the pitch-black room.

He tugged on a shirt and found his knife.

He kicked at the screen and put a leg through the first-floor window.

Barefoot, he stepped out onto cool, damp grass.

The power had to be out. There were no lights

anywhere.

He made his way cautiously to where he remembered the ice machine was between buildings.

Heavy boots scratched on gravel and pavement.

He followed the sound and ended up peering around the corner into a darkened alley between the two buildings.

A trouble light flicked on.

The feeble glow was enough to illuminate the man bent over Bobbie's back. His weight forced her over the ice machine.

She struggled to escape the grip of a second man grabbing at her wrists.

She got one free and slapped and scratched until her arms ended up completely subdued.

The man behind her pulled at her pants and forced them down.

The second man covered her mouth and pushed her face against the wall.

Bobbie's head twisted and turned beneath his grip as she struggled to call out.

A loud grunt escaped as Bobbie bit into a hand.

A fist came up and smashed into the back of her head.

She banged against the cooler, collapsed, and went limp and silent.

The battery-powered trouble light flickered and died in the same instant.

The knife slipped out of its sheath. It fit his hand perfectly.

In half a dozen barefoot silent steps he was at the assailant's back.

He smashed him in the head with the butt of the knife.

He didn't go down.

He didn't let go, either.

For good measure he gave him a solid blow to the temple and he thumped onto the asphalt.

His partner didn't notice the commotion. He was too engaged in trying to drag Bobbie's underwear below her knees.

He realized he had company. He released Bobbie and turned his attention to Jim.

It was too late.

Bobbie slipped from his grip and planted herself on the ground.

Jim twisted and drew back and then extended the arm holding the blade.

It plunged into the man's side.

Somehow, he managed to hold off thrusting it all the way to the hilt.

A groan, and then another and the rapist collapsed beside his partner.

Two heel kicks to two heads for spite and it was over.

He pulled Bobbie up and surrounded her in his arms.

"Come on, sunshine. It's time for bed. The next time you want to go for a walk in the middle of the night, wake me first. I'll write you a note, okay?"

She didn't see the humor.

"Not in your lifetime."

"Of course not. And look where it got you. If I hadn't heard—"

"You don't seem to appreciate my methods. I

had everything under control. I was biding my time to make my move."

"So that's why you're leaning on me shaking so bad you can barely stand on your own?" he said.

"Pretty much. Can you help me back to the room?"

The trouble light flicked on for an instant, illuminating a faint smile.

He shook his head, figuring that was all the surrender he'd get. HIs arm circled her waist.

At the door, Bobbie halted, waiting.

Women. A man can't live without them.

He picked her up and carried her through the door.

"Are you going to call an ambulance?" she asked.

"Why? He only got your underwear to your knees. Are you trying to tell me he got to home base?"

"You knifed him."

"Nah. I only stuck it in part way. And you seem to be doing all right. No sense circling the wagons for anyone to spot."

"You're a good man. Now set me down. I need to shower."

He went back to bed.

When he woke up, Bobbie was beside him, clinging and snoring peacefully.

Damn but he wished he had a camera phone.

He'd play the video after she declared she didn't snore.

CHAPTER 26

Bobbie Dawson only meant to get ice. How was she to know a motel pervert would be on the lookout for a victim? And there were two of them. They moved so fast she barely had time to react.

She tried, though.

Dammit to hell.

She swung too late. Her arms were forced down and her fist had no travel.

She tried a kick.

Couldn't get leverage.

Already the men had her off balance.

She couldn't get a foot back far enough to do any real damage.

She reached for a knife before remembering she had left it in the room.

Her struggling was in vain.

She twisted and managed to open her mouth far enough to bite the shit out of the finger slipping into it.

The hand pulled back and she screamed and had her head bashed against the ice machine for her trouble.

Her ass would be up for grabs in another minute if it took even that long in the dark.

Damn the power failure, too.

And then Jim stormed the hill. He kicked ass and took names and it was over before she knew it had even begun.

The only thing is, he stuck a knife into one of them. If he bled out, they'd be in deep shit.

Then she remembered the power was out. There'd be no CCTV tape on the news at eleven.

She ended up shaking so bad Jim had to help her to the room.

She made him pay for being late. She forced him to carry her through the door.

"We need to check into a better class of motel," Bobbie said.

"No prob. You pay next time."

Point made.

And she was just happy to be here.

She headed for the shower. When she came out, she collapsed on the bed in nervous exhaustion and fell asleep snuggled against her savior.

Warm and safe.

Jim didn't want to push the woman. He pushed anyway. He needed to know.

"Your brother's friends. Who are they?"

Bobbie pulled at the sheet to cover her naked breasts and sat up. It was as though she was attempting to shield herself from the interrogation she knew was coming.

"All our friends were neighborhood kids. We

hung out at one time or another with everyone. Some moved apart as we got older. Ray kept up with the two who ended up taking government jobs and the guaranteed security for their families. My brother didn't want that. He wanted something better for himself."

Jim said, "Did he ever stop to figure out how he'd do that?"

"I don't think so. That's why he was still living in the basement. Maybe his two friends figured out a way to feed him a crap line about having money to do all the things he wanted. They probably told him all he would have to do is make a few trips across the river."

"Yeah. I think we know how that goes. They would eventually get gold stars for busting a supply chain. Whether it was a friend or a cartel."

Bobbie looked at him like he was a traitor for even suggesting it. For her own good he went on.

"Ray is taking all the risk. Whether he got discovered by his friends, or by a drug-sniffing dog, he'd be done. He might have leverage if he turned in his border-guard friends. Maybe not."

Jim could see the wheels turning.

Bobbie said, "He's loyal. He'd never rat out friends."

"In that case he'd do serious time. And your parents would lose everything they ever worked for as proceeds of crime. It would take too much money and time to get it back."

"Well, you're a Mr. Negative." She patted the bed. "There's room for you here, you know. You don't have to sit all alone way over there."

He wanted to get away. And he wanted Bobbie to at least take time to consider what he said. "There's a little takeout place next door. I won't be long."

She smiled and wriggled beneath the sheets.

"I'll be here keeping everything warm."

Jim was gone for twenty minutes, max.

"Bobbie? You here?"

No answer.

The room was empty.

Damn the woman and her disappearing act.

He'd only been half-serious about writing notes for her.

He pushed open the bathroom door.

Nothing.

Someone had to know where they were. Or where Bobbie was. He had no idea whether he fit into their equation or not. Probably not, since he was left behind to try and figure it out. It looked more and more like last night's attack had been a prelude to today's disappearance. If he hadn't heard her scream—

It didn't matter.

Bobbie was still gone.

Jim wolfed down the food and burned his mouth with the too-hot coffee while he shoveled clothes into their bags.

On the way to the car, he stopped at the front desk. The clerk hadn't seen anything. If he had, Jim figured the man wasn't about telling him anything.

He knew from the clerk's empty, shifty eyes staring back.

He was on his own.

He opened the motel room's door.

Before stepping out, he took a studied look over the lot.

There was nothing out of the ordinary, and he made his way to the car.

Drove in circles, waiting to find a tail.

Hoping he would. It would give him somewhere to start, at least, if he could put the finger on whoever it was.

Where would Bobbie end up?

The safe house turned into a money and drug drop was a good bet. While he sat watch, he wracked his brain. Friends. Neighbors. Buddies. Could it be that obvious?

He quit the stakeout and headed for what he thought might be a better opportunity.

Jim pulled the car in back.

Bobbie's parents were long gone, having finally listened to her reasoning.

He loaded up with his handgun and a knife.

He jimmied the door, walked in, and locked it behind him.

In the living room, curtains covered the huge window.

He dragged a chair into position, lifted a corner of the curtains, and settled back to watch and learn what he could from neighbor Terry's former residence.

If he was any more comfortable—

Jim's chin sagged onto his chest and he woke with a start. He peered out the window in the dark. Across the street, two coverall-clad men resembling yesterday's border guards were leaving Terry's place. They were definitely the two Bobbie helped him scope out in the parking lot.

He began following on the off chance they might not be going to or coming from work.

He ended up tailing them to something called Dos Amigos. It turned out to be a sketchy-looking storage facility not far from the Express Bridge. They disappeared through the door, most likely on their way to an inside unit.

His problem became one of finding out where it was and what the storage unit might contain.

While he was trying to figure out how he'd accomplish that, he realized he needed to return to Bobbie's place.

It dawned on him that Bobbie just might be sitting inside Terry's lookout house across the street. If that turned out to be true, he'd slap himself for being so stupid as to not consider it in the first place.

Besides, the house would be a lot easier to get into than an unknown storage building.

CHAPTER 27

Jim Nash stepped out of Bobbie's place looking like he was taking a nighttime stroll. He angled across the street and ducked into Terry's back yard. He tried the door. It opened without a struggle. The place had to be abandoned. Bobbie couldn't possibly be inside.

He took a chance, flipped on the lights, and wandered from room to room.

There was no sign of her.

He closed and locked the door and crossed the street. He leaned back on the sofa kindly provided by Mr. and Mrs. Dawson and closed his eyes. In no time he was slumped over and dreaming of lakes and forests and chopping wood.

Bobbie wasn't a part of the dream.

There was no sense trying to figure out what Bobbie was becoming. It was an impossibility. He only knew he cared for her too much to leave the woman out in the cold.

Her kidnapping had to mean that she'd become too close when they took a look at the border parking lot. Now that they knew who was involved, it had to be a straight shot to locating her brother.

The problem was, he had absolutely no idea where to start. And now with both Bobbie and her brother missing, he was in the midst of double trouble. His feelings for her made it all the more urgent to find a solution.

He made his way to the Dawson living room and the view across the road.

Every room in the downstairs was lit up like a bowling alley.

He was certain he had turned out the lights when he left.

He tucked his automatic into his belt and strapped on the knives.

Being prepared was something he believed in long before he got into whatever he was into with Bobbie.

He put on his best smile, knocked on the door, and waited. He knocked again. The woman who opened it was gorgeous. Dark-skinned, with black hair. Mexican by the look of it.

He blinked, stuttered, and introduced himself.

"I'm a friend of Bobbie's from across the street. Have you seen her around recently?"

Lame-ass, probably, but would it work?

The woman smiled and opened the door wide.

He managed to get a quick look. Everything appeared to be as he had left it.

"If you're staying at her place, why don't you know where she is?"

The woman had him there. She must have been watching, too.

"We had a fight and she stomped off into the

night. I thought—"

"Welcome to my world. I've been keeping an eye on this place waiting for my ex to leave. By the look of it, he's gone. Thank goodness."

"Yeah. Well, if Bobbie should show up—"

"I'll let you know."

She closed the door in his face.

Before he made it to the end of the walkway, the door opened again.

"Why don't you come in? Maybe we can help each other."

Since waterboarding her partner out of town, he didn't think so, but why not? He might learn something.

Jim said, "Where did your ex take off for?"

"I don't know and I don't care. Now then, let's talk about you."

The handgun leveled at his chest was an eight-shot hammerless. It was used mostly for close-in, quiet work. As in putting one in the back of a head, up close and personal.

The single shot would be quickly followed by a second to reinforce the first.

He didn't like it in the slightest, especially if it was going to be his head in the close-up part of personal.

If she wanted him in there, she'd have to drag him.

He kept to the doorway, unsure of what might wait inside beyond two in the back of the head.

CHAPTER 28

Jim Nash was out of options.

His eyes were riveted to the hand holding the pistol.

He eased past the woman, careful not to make any sudden moves.

That this woman knew he had been across the street said she had at least one dog in the race.

"You go first."

He thought he'd get an argument from the woman.

Instead, she confirmed something for him. Ray wasn't only missing. He had been killed. Mexican style. Cut up and parted out to places unknown. There was no doubt. The woman witnessed it.

He couldn't be sure she wasn't lying, but for now, he took her at her word.

Jim said, "What about Bobbie?"

"We're still looking for her," she admitted.

The glance said something else.

Still looking?

Just who was this woman?

Jim said, "So then, the cartel hasn't found the

drugs yet. Do they think Bobbie has them?"

It was a gamble, but he just shot his wad. If she took him at face value, maybe she'd think he knew more than she did. Maybe she'd hand him something on a platter. Hell, he'd take anything right about now.

Jim threw one last line out of his sinking boat.

"What about those two border guards? They're in this up to their necks."

The woman's eyes widened for an instant and there it was. He had something. He was certain. But what?

He threw out another morsel for luck. It couldn't hurt. "They've got a storage unit over by the puente viejo. The old bridge."

He held out hope. The woman didn't know where Bobbie was. Maybe she'd run off, thinking she could do better on her own. And maybe she could. But if Bobbie was about taking on a cartel all by her lonesome, she was in for an education she wasn't prepared to get.

"Will you take us there?" she asked.

Us?

So now they were a team.

He considered for an instant—not long enough to think it through, but at this point, he didn't care and didn't have time. He was desperate to find Bobbie.

Jim said, "We'll go in my car."

But not right away.

He headed down the alley behind Bobbie's place and drove them straight to the old safe house. It wasn't hard to talk the sicario into backing him up. She had the gun.

He kicked the door open.

Nothing. It was abandoned.

He did a desultory rummage through a couple of cabinets and came up empty-handed.

"Your car is the drug car. The one from which the drugs were taken."

For sure someone in the know had filled the woman in. If she knew everything, then Ray had escaped with a boatload of coca. No wonder he'd been parted out so fast upon his discovery.

The cartel had to send a message. Part two of the message was family next. He hoped he'd be able to do something about that—if it wasn't too late.

Jim pleaded ignorance and let the woman go on.

"Ray was an amateur as a smuggler. He only wanted to make money and quit. He was an amateur as a thief, too. He approached his two border-guard friends about doing one run and then cashing in. Unfortunately for Ray, the guards are on our payroll."

So that was it. Simple yet effective. They were greedy bastards to boot. He was proved right. They kept an eye on the product when it crossed the river. Ray hadn't known that. So maybe Ray wasn't the drug thief after all. Maybe it was the guards who used Ray to throw off suspicion.

He pulled into the storage unit lot and together they made for the tiny office. The woman said something in rapid-fire Spanish he couldn't understand. She caught the key the attendant tossed her way and they headed down a dimly lit corridor.

He wanted to bring up the rear. She wouldn't allow it.

We stopped at the door and she handed over the key.

He wasn't prepared for what he saw when he unlocked the door and opened it.

"Jim. You found me."

The voice was the last thing he heard. The stars came out and the pain started as he collapsed in a heap on the cement floor. Before his eyes closed for good, he recognized a tub full of water and a bench seat. It wasn't rocket science to know what had been going on in his absence. Now that he was present and accounted for, he'd probably get the same treatment.

Jim came to tied to a chair.

A sliver of light coming through a crack in the cheap siding revealed Bobbie in the same situation. Wet leather bindings. They would shrink and tighten as the leather dried. It could be a long, slow torture if it ended up around a neck. He tried moving his and couldn't.

"Is she gone?" he asked.

"As soon as she tied you," Bobbie said." Where have you been?"

"Looking for you. Mostly. Where the hell did you go?"

He didn't get an answer. Why was he not surprised.

Jim said, "I don't mean to change the subject, but can you wiggle your ass over to that tub of water? We need to tip it over."

They did better than that. His chair tipped in.

Bobbie screamed.

Somehow, he ended up on his back, submerged in five inches of water. That was all right, though. As long as he didn't open his mouth, he could keep his nose where it needed to be.

That didn't stop Bobbie. She kept on calling him every name in the book.

With his ears below the waterline, he could only pick out the occasional word. She had to be happy I couldn't talk back.

He struggled to work at hands and wrists submerged in the water. He twisted and turned at the leather bindings. He managed to work a hand free. Numb and weak, his fingers went to work on the knots keeping his ankles bound to the chair.

Freed finally, he went to work on Bobbie and had her free in minutes.

Jim said, "Are you happy now? You can slug me if you want."

She drove a good one into his shoulder.

"That's for taking so long to find me. And if you hadn't been listening to me while you were in that tub, I'd give you one for the other shoulder."

He flicked on the light and she let him have it with another one for good measure. "That's for the silly grin on your face. Now let's get out of this bachelor suite."

He chose not to let Bobbie know her brother had most likely been killed in the room they had escaped. He couldn't help the sin of omission. He wanted to let her keep a measure of hope, at least for now.

He cajoled the car keys from the desk man and three of us marched to the room we just vacated.

Jim said, "It'll only be for a little while, friend. I'm sure one of your many compadres will be along shortly to let you out. In the meantime, there's plenty of water if you get dehydrated."

He grabbed Bobbie's arm, pulled her out of the

room, and locked the door.

"We can't leave him in there. What if nobody comes?"

He gave her the evil eye.

She gave it back just as hard.

"Look. We could still be in there. As it is now, we're out here. Doesn't that make you even a little happy? Don't thank me right away. Think about it for a bit first."

He thought her look softened just a little.

"Well—"

"All right then. Now come on. We don't have all day," Jim said.

They suited up in the lobby with the handgun he discovered beneath the front desk.

He offered Bobbie the baseball bat he found beneath the desk.

She declined.

In any case, they were ready for bear.

All they had to do was find one.

CHAPTER 29

Bobbie Dawson didn't realize it, but she wasn't thinking about anything but her brother, Ray. He was all she cared about. He had to be alive. It never occurred to him that Jim could be lying. Why would he?

Sure, she was upset about locking the manager in the storage unit. What if no one else knew? What if no one came back? Jim didn't appear all that concerned.

And then she remembered. Jim hadn't started on his own mission to find the killers of the women that had been taken from him. Perhaps that was why. She'd not given him a chance. Or a choice. Instead, she had coerced him into helping her.

That he might see her as dragging him down only made her feel worse about stealing his time. If she had it to do all over again, would she do it the same way?

Probably.

It was all about her brother. She was selfish that way. If they found Ray, she'd be able to dedicate time to Jim's search.

But not before.

She turned down the baseball bat he offered.

"I'm clumsy that way," she told him.

As usual, he ignored her and they got in the car. The bat ended up in the back seat.

Jim said, "We need to talk, Bobbie."

It was past due. A long time past due.

She waited, an expectant look on her face. He didn't want to do it. Her reaction wouldn't be good. In fact, he feared it might jeopardize everything.

"It's about Ray." He steeled himself for what he had to tell her. He couldn't keep it from her any longer.

"What about him? Did you find him? Where is he?"

He couldn't bring himself to look her in the eye. He thought she probably knew why. It still wouldn't be easy.

"They found him, didn't they?"

Jim nodded. He still couldn't bring himself to look at her.

"Is he dead?"

He said it anyway. "Yes. Ray is dead." Who was he trying to convince?

"Do you know where he is?" she asked.

"No. Are you sure you want to find out?"

Bobbie didn't hesitate. "Yes."

But did she really? Even while he was crawling through a lime pit in Mexico filled with bodies, he prayed he would never have to see anything like it again. And he didn't want Bobbie to experience anything like it. He cared too much for her.

"One more thing. Your parents can't come home until you let them know it's safe. Did you tell them?"

"Not directly. Should I?" she asked.

"Yes. There's a sicario—"

"A sicario?"

"A hit man. A woman in this case. She's holed up across the street in Terry's house. Waiting. She told me Terry was her husband. That he'd taken a trip. By the sound of that, I'd say he's dead, too."

"We need to find Ray's two friends. Maybe they know something," she said.

"Bobbie—" He hesitated. This was becoming more difficult the longer it went on. "They're part of it, too. The sicario—the woman who brought me to join you in the storage unit—told me about them."

She sighed.

He thought she was going to cry. Instead, she asked for a knife.

"I thought you didn't want one."

"I changed my mind."

We backtracked to the motel. She tucked the knife into the small of her back, just as Kara had done so many times. She pulled her shirt out to cover it.

"The sicario keeping an eye on your place has to know more than she admitted. I'll start with her. That we escaped her jail cell should be worth a surprise or two."

"Then what are we waiting for? Let's go."

"You're not going," he said. "You'll be busy convincing your parents to stay away."

"Like hell. Take me or we're done."

Bobbie's steely-eyed glare said he'd better pay attention.

"All right, but you need to know—"

"I don't need to know anything. I've got it figured out. Are we going, or do I have to do it alone?"

Jim knew she was bluffing, but hell, she was doing a good job of it.

Bobbie went in through the back of Terry's house.

He picked the front, just because. He should have known better. It took him two kicks before Bobbie swung the door wide from the inside.

"You need a stronger leg."

"Where is she?"

"While you were leaning on the door making all the noise, I came up behind her and cold-cocked her. One punch. Don't worry. I used duct tape. She's sleeping it off in the kitchen."

"Did you search her?"

Bobbie beat him to the kitchen.

Her sparring partner on the floor was cutting at the tape on her ankles with a small knife. Blood streamed from her nose. Her shirt was ripped open. She looked up and Bobbie dispatched her for the second time with a rap on the head. The woman slithered on the floor before going into a deep sleep.

"First thing you do is search. Where's her hardware?"

"I'm sorry. I'll know for next time. Hardware?"

Jim said, "Firearms. Hand grenades. Knives. AKs. Anything."

"Her phone's over there. I don't know about the rest of it."

"Then go and look. And then look again."

There was no way he wanted this one to get away.

"I'll keep an eye on our prize."

Metal scraped and clunked as Bobbie rounded up the firearms in a blanket.

"Way to go, girl. Now load all of it into the car." He handed over the keys.

"Who'll be your slave when I leave you?"

Jim said, "Stop whining and sniveling and just do it, woman. I've had about enough."

She gathered an armload of weaponry and carted it out the back door to the alley.

He found a duffel and stuffed it with the rest.

"All right. We're done. How do you want to work this?"

Bobbie said, "What do you mean?"

Our prisoner moaned and began a weak struggle against her bindings.

"Who's driving? Who'll be keeping an eye on little miss muffin?"

Bobbie kicked the woman unconscious and used the opportunity to wrap her in more tape.

"I guess that answers that."

She picked up the woman's feet and dragged her out the back door. The sicario's head sounded like an out-of-control watermelon rolling down the concrete steps.

"Keep her alive, will you? We need her a bit longer."

Jim went back inside, searching. He located a cooler and filled it with water. He added a towel and hauled it to the car.

Bobbie's head shook in disbelief. "I wondered what took so long. You raided the place for beer."

"Sort of."

CHAPTER 30

Bobbie was beginning to realize that she didn't know anything. Furthermore, Jim wasn't talking. This woman—this sicario—the cause of it all, wasn't talking, either. She was occupied in the kitchen, trying to get out of her tape job.

Recognizing that she was clueless about whatever the hell they were doing, she stood over the woman stood over her. She kicked and then gave her another one to be sure.

The tape came off the roll with a tearing sound. She wrapped her in more and prepared to drag her out to the car. She was sure to stay silent and secure now.

Jim wanted her to collect the woman's weapons. She didn't know she'd have more than one or two. It shocked her when she collected an armload. She had no idea.

She palmed the phone and slipped it into his pocket.

She picked up our prisoner's feet and struggled to drag her out the door to the car.

Jim was no help until her head started to bounce

on the steps. All he had to offer was an admonition not to kill her.

When he finally came out of the house carting a heavy cooler, she didn't know what to think. Why would he want to bring a cooler full of beer?

To their advantage, dos amigos from the border patrol appeared to be still missing from the storage building's small office. They had the clerk tucked away. Together they dragged the sicario out of the car and into the empty office.

Jim flipped the switch to light up the long hallway.

He left Bobbie to return to the car for the bag of weapons. He took another trip to retrieve the cooler. He locked the office door and hung out the closed sign. Unless someone had a key, they would be alone.

Bobbie yanked the tape from the sicario's mouth.

The woman didn't appear happy at the prospect of being within the same tin walls and ceiling where she had left them to rot. Perhaps she could take comfort from the presence of her amigo, still alive, on the floor.

"He was talking to her in Spanish so I cold-cocked him and taped his mouth."

"So he's not dead?" Bobbie asked.

"Not yet."

She pointed at the woman.

"Her name is Yesenia," he said.

"South American."

"I guess."

Jim looked at Yesenia.

She stared back, her face cold and blank. She definitely didn't want to be there. There was no doubt. "Si. Colombia."

Two words so far. Maybe she thought she'd be able to talk her way out of whatever it was she was knee deep in.

"It looks like we've got us a real live Colombian hit-woman, Bobbie."

Bobbie's duct-tape job kept the woman subdued. Sweat covered what the tape didn't.

"We need to cut some slack in the tape. I want to sit her in the chair."

Bobbie went to work with the knife, slicing through the tape at the knees and waist. By the time she finished, the woman was turning a deep red in places.

It wasn't enough to concern him. A little blood went a long way.

"So. Yesenia. I'm Jim. Your captor is Bobbie. She did one hell of a job, didn't she? Maybe you know her brother."

Yesenia looked at Bobbie and lobbed spit at her feet.

Bobbie raised a fist.

To say she was pissed would put it mildly.

He grabbed her arm and spun her around.

Bobbie's eyes bored into his. "Not yet. Soon. I promise."

He dragged the cooler closer and popped the top. Water sloshed.

"Water. I thought you brought beer," Bobbie said.

Without hesitating, He dipped the thick towel in

the cooler. It came out dripping wet and a lot heavier than when it went in.

Yesenia's eyes grew large. She knew what was coming.

He squeezed it for effect. Water streamed from the towel and splashed into the cooler.

"Okay. It's time."

Jim dropped the wet towel over the woman's head. He kept it away from her face. "Punch her in the gut."

Bobbie drove her a good one.

The sicario gasped and he released the towel. It dropped against her face.

"You complained about how I treated Terry. Isn't this more humane? She's nowhere near the water."

"You're not asking any questions," Bobbie said.

"Never satisfied, are you?"

Jim pulled the towel off.

Yesenia gulped fresh air.

He made sure she could see him dunking the towel a second time.

"Punch her again."

Bobbie laid another one into the sicario's gut.

The woman managed to draw two good breaths before he draped the towel over her face.

"You're getting good at this."

He kept the sopping wet towel against Yesenia's face, letting her suffer for a little longer before pulling it off. The results were the same.

"Once more."

They went through the exercise.

Yesenia sputtered through the soaked towel.

"No mas. No mas."

"Third time's the charm."

He didn't pull the towel off right away. He wanted the woman to have time to think between her attempts to draw in panicked breaths of air.

"One down, one to go."

He looked over at the storage facility's front-desk jockey, huddled in the corner. He was wide awake now. His eyes were even wider.

Jim pointed. "El siguiente. Number two. Next."

It was all the encouragement the poor soul needed. He began shaking like a man who needed a drink. He started to sing like a long-vanished canary in a coal mine.

Yesenia didn't appear to be so happy, but she was in no position to complain. Although she tried. Finally, her threats worked and she cowed the man into silence.

Then it was Bobbie's turn.

She taped Yesenia's mouth and gave her one in the gut. For good measure, she made sure the woman caught one on the nose, too.

Wheezing and twitching, Yesenia tried to catch her breath through a bloody nose.

The desk jockey didn't know a lot, but his song was good enough.

He was happy he didn't have to apply any pressure. He wasn't so sure about Bobbie. It looked like she wanted him in the dunk tank just because.

He left Bobbie with the prisoners.

None of them were in any condition to do any damage. He knew, because he checked before he left for the office.

After flipping through a few pages in the registry,

he headed back. He wanted to ask Bobbie if she recognized any of the names. He wasn't gone long. In fact, he remembered looking at the clock on the office wall.

By the time he returned to the storage room, it was too late.

CHAPTER 31

Bobbie Dawson thought she'd help Jim out while he went to the office. It wasn't anything more than that.

At least, that's what she wanted to believe. It's what she ended up telling herself.

She wanted to speed up the process so they could get out in a hurry if they had to.

She dragged the cooler in front of Yesenia. She offered no resistance. She couldn't. She was taped.

She forced Yesenia's head into the water-filled cooler.

There was a noise. The desk clerk, maybe. Or Jim's steps, echoing off the tin walls as he walked away.

Wondering if he would come back.

She remembered saying something to the man on the floor. The desk jockey. Shut up, or be quiet. Maybe she kicked him. Or all three. She couldn't remember.

By the time she turned back to Yesenia, it was too late.

She didn't do it on purpose. At least she didn't

think so.

Jim wasn't so happy. Or so convinced when he returned with the register. He wanted to show her the names, thinking she'd be able to recognize if the unit belonged to any of Ray's friends. If they could tie them to the unit, it would go a long way to setting them up for a fall. And just maybe they could find out about her brother by threatening them with being revealed as drug dealers.

"Jesus, Bobbie. I leave you alone for five minutes and you end up missing, kidnapped, or you kill someone," he said.

He certainly had a way with words. It was making her feel even more shitty.

"I pulled her head up. I swear I did. I didn't want her to drown. It wasn't on purpose. I wanted to find out if she knew anything about my brother. I looked away for a minute. Maybe two at the most."

Okay, so maybe five. She wasn't counting.

She would deal with Jim later.

That, and probably a lot more she knew nothing about.

Jim opened the door to the unit.

Bobbie froze mid-step and stared at him, wild-eyed. She buried her face in her hands and bowed her head and sobbed when she could fit it between the shaking.

He couldn't have been gone more than a few minutes, yet Bobbie was in a state of near panic.

Yesenia was on her knees, bent over the cooler.

"Jesus, Bobbie. What the hell did you do?"

Yesenia's head was face-down in the cooler.

Bobbie looked crazed.

She paced, back and forth, from one wall to the other.

Hyperventilating.

Sobbing.

"What does it look like? I asked her if she killed my brother."

So she didn't believe him when he gave her the same news.

"Why didn't you pull her out of it? You didn't have to leave her like that. Jesus."

"Yes I did. I asked. She couldn't wait to tell me."

So now she had the truth about her brother from the person who'd killed him. She wasn't handling it so well.

"I couldn't wait to make her pay. In fact, I made her pay and pay and pay."

Yesenia wasn't moving. She paid, all right.

He pulled her head up. He already knew there was nothing to be done.

"What are you going to do about desk-boy over there?"

He groaned and twitched.

"I made sure I didn't have a witness. I cold-cocked him."

They were deep in the shit now.

A dead sicario would be replaced by a team of two, or even four.

Bobbie had no idea.

Could he blame her? He was hell-bent on his search for the killers of his unborn child and two wives.

Still, where would they go from here? Would Bobbie still want to help with his search? Or would she disappear by hitchhiking to nowhere on a lonely road?

"I'm not done yet, Jim."

The determined look on her face spelled trouble in all caps.

"The son of a bitch that put me up to this is going to pay, too."

Sailboat guy.

He didn't tell her he'd once owned a sailboat. Hell, he couldn't even swim. She wouldn't believe him anyway.

"How do you intend to track him down?"

If sailboat guy was the one who put the sicario on her brother—

And if he had ears on the ground and—

He'd be finding out soon enough something was up. Would he still be waiting for Bobbie? Or would he be searching for her, intent on eliminating her?

"You need to tell me about him, Bobbie. What were you thinking?"

"I was thinking like you before I even met you. I wanted to find out what happened to my brother. Now I know."

"But are you sure?"

He knew he had to be sure.

"Remember when you showed me Terry's phone with that text message?"

He did, but it didn't seem important at the time.

"I recognized the number. It was the same

number programmed into the phone I had. Until you forced me to toss it."

So she was being tracked. That's why they were followed after he picked her up at the gas bar. It didn't explain why they were attacked on that same road.

"We have to get out of here. Right now. We're ditching the car, too."

He already knew she'd be heading north to her friend's boat.

"It's a red flag that those two border guards could use against us. If we have to go through one of those extended checkpoints that the government has so proudly allowed sixty miles inland from the border, we're in even more shit."

"So what are we going to do with the guy in the corner?"

"For starters, we're not going to kill him. We might be home free on the sicario. Fake travel documents and all, she'll never be traced or identified."

Bobbie's hands went to her hips, still shaking and exasperated.

"Look. You've grown up a lot in the past two days. Too much, if I know a thing or two. It hasn't set in yet, but you're going to collapse. It's only a matter of time. You can damned well trust me on that."

The look of sorrow that crossed her face disheartened him even more.

"So that's one reason we're not killing him."

"Fine. What are we going to do?" she asked.

"We're getting out of Dodge. We need a new

car. What do you say to cruising the parking lot at the border and looking for keys?"

They ditched the car.

He let her do the search. She came up with a brand new sports car.

He transferred the bags to the small trunk and they drove off.

"What the hell took you so long?"

"I wanted air."

"Woman, you're going to be the death of me yet."

"I hope not. I was just thinking of changing into something light and frivolous to show off for you. Pull over."

They weren't even a mile from the puente viejo.

Crazy is as crazy does.

Jim did as he was told.

Bobbie jumped out of the confines of the small car, changed by the side of the road, and got back in. She lifted the skirt to her thighs and smoothed it.

"There. This ought to take the collective minds of the border patrol off of anything that matters."

She was right, too.

The tops of Bobbie's perky breasts peeked out from a sheer blouse. Not to mention what her nipples were doing.

He grinned and shook his head. She did what only a woman could do. She grinned right back, not shy in the slightest.

Drive, she said.

So he drove.

They stopped for the checkpoint.

Leering eyes of the green-clad male leaning in through the window distracted him from anything beyond a cursory question.

He waved them through.

In the mirror, his female partner's lips moved furiously, wasting her breath to give him shit.

Bobbie said, "Told ya. Nothing to it."

CHAPTER 32

It came on suddenly, like the flu, maybe.

Or like she'd eaten something bad. The one time she needed a window down and almost didn't make it.

She jumped up on the seat on her knees and hung out the window before throwing up, and then threw up again.

Jim pulled over to the side of the road, all concerned, like he cared. He probably thought she was pregnant, except they hadn't been together long enough for that part of it. Maybe in a month.

She gagged and coughed and spit and heaved until she had nothing left to give up.

He moved the car forward a bit and got out and walked around to her side.

"I was wondering when it would happen."

She dry-heaved, just because she couldn't stop. A long string of saliva hung out of her open mouth.

He poured water on a t-shirt, bent down, and gently wiped at her face.

"Shit. That's one of my good shirts."

Why was she concerned about a cheap shirt? It

didn't seem all that important. Then she remembered what he said.

"When what would happen?"

She heaved one more time for good measure. She sucked for air and breathed in, again and again, panting almost.

"It's your delayed reaction to what happened back in the storage shed."

She looked up at him. She guessed he looked concerned. He was certainly anxious.

"Don't stop breathing. Keep them deep."

He handed her the bottle.

She rinsed and spit and rinsed again.

She chugged the water and gagged again. Somehow, she managed not to throw up through hiccupping. She kept the water down, too.

"It was an accident. I told you. I didn't mean for anything to happen to her. I got distracted and I never noticed—"

"I believe you, Bobbie. It's normal."

She looked at the man like he was crazy. "Normal?"

"Yeah. It's normal. The reaction, I mean. That's what's normal."

"Well thank goodness for that. How would I sleep at night otherwise?"

His look changed instantly to one of concern. "You're going to have problems. I can guarantee that. Fortunately—"

She interrupted him again. "Fortunately? What's fortunate about it?"

His hand went over her mouth, forcing her to shut up. She couldn't breathe. She choked and almost gagged before he pulled away.

"I was going to say that it's fortunate that you have me to comfort you and explain how it's going to go. Eventually, you'll dream and scream and wake up and dream again and wake up again. In a cold sweat. In a warm sweat. In the summer. In the winter. To say you're going to need some counseling would be an understatement."

Oh great.

"How's it going to go when I admit to a psychiatrist that I murdered someone?"

"If I have anything to do with it, you won't have to. It could be a car accident, or someone falls off a balcony while you were there. You'll figure it out," he said.

Or she could just ignore it all.

"The one thing you can't do is ignore it."

There went that idea.

Bobbie reached for the mirror. She checked her reflection and adjusted her hair. Her fingertips traced the outline of the dark circles beneath her eyes.

To say he was worried about her would be an understatement. Now that the delayed reaction was over, it would continue to be a struggle for her going forward. And like a woman, she went for the makeup to cover her pale face and the dark circles.

"Damn the wind and the heat and the humidity."

She rustled through her bag, took another look in the mirror, and put it all back.

Hell, she didn't need makeup. Ever.

So he had to open his big mouth.

"All you need is a little lip gloss."

For his trouble, he got the look that women hand out when they think they have all the answers. And then she must have changed her mind.

Bobbie went back to work with the makeup.

He went back to paying attention to the road.

He also went back to worrying about the woman. She'd puked her guts up, but it was only a symptom of what would be coming. When they stopped, he'd try again to explain it all.

Would she listen?

PTSD.

Bobbie was no killer.

She knew what happened in the storage unit was an accident.

So did he.

Unfortunately, it didn't mean she wouldn't continue to be affected by it.

He could do all the talking in the world, but it wouldn't help her. She had to help herself.

Would she?

Time would tell.

CHAPTER 33

Bobbie Dawson looked across at Jim. There was no way in hell he would want anything to do with her now. How could he? She had been responsible for a death. Yes, the woman was a killer. Yes, she'd been sent to find and kill her brother, Ray. And yes, she had been working up an appetite to kill Jim, too.

And maybe even her.

So, what was the big deal about it?

All right, maybe she should have been paying more attention in the storage unit.

Maybe Jim shouldn't have brought the cooler of water. He knew what he was planning.

She should have put a stop to it.

Did she really believe he was bringing a cooler full of beer along for the ride? For real?

Sure, Jim put Terry through the shower in the apartment above the garage. But she had walked away then, too.

She couldn't put any of the blame on Jim. Could she?

She'd been the one who stopped paying attention in the storage unit. And someone died. How could she possibly live that down in Jim's eyes? He had to be disgusted with her lack of attention. It had ended in death.

And it was all her fault because she wasn't up to the task.

How would she ever live it down? She loved Jim, but there was no justification for what she let happen to that woman. It was all on her.

All of it.

And now she would have to live with it.

She pretended she had to go to the bathroom. She asked him to pull over in a rest area and made for the facilities.

She pulled out the phone she pocketed at Terry's place.

She flipped it open and knew right away it belonged to Yesenia, the sicario.

She punched the button and waited. It went to voicemail.

Bobbie said, "Kennedy. I'm coming for you. And I'm bringing help."

Hesitating, only for a moment. Wondering. And then, finally, knowing.

"I'm going to kill you. I'm going to kill anyone associated with you. I'm going to kill your wife. I'm going to kill your children. I'm going to kill your pets. When I'm done killing, I'm going to burn down your house and everything in it."

She hung up and tossed the phone into the shitter. No doubt it would end up wherever shit ended up, downhill and far from where it was launched.

She wanted Jim to be proud of her. She didn't tell

him what she did, but still—

Bobbie returned to the car and settled in the seat. Put her feet up on the dash. Tried not to think any more. She turned on the radio, dialed up some rock and roll, and cranked up the volume.

It didn't do any good. Trying was not doing, and her brain was still going a mile a minute, filled with disgust and disappointment for being so naive that she thought she'd be able to find and rescue her brother on her own.

She needed Jim. He didn't need her. And he sure didn't need a wild card that he couldn't depend on or control. The sooner she got away from everything, the sooner he could get back to solving his problems.

Bobbie said a silent prayer. She already knew it wouldn't do any good.

And what the hell were the blinking lights behind them?

Bobbie's gaze went from the side mirror to Jim and back.

"It looks like la migra is on our tail. You better let them go by," she said.

Jim slowed and eased onto the shoulder of the narrow two-lane highway and stuck an arm out and waved them past.

The green and white Jimmy slowed and stayed even with them.

An arm hung out the open window. An automatic leveled a big, round muzzle in their direction.

His eyes went just as big.

He didn't need to be told twice. He slowed and stopped on the side of the road and turned to Bobbie.

"The bastards were too lazy to use the siren. It's like they wanted to make it look like we were running."

She turned to look and recognized the men. "It's Ray's two border guard friends."

Weapons drawn, the duo rushed the passenger door in a noisy scramble of boots on pavement. The door opened and two pairs of hands yanked Bobbie out. They dragged her, kicking and punching, toward the Jimmy.

She fought hard, swinging, kicking, yelling, to no avail. She ended up dumped in the back.

Two gunshots and two flat tires later, Jim was left to rot on the side of the road.

Stranded and without water, he rummaged through the trunk and dumped Bobbie's bag. He hastily threw her clothes in with his.

He figured on an AK and a couple of mags for backup to go along with his automatic and the knives.

Better safe than sorry.

He waited in heat and humidity and scorching sun beating down.

No one stopped.

It was an hour.

And then another.

A passing bus heeded his thumb and growled to a halt. The door hissed open.

He shouldered the bag and climbed aboard.

The bus took off and he shuffled unsteadily to the empty rear.

He settled in for the long haul in the noisy, hot, and dusty bus. The humid air had so many smells he was almost afraid to inhale.

He stayed with his bag rather than take a chance on carrying it into the coffee shops during stops.

As they got farther north, he approached the driver and made inquiries about getting back to Diamondhead.

The driver said, "You change buses in Houston. Diamondhead is a regular stop. Just been added if I remember right. You can check at the counter."

Nice.

He was about to retrace his steps. If only he'd taken Bobbie back to the sailboat when he learned about it, they might have made more progress.

Would she be there? Were the two border guards so stupid they thought they could confront her by returning the woman to her tormentor?

Was it Kennedy?

Was he the man in charge of the whole thing?

He had no idea.

He only knew one thing.

He needed a drink.

Bobbie was going to have to wait.

In Houston, he checked into a motel on the seedy side of the strip.

He strolled across the street to the liquor store and rescued a bottle of Crown Royal. If he was going to drown his sorrows, he wanted to be sure the sorrows enjoyed the best.

Alone in the room, missing Bobbie, he unloaded the duffel of its contents and went through everything.

Bobbie's clothes went back in, neatly folded in the plastic bags he picked up at the liquor store. He discovered she still had one colorful, filmy skirt that she hadn't yet worn. He hoped he'd see her in it soon enough.

At this point, he wasn't counting on it.

By the time he got to the rest of it, he was exhausted, physically and mentally.

He rinsed a glass and polished it with a thin, gray towel laundered too many times.

He filled it with three fingers of rye and leaned back against the pillow on the bed.

A million thoughts circulated. Most were about Bobbie.

Could he find her?

How?

Would she be at the marina in Diamondhead?

Why would the border guards have kidnapped her in the first place?

Did they suspect her of having the drugs?

If she did, was finding her brother only a ruse until she could make good her escape with the drugs?

Was she in a partnership with the guards?

Or maybe she was partnered up with her brother.

CHAPTER 34

Jim's eyes opened to focus on the glass parked on the night table. Three fingers of whiskey stared back. That had to be a good start to the day.

He jumped out of bed and placed a gray towel on the table. He removed the AK from the duffel bag, put it on the towel, and began field-stripping it. He promptly pinched his thumb on that damned receiver button. Obviously, he hadn't been doing it often enough—which was probably a good thing.

He reassembled the AK and went on to the automatic.

Done and done.

He stepped out into the early morning's cool, humid air. It would turn to hot and humid by noon, but he'd be out of here by then and well on the way to Diamondhead.

He closed the motel room door behind him, shouldered the bag, and headed out on foot.

An ambulance screamed by on its way to a hospital. He watched it slow and turn several blocks down. By the time he caught up, he knew where he'd find a new truck.

He cruised the hospital's parking lot, on the lookout for unlocked doors and keys stashed behind visors or floor mats.

By the time Jim pulled out of the lot, the sun was over the horizon, and he was the proud possessor of a two-and-a-half door truck built in the late 90s.

He squinted into the sun until he hit the east end of Houston and a gas'n'go for a bag of burritos and two pairs of sunglasses. He added a couple of ball caps and dark gray hoodies for good measure.

Steady driving would get him to Diamondhead in an easy eight or so.

He had a look in the truck for a GPS and came up with an older model stashed in the jockey box. The charge looked to be good.

He pinched and scrolled until he spied Diamondhead, about four hundred miles away. Satisfied, he reached into the paper bag and attacked a still-hot burrito.

It was the most he'd eaten in what felt like forever.

A couple of hours in, his stomach began rocking and rolling. He pulled over and purged and rinsed with water. He splashed some onto his face for good luck and climbed back in.

He one-handed the paper bag over the side onto a breakwater.

Fish food at high tide.

As much as he wanted to push it, the speed limit whispered his name. He was in a stolen truck. He wanted to lessen the odds as best he could. Mostly he kept to a couple over and he must have been a good boy.

No cops.

No roadblocks.

His guts settled and he was looking forward to recognizing the green and white sign calling out Diamondhead. It appeared, finally, and he joined the off-ramp and exited right onto a road headed to a yacht club. He did another right from a roundabout and found himself driving toward a small airport.

A private jet appeared through the trees on the tarmac. A cartel plane, maybe. Whoever owned it had to be a cheap bastard. It looked like you couldn't stand tall and upright in it.

He turned and doubled back. On the way he eyeballed the harbor. It was small. Plenty of vacant trailer pads. A couple of parked cars. But no sloop.

The yacht club parking lot had a few cars. He figured on scoping out the place from the inside.

He turned back to the deserted mini-mall. A small gas bar at one end was all it had to offer. He parked the truck out of sight and stashed the keys for an out, just in case. He pulled a blanket over the duffel in the back seat after donning a fresh button shirt.

He humped it to a sign at the yacht club pointing to a restaurant. He wouldn't look the part of a moneyed member, but he might buy enough time to learn something. No way in hell did he want to storm grandma and grandpa's pride and joy with an AK in one hand and a bag of burritos in the other.

By the time he got around to looking, the yacht, if it had ever been there, was gone.

It took a minute for Jim's eyes to adjust to the subdued lighting in the bar. When they did, sunlight reflecting through a huge expanse of glass overlooking the wharf and the water blinded him again.

A handful of customers occupied tables. Rivers of water from icy drinks dribbled onto tabletops. The bar was disturbingly unpopular with so few customers.

It was disturbing because the woman behind the bar was a real looker. Long and leggy, with a skirt that had to be spray-painted on before she left for work.

He paid attention to the eye-pleasing sway as lengthy legs and a quick stride caused her high-heel sandals to click-clack across the tile floor on the way to a table.

On her way back, she caught him looking.

An inviting smile looked back.

Breasts threatened to break free of buttons keeping them behind her blouse.

Once she got behind the bar, she turned with another willing smile and looked across the room with a come-hither look.

He took a look at her clientele and knew right off not a one was under seventy.

She came hither instead, smiling like there was no tomorrow.

"What'll it be, sailor?" she asked.

He grinned like a kid in a candy store. It was all he could do to wait until she looked away so he could get a better look at the goods.

She must have known, because she didn't look away.

"I'll have a sweaty Sol."

She nodded, and the torture was over. She bent to

retrieve one from the cooler.

He leaned in to better the view. There were no lines beneath the tight blue skirt that he could discern.

She slammed his beer down on top of the bar and popped the top.

Foam ran over her hand and down the bottle.

A measured shove sent it in his direction.

"Would you like anything else with that?"

He looked just long enough to read the woman's name tag. It was a perfect excuse to check out her breasts now that they were closer. He didn't expect she was fooled by the old trick. She looked too experienced for that.

"How about a little conversation, Diana?" he asked.

She looked over the almost empty room. "I'll be back in a minute. Don't go away."

Fat chance.

She strode off purposefully, rolling her hips with each measured step.

She had to know he was looking.

She circulated around the tables, filling a tray with half a dozen empty glasses and bottles while collecting the cash, all while swiping a rag to soak up the drool.

The woman wasted no time getting back to the bar.

She deposited her tray and took a seat beside his.

She made sure he was looking before crossing long, shapely legs. She swiveled back and forth on the bar stool, hitting his shin with a rhythmic foot. She took her time uncrossing her legs for effect.

Jim took a quick glance in the appropriate direction.

It seemed to please her.

It surely pleased him.

Jim said, "Are you comfortable now?"

"I am. Are you?" she asked.

She did the leg thing again for good measure.

Damn but she had some legs. He was almost forced to forget why he was in the place.

He took a long swig of the Sol, and then another. He drained it and the name tag that said Diana went behind the bar and returned with another.

This time, her legs stayed put, but he didn't mind. He already had his look.

And Diana knew it.

Jim said, "I was wondering about a sloop that might have been parked next to one of the pads. The one where the cars are parked."

"I remember it. They untied late in the morning."

"Today?"

"Yes. I think I overheard them talking. They were expecting another crew member to arrive at some point. Would that be you?"

Jim took his cue from that. "It is. I hope I haven't missed out."

"They'll be back first thing tomorrow, if I recall. You can probably sign on then. Have you got a room somewhere?"

Three men walked through the door. They scoped out the room, eyes hesitating when they caught sight of Diana.

Or maybe they were on the lookout for him. He couldn't be sure, given how he'd been drawn to the woman as they must have been.

"Excuse me. Customers," Diana said. She smiled and stood up.

Both breasts brushed against his arm just long enough to let him know it was no accident.

Perhaps he had a place to stay after all.

"Don't go away."

CHAPTER 35

Diana smiled, and he didn't go away.

She halted at the table with the new customers. Lips moved, but with the air conditioner humming in the background he couldn't make out a word. Three pairs of eyes looked him over. He turned and swiveled on the barstool and concentrated on the mirror behind the bar.

He didn't see Diana until her lips moved against his ear.

"It sounds like they're looking for you."

Two men grabbed his arms and pinned his hands to the bar.

A third drove a fist into a kidney.

He squirmed and attempted to topple to the floor.

They weren't having it.

An arm went around his neck, tightened, and held him where he was.

Two of them propelled him in the door's direction.

He couldn't put up a fight. He was moving too fast on his feet, and his arms were locked behind.

Outside, one locked his arms while the other two rained down blows hard enough to put him on the ground.

Boots kicked, connected to bone, and withdrew.

Car doors slammed and tires pealed on asphalt as the threesome departed in a hurry.

Dazed from the beating, he allowed a sympathetic Diana to help him get up. He leaned into her and steadied himself against a wall.

"You're a mess."

He leaned a little too hard, almost taking her to the ground.

"Help me get you to my car."

He let her lead.

She opened the back door before checking her phone.

"I'll be off in half an hour if you can wait.," Diana said.

"I don't think I have a choice."

She surrounded him with an arm and he leaned against her on the way to the back seat. She eased him down and he groaned.

"You should see the other guy."

"Yeah. I was there, remember? You didn't get in a single blow."

Diana chuckled before rolling down the windows and heading across the pavement to the bar.

He was so out of it he forgot all about watching the woman walk away.

The last thing he remembered was the odd man out. He was the one who offered up the jack stand when they were on the side of the road with a flat tire. It was the same man Bobbie had been chatting up while he changed the tire.

He had to be Kennedy. Was he the one Terry texted? Was he the man who assaulted Bobbie before sending her out on her mission to recover her brother or the drugs, or both?

Too late. He passed out and only came around when Diana shook him awake.

"Get up. We're home. Five steps and we're there."

Easy for her to say.

She didn't tell him they were five steps almost straight up.

He groaned and let her help.

The woman's breasts felt just as fine as they did in the bar.

Jim couldn't avoid them.

Nor did he want to.

Hot water was filling the tub. Jim couldn't say he was unhappy to hear that.

Diana unbuttoned his shirt, went to her knees, and unfastened his belt.

Tugged down his pants.

Her eyes hovered before finally looking up.

"Well, that's encouraging. Now get in."

She struggled to pull her shirt past firm breasts without unbuttoning.

Her skirt dropped next.

Commando.

That's why there was no line.

Diana stepped into the tub, not shy in the slightest.

Jim was unsure where to park his eyes, only

because there were too many possibilities.

She eased down to share the water.

She soaked a sponge and squeezed hot water over his aching body. He only groaned and sat back.

Diana's breasts weren't quite covered by the soapy water. They bobbed and weaved with every motion.

"Nice."

She smiled and reached between his legs.

"You're not so bad either."

Both hands went to work. She was enthusiastic, to say the least.

"Stand up."

He was already standing up and she knew it.

Not wanting to disappoint, Jim did as he was told.

She reached with both of hers, using them to encourage the reaction she seemed to need.

"Even better."

Outside the tub, she helped him dry off before leading him to the bedroom.

The rest of her body was a match for the legs that had so enamored him at first.

It wasn't a gentle push that ended up with him flat on his back on the bed.

He groaned anyway, and it wasn't for effect.

She threw a leg over and without hesitating, guided him between her legs.

He settled back for the ride.

She hovered, leaned, and he was forced to enjoy hard-tipped breasts pressing against his face.

He opened his mouth and was immediately rewarded with warm, swollen nipple.

Jim woke to the smell of breakfast.

She forced him to wait when they discovered unfinished business from last night.

Long legs surrounded him as she allowed him to become lost in her once more.

The pleasure was short-lived.

"Jim? It's time. Eat it and beat it. House rules."

Her house, her rules.

He ate it and left it.

Diana didn't bother turning on the lights.

Perhaps she didn't want to encourage either of them any more than she already had.

CHAPTER 36

Bobbie checked the side mirror. The green and white immigration Jimmy reflected back was going to be trouble. The grill filled the side mirror. It was close. Checking us out, probably. It had to be Ray's border guard friends.

She warned Jim about it, about who was likely inside, as it continued pacing. Then it pulled up alongside on the two-lane highway.

Jim slowed and pulled over, thinking they wanted to pass.

The Jimmy slowed and kept even.

The handgun out the window was aimed right at Jim.

She screamed, terrified that he was in the line of fire and what might happen if the trigger finger slipped.

If the gun went off.

Jim hit the brakes and screeched to a halt.

The Jimmy halted beside them.

Jim sat still, hands on the steering wheel.

She mimicked him and placed hers on the dashboard.

The Jimmy's passenger covered the driver off as he got out and walked behind our car.

He flung open her door, grabbed her by the hair, and she ended up on the ground.

The punch in the gut made sure she didn't scream a second time.

He dragged her around to the Jimmy on her ass.

Frightened and off balance, she couldn't manage to get in a kick or a punch. She managed another weak scream before a fist to the back of her head quieted her a second time.

Bobbie's attacker must have thought he had her under control.

He leaned over and checked the back of their car.

His mouth opened and he was about to say something when she took her chance.

She rammed the back of her head against his jaw.

His teeth slammed shut with a satisfying clunk.

Pissed off as he was, she managed a punch and a kick before he smacked her in the gut with a roundhouse.

She couldn't breathe. It was all she could do to stay upright.

He shoved her into the back and made sure her head banged the door when he closed it.

She knew for sure these two friends of her brother were part of Ray's problem.

They had to be.

Trapped and scared, she looked for a door handle.

Slipping out the opposite door wasn't an option.

There was no way out.

Gunshots sealed her fate.

Stunned, she crawled to the window, expecting to

see Jim on the ground, dead or bleeding out. Bleeding would be the least of it.

She raised her head over the door, afraid.

Jim wasn't on the ground.

He was standing.

She almost cheered.

No blood.

At least he hadn't been the target.

Then she saw the flat tires and knew.

With no way to be chased or followed, she was definitely in more than ankle-deep crap.

Where would she end up?

Would Jim find her?

Would he have a clue where to begin?

Had she told him about Diamondhead and the sailboat when they first met?

Was that where she'd end up?

She couldn't remember any of it.

It was a long drive for a couple of former friends to haul someone who threatened their discovery and their drug dealings.

Perhaps they thought she knew where the drugs had gotten to.

Maybe they knew what happened to her brother.

Or just maybe they thought she had the drugs.

If she could convince them, they could exchange information.

She couldn't trust them, but maybe she could bluff them.

And she tried.

She really did.

It didn't do any good.

The more she talked, the more they kept silent.

Maybe she was telling them too much.

She hoped they'd think they were on the verge of being discovered.

Nothing she said got a reaction.

She gave up.

Bobbie dozed fitfully off and on in the back of the hot, dusty Jimmy. She daydreamed of Jim and burritos and the kindness he'd shown when they first met. She'd have done anything for a burrito, starved as she was.

She woke up shaking her head at the crazy dream. Food and Jim, not necessarily in that order. The man and his favorite road food was on her mind even when her life was being threatened.

Damn the man.

How could she still be thinking of him after everything that happened? Would he be coming for her now that they were separated? She'd screwed up in the storage unit. He had to think she wasn't worth the effort now she was out of sight.

Out of mind.

And she was out of her mind with worry about her fate with these two.

After what seemed like forever in the back of the Jimmy in the heat and sticky plastic seats, it slowed

She looked out the window.

The bay stared back, stretching out to infinity.

They yanked her out of the Jimmy and pushed her toward the sloop still tied off on the finger where she had left it.

She was back where she started. And for what?

They dragged her to the yacht and tossed her below.

The hatch slammed shut and she was in complete darkness.

Ropes hit the deck.

The engine fired up.

They were headed somewhere.

After about an hour, the engine stopped.

The anchor rattled and splashed.

So maybe they weren't so far offshore.

Bobbie curled up on a berth and tried to sleep in the hot, sticky yacht's interior.

The sound of a powerboat on a fast approach interrupted nap time.

A boat bumped, and then it tipped as at least two men stepped on board.

Voices argued and the hatch slid open.

A body bounced down the steps, grunting all the way.

The hatch slammed shut and left her in darkness.

Even the portholes were covered over.

She stumbled out of the berth, hands outstretched, searching for the table.

Someone's labored breathing kept her alert.

Something moved.

Whoever had been tossed down the stairs was conscious.

"Who's here? Jim? Is that you?"

It couldn't be. He'd given up on her for sure when they were separated. He had to. Even if he hadn't, how did he get here so fast? Impossible.

Was she starting to go crazy?

"Bobbie?"

She recognized the familiar voice immediately.

"Ray! Are you all right? I thought you were dead.

Where have you been? How did you get here? What's going on? You're not dead."

In the dark, Ray found her and threw his arms around her and lifted her off her feet. He hugged so hard she couldn't draw a breath until he set her down.

Bobbie said, "I've been looking for you for days. Are you all right? They told me you were dead. What happened?"

She talked non-stop.

She told him about Jim and how they met and searched and about Terry across the street from their house being an informant paid by the cartel and their parents having to leave and the sicario. She left out the part where she let the woman die.

"Sis. Slow down. You're talking a mile a minute, as usual."

"I know. I know. I'm so happy I found you. Are you all right?"

Would Jim ever find them?

Would he go back to his own problems and leave her behind? She couldn't blame him if he started hitch-hiking in the opposite direction just to be rid of her.

Tears rolled down her cheeks and she started sniffling.

Ray said, "It's all right, sis. Calm down. We're safe for now. You better make sure you tell me about it this time. And who's this Jim again? You've been talking so fast it's all I can do to understand you."

As usual, her older brother was willing to listen.

Did she want to start from the beginning?

How much time did they have?

CHAPTER 37

Jim Nash rode in Diana's car in deafening silence. He thought about thanking her for the previous night's debauchery and great sex to break the ice. Instead, he thanked her for rescuing him.

Beyond that, it was obvious she couldn't wait to drop him at the gas bar where he'd left the stolen truck.

She didn't bat an eye as she pulled into the gas bar to let him out.

"One time only, Jim. Thanks for the good time."

Okay. So she thanked him for the good sex.

At least, that's the way he heard it.

She drove off without looking back.

He knew, because he checked.

Jim limped to the truck, opened the door, and pulled himself in using the steering wheel.

He wrestled with the armrest as he eased onto the driver's seat.

He didn't bother to close the door. He couldn't, anyway. He was too stiff and sore.

He flipped the seatback down, closed his eyes, and slept the sleep of the dead.

It was almost mid-day when he was forced to vacate the truck and the sweltering heat and humidity. He limped his way to the restroom and splashed cold water on his face before making his way to the counter and a lukewarm burrito.

He choked it down with gas bar painkillers and chased it with bad coffee.

He groaned as he pulled the heavy duffel out of the back seat. He manhandled it over his shoulder. He wasn't sure if it was because of the beating, or punishment for satisfying Diana's needs and a few of his own.

Before long, he had the marina gate house in sight. Flags flapped and snapped in the strong, gusty wind blowing ashore.

He made his way to a small, fenced boat storage area he had scouted out the day before. Trees and low scrub facing the concrete pad would provide good cover while he kept watch. He stayed alert and angled toward it. It wasn't so thick he had to fight his way through to the fence.

He made his nest, settled in, and sat down to wait.

The burritos did their thing and forced his eyes closed. He needed the sleep.

He needed to keep an eye out for the sloop, too. Every so often his head snapped to attention and he looked around to end up swatting at flies.

When swatting flies became boring, he busied himself by taking inventory.

Plenty of firepower.

Plenty of nerve.

Plenty of damage left over from yesterday's beating, too.

Needing to know if Bobbie was aboard the sloop.

Not wanting to be here if she wasn't.

He faked a couple more desultory swats at the flies and settled in for the long haul.

He was in a good spot. The location gave him a clear view of the only pad in the marina with cars. It didn't occur to him it might not be Bobbie's yacht he was looking for, and he grew impatient.

Jim's eyes closed again thanks to the food and heat and humidity.

When he woke, he discovered a nice-looking sloop tied off on a finger of the wharf. It looked lonely all by itself. It had to be the one. Isolated. Just far enough from the main building and looking about right.

He didn't know what he was expecting.

Maybe Bobbie on deck, waving frantically.

Impossible, though.

How could she know he was here?

Was she even here?

Two parked cars commanded the concrete pad where a trailer and snowbirds would sit in the winter. Beyond that, there was nothing but the wind rustling leaves and flapping flags.

Fed up with the lack of action, he changed into a clean shirt and made his way to the yacht club lounge.

He checked before entering. There was no one from yesterday's one-sided boxing match.

Diana looked up and smiled from behind the bar. "You don't look too bad. I could dim the lights and you'd look pretty good."

"From what I remember about last night, you

look too good in any light."

She blushed a bright pink. Maybe the veneer of toughness she presented wasn't so thick after all.

Diana said, "Keep it up with the flattery and I might invite you back."

Absentmindedly, his hand moved to a shoulder and rubbed. His subconscious knew what would happen if he got involved with this one and Bobbie ever found out.

"That's a sweet-looking sloop tied off on the finger. Any idea who owns it?"

It didn't make him feel any less guilty about changing the subject.

Diana said, "I noticed it when it first came in a few days ago. A man and a woman. The man was a lot older. I think the woman jumped ship. He's been here ever since. He comes and goes in his sloop, all by his lonesome. He eats here. If he wasn't so old—"

Diana looked into his eyes, and her face softened.

"You aren't so old."

Judging by the yacht club's aging customer base and Diana's hustle, he figured his chances were good. He returned her gaze rather wistfully until he was forced to remember her words from this morning and why he was here.

"So what's up with it? Has the guy mentioned how long he'll be staying?"

Diana cast a roving eye before replying.

Jim felt like a side of beef hanging on a hook, waiting for a buyer to nod approval.

She nodded. "The same cars come and go. It looks like he's having meetings with people. More than that, I don't know. He doesn't say much when he's here. He tips well, though."

He thanked her and fished for a twenty. He pushed it across the bar.

"Why do you want to know? Are you going to blow up this one, too?" she asked.

Diana's face turned pale before reaching to palm the twenty.

He attributed it to a lack of sleep they shared from the night before.

A hand reached into the top of her blouse and tucked the twenty into the bra he had watched her put on this morning.

The woman didn't need a bra.

She probably didn't need the twenty, either.

Diana regained her composure and it was time to go before he got into more trouble than it was worth.

He pushed off the barstool and headed for the door.

"Come back any time. I'll be here."

But not for long.

He wasn't looking forward to swatting more flies in his hideout.

He'd rather be swatting at Diana.

If it weren't for Bobbie, that is.

CHAPTER 38

Jim wasn't so busy killing time in the bar with Diana that he didn't notice the single car rolling onto the concrete pad beside the sloop. A second screeched to a stop beside it.

A tall, gray-haired man exited and stretched.

He recognized him. Kennedy. From our flat on the side of the road. It had to be. He hesitated, looked around, and headed for the boat.

A third vehicle approached.

He recognized the border guards, still in their coverall uniforms. They must have ditched the government Jimmy. Too bad. He'd set fire to it just for spite if he could find it.

There was no sign of Bobbie. They had ditched her.

He wanted Bobbie to be only as far away as the sloop.

Kennedy took his time with the two men. In an obvious fit of temper, he began pointing and gesticulating wildly. He had to be pissed off about something. Was he handing out shit for the screwup the pair left behind in Brownsville?

By the time Jim made his hiding spot, he was too far away to hear anything. The words didn't carry in the wind, nor could he make sense of what was happening.

Perhaps they were taking shit for bringing the girl back to the scene of the crime. According to Bobbie, this was where she took a beating and handed somebody's balls to them on the toe of her boot. They had to be the balls belonging to the gray-haired man.

He had picked Bobbie up a bit to the north. Since then, they'd been tested and survived. When it seemed like they might have a chance, she was taken from him. Yet another woman destined to enter his life, linger for what seemed like an eternity, and then disappear without a trace. At least this one hadn't been killed.

Or had she?

If Bobbie was alive, she had to be in trouble, else why would they have taken her? Did they think she knew where the drugs were? Did they think she might have them? Had they found out that she'd left a dead sicario back in Brownsville?

Maybe the desk-clerk witness left behind spilled his guts. Bobbie's days would be numbered if she gave up what they wanted to know. But did she have the drugs?

He didn't want to think so. Still, he couldn't be certain. He didn't know if she was even on board the yacht.

While he contemplated all of that, the hatch door banged open. A flash of light shattered his daydreaming. He waited, impatient. A woman stepped onto the deck.

He recognized her instantly, even from the distance.

Bobbie was wearing the same clothes she changed into before she was hauled out of their car and forced into the Jimmy. She didn't look happy to be here.

They were even, though.

Neither was he.

A man joined her on deck.

He didn't look familiar.

They hugged for a moment.

Both squinted over the water.

Friends?

Lovers?

Someone she was working with?

He'd shared that woman's bed. It didn't mean he owned her. Or that she owed him anything. But he felt something more than lust when they were together. Although, the lust wasn't so bad, either.

Jim didn't know whether he should be disappointed or angry, so instead he sat back and waited for the cars to disappear.

Bobbie remained below with the stranger, staying out of sight. He wondered if she thought he might be close. Or if he was still searching. And if she thought he was, could she be hiding out on him?

He had enough.

It was go time.

Jim unzipped the duffel and retrieved a knife. He strapped it to a leg. He tucked the automatic into the small of his back beneath a sweaty shirt and shouldered the bag.

He made his way nonchalantly toward the

moored yacht, hoping he looked like a crewman who'd been on a bender showing up late for work.

Up close, it was a nice-looking boat. Almost a twin to one he was once very familiar with. Newer, though. Well-maintained, by the look of it.

He wondered who did the work. Bobbie? Perhaps. She told him she had crewed on it. She never said for how long.

Gulls swooped and screeched.

The yacht club flag flapped in the stiff breeze blowing in off the gulf. Water lapped at the sides of the yacht, another familiar sound from his past. The sloop rocked naturally in the swell making its way into the finger of water.

It was a pretty sweet yacht. One day he'd like to own something like it. Inexperienced sailor that he was, Jim knew he'd never be able to sail on his own.

His daydreaming halted the instant he stepped aboard. The yacht eased over slowly and righted.

Water continued slapping gently against the sides.

"Hello?"

He recognized the voice immediately.

"Is anyone out there?"

Below, someone moved.

The hatch slid open.

Bobbie stepped up and looked into his eyes.

"Jim. What are you doing? How did you find me? How did you get here? I thought I'd never see you again. You have to get away. They'll be back soon."

Jim took Bobbie in his arms and she relaxed against him, shaking uncontrollably and sobbing.

He held on tight.

She tried to quiet her sobbing, but it only

contributed to the shaking.

"Whoa. Slow down, woman. You must know by now sniffling isn't allowed."

She punched him in the shoulder because she could, but for once it was gentle.

Maybe she had mellowed since we lost one another.

He dumped the duffel below deck and jumped ashore to untie.

He turned on the fans to rid the engine compartment of fumes.

They drifted free in the finger's calm waters.

"What are you doing? You can't steal it. They'll find us again."

"Why not? Who's going to stop us?"

He looked for vehicles and hoped no one was on the way.

Jim said, "I brought you a change of clothes. There are some slightly warm burritos in the bag if you're so inclined."

Bobbie shook her head and mumbled. "At a time like this you think of food?" She hesitated before going on. "Sunglasses too?"

"You betcha, baby."

She dived below and returned with a handful of clothes.

"Nice hoodie. You planning on going gangsta on me?"

"I thought once we got out to sea I might have some time, yes."

Cars raced onto the pad and screeched to a halt beside the yacht.

A familiar figure standing in the clubhouse

doorway watched it go down. She must have made the call. Perhaps Diana already had her ride out of town lined up.

Three men exited the cars in a hurry. All three were reaching around for whatever was tucked into their belts.

"Throw up the duffel, baby. I need to find something in it."

Bobbie did better than that. She carried the heavy bag over and unzipped.

He pulled out the AK, slipped a taped cuerno de chivo home, and racked.

"Get below, woman. There's going to be a bit of trouble in paradise."

CHAPTER 39

Bobbie felt the sloop rocking gently in the sheltered finger. The yacht shifted. Mooring lines tightened and went slack. Fenders squeaked.

Faint steps began at the bow and traversed the deck. She hoped it was Kennedy. She sailed into port with him—how long ago was it now? It felt like a month.

She could deal with the man. He was a lot easier on her than the others. Perhaps he would tell her what was going on.

Bobbie slid open the hatch. Blinding sunlight assaulted her eyes. She blinked and squinted and realized she was face-to-face with another human being. It was Jim. In that instant of recognition, she grinned like a woman saying yes to a marriage proposal. "How? When? Where were you?"

A huge smile looked back at her. It took effort to stop with the questions.

"Nash is back in town, baby. That's all you need to know."

He took her in his arms and she felt safe all over again.

He gestured to the bag. "Stow this below deck while I release the lines."

He and dropped the bag at her feet.

She didn't ask what was inside. If she knew him, it was an armory. The heavy bag almost slipped from Bobbie's sweaty grip as she hauled it below deck.

Topside, Jim had the fan going.

They were drifting free in the finger.

Cars braked to a screeching halt on the concrete pad beside the yacht.

Danger in Diamondhead.

It sounded like a movie title, but she wouldn't be hitchhiking her way out of it this time.

She called to Jim, busy at the helm. "They're back."

It suddenly dawned on the men that the yacht was floating free. Their pace quickened as they tried to catch up before the yacht cleared the dock.

Jim didn't appear the slightest bit troubled. He carried on like it was nothing.

"Can you get the duffel for me in a hurry? There's something I need."

Bobbie flew down the stairs and struggled to haul the heavy bag topside.

She searched through it frantically, looking for the automatic she knew would be there.

Jim pushed her hands away and went for what she thought he called the AK.

He withdrew two magazines covered in duct tape.

She was ignorant, but she wasn't stupid.

The men on the receiving end would be in for a shock.

"You're not leaving my sight ever again, woman. Never ever."

She gave him the look and he grinned like a fool.

Come to think of it, she did, too. This time, she let him give the orders while she paid rapt attention.

Jim said, "What you're looking for is tucked into my belt."

Bobbie did as she was told. No way was she going to screw things up now that Jim was back in her life. She busied herself trying to yank the pistol from his belt without shooting him.

Jim went to work with the AK. He slipped one of those huge magazines into place and started doing what the weapon did best.

He fired short bursts.

Brass clattered onto the deck.

Some splashed into the water.

Ashore, lead kicked up shards of cement and lead ricocheted.

The gunfire forced the armed men back to the cover of their vehicles.

It wasn't like a movie or a television show.

They sheltered behind the engine block, and for good reason.

Doors and anything else wouldn't do.

Jim had a standoff going on.

Judging by the shouts, his opponents weren't happy about it.

She thought they were doing pretty good.

Jim went back to handling the yacht.

He steered out of the finger and into open water.

Ray came topside. He spotted Jim and without hesitating, rapped him on the back of the head.

Jim dropped like a collapsed sail boom and stayed down.

"Ray. It's Jim. Damn you to hell. Why did you do that?"

The guilty look on Ray's face made him look like he was ten years old all over again. "How was I to know? You never told me about him."

"Now you know. Take over piloting this thing while I try to talk him out of killing you when he comes to."

Typical woman.

Bobbie just wouldn't listen. Instead, in the thick of things, she flipped up the back of his shirt and tugged at the automatic tucked into his belt. It was a miracle it didn't go off.

He was impressed when she checked the magazine.

"We're a team or we're nothing. Don't ever order me around again," she said.

He couldn't disagree. She had a loaded handgun filling her hand. While it wasn't pointed in his direction, it could have been.

He grinned a shit-eater in her direction. "Yes, dear. Anything you say."

Jim aimed at the feet of the advancing attackers and pulled the AK's trigger for a short burst.

Flying lead kicked up cement.

It put the fear of the rifle known as the African credit card into them. They scattered toward the cars and halted their retreat by taking shelter behind engine blocks.

With a move like that they definitely weren't amateurs.

"Can you back this thing up and get us out to sea? I'll hold them off as best I can."

A shadow appeared in the corner of his eye.

Bobbie screamed. "Ray! No!"

It was too late.

The AK slipped and clattered to the deck.

Jim thumped down beside it like a side of beef.

When he came to, his head was against Bobbie's familiar bosom. Her arms were around him, too, but he didn't notice that right away. He nuzzled comfortably against both breasts and grinned.

She almost dropped him.

"You're faking it. You are a wicked bad man, Jim Nash."

"Not entirely." She allowed him to continue play-acting. Maybe she was enjoying it, too.

Then she pushed him away.

Bobbie said, "You're sure you're all right? Ray gave you a nasty wallop."

"Ray? Your brother Ray? I thought—"

So they brought both of them here. They had to be thinking brother and sister were a team working to steal the drugs.

"So did I. Until we discovered each other on board the yacht. We were waiting for the right time," she said.

"The right time to do what?" he asked.

"I don't know. We didn't have weapons until you showed up."

"Lucky for you. I didn't think I'd find you."

He pressed his head against her and waited.

This time, she didn't push him away.

The sound of the engine convinced him were away from the wharf and headed for the breakwater. "Who's driving this tub?"

He struggled to stand. Ray's wallop was worse than he thought.

Unsteady on his feet, he made a grab for Bobbie and then the jackline to keep from going overboard.

Bobbie grabbed and hung on, steadying him. "Ray. My brother. He's a professional sailor."

"Good to know. Can he teach me to swim, too?"

Bobbie helped him below and convinced him to climb into a berth.

He closed his eyes and Bobbie went topside.

It was pitch black when he came around. The rap he took on the side of the head did more damage than he suspected.

Jim struggled up the stairs to face howling wind and flapping sails. Wobbly and disoriented, he kept a hand on the jackline for support.

The sloop in full sail charged through the waves, drenching him in spray. He leaned against the rigging for support.

"You better strap in, Nash. It's going to get a lot rougher," Ray advised.

As far as he was concerned, it was a lot rougher already. The rocking sailboat tossed him from one side to the other. He hung on, only barely. Bobbie helped him into straps and fastened him in.

"Where are we headed?" Jim asked.

"We'll moor her off Playa Bagdad," Ray said.

"Playa Bagdad? Why there?"

"We heard that's where you need to be."

"Well yeah. Maybe. But you don't have to hole up there on my account."

"Yes. We do. There are a few things we're not telling you."

Jim took a chance. "What about Brownsville?"

He already knew that would be a no. After what they left behind in Browntown, as Bobbie called it, here was no chance in hell any of them would be welcome back there.

"We burned that bridge too well."

It took him a minute. "Yesenia."

"Yes. And Terry, too."

Jim was the one needed convincing. At least they realized it. He let it rest. He had nothing.

Playa Bagdad wasn't far. Still, it had nothing resembling a harbor. A sand beach and a collection of bodegas for sunbathers and locals who wanted to do some beach shopping were about it. At one time, the place had figured in one of his escapades with just about all the women in his life. Whether he considered that operation a success was another matter.

He had to admit he was happy Bobbie found her brother alive. That he'd given him a good one on the side of the head didn't bother him any more than the pain and suffering. How would Ray have known he was the good guy? He had showed up out of the blue, after all.

Now, with her brother in tow, they were headed for Mexico. By boat. By sailboat.

Was that taking the slow train, or what?

Jim headed below to make sandwiches in the well-equipped galley. It would give him a chance to think things through without having Bobbie, finally safe and sound, to distract him.

Tampico owed him. His old operation had gone south in a hurry. Two close friends had been killed. One betrayed; the other, his lover, ambushed and killed. Corrupt and dangerous as the city was, it looked like it was the place he needed to be. The trouble was, he knew nobody. He had no connections.

From what he knew, warring cartels had taken the place over. It was still going on, hot and heavy as ever. America hadn't stopped buying drugs or supplying the cartels with weapons.

Did he want to take Bobbie and Ray into something like that? He already knew the answer. If we went, they'd be his only allies. He didn't think either of them—inexperienced as they were—would be up to the monumental task.

The only thing keeping him going was the knowledge that Bobbie's brother finally showed up. It was time to confront her before it became too late for any of them.

And it was time to think about his own reasons for the vendetta he was convinced would solve all his problems concerning his past. He couldn't possibly allow Bobbie and her brother to shoulder the burden for anything he had to do.

That was for him alone.

If he was successful, maybe Bobbie would be waiting. If he wasn't, his feelings for her wouldn't matter in the slightest. He had to set her straight. He had to get her to understand that his fight wasn't her fight.

If anything happened to her, he'd never forgive himself.

CHAPTER 40

Bobbie Dawson ended up cradling Jim in her arms, waiting for him to come around after her brother, Ray, cold-cocked him with a blow to the side of his head.

When he finally did begin to come around, Jim went full perv on her—not that she minded. It was relief coupled with joy at having him with her, finally.

She found herself subjected to the man's face tucked into her breasts.

He nuzzled and sighed and she grinned like a woman on her wedding night.

She tugged his head away and began chastising him anyway.

He squinted up at her with a forlorn look and she had to give up when his grin mirrored her own.

"You're incorrigible. What's a girl to do?"

Bobbie shook her head and gave him another chance. To no avail.

Jim said, "That bump on the head isn't so bad. Help a man up."

He was still dizzy, and not in a good way. He made a grab for the jackline, attempting to steady himself.

At the same time, he let go of her and for a split second she thought he was on his way overboard.

"You need to strap in or go below, Jim. Now."

He wasn't having any of it. "I'll be all right. I just need another minute."

She gave him more than a few, but she didn't leave him until she forced him into a life jacket. How could she let the man who rescued her fall overboard, even if he could be frustratingly stubborn?

When she was satisfied, she went back to Ray and lit into him like there was no tomorrow.

Ray held up his hands in surrender. "You're in love with that man." It was an accusation.

Bobbie mumbled and went beet-red and mumbled some more.

"All right, sis. It's your funeral," Ray said.

That was the final straw.

"My funeral? What are you talking about? You're the dim bulb that came up with the idea to steal cartel drugs for a payday. What did you think was going to happen? Even if you never saw another news headline in this part of the world, surely you had to know what would happen. You put our entire family in jeopardy. And now you're telling me that Jim is bad for me?"

She caught Ray looking at Jim. She wheeled and gave him a look that could have felled a lesser man. He just grinned and shook his head and knew better than to utter word one. She might have tossed her brother overboard if he had.

Jim came up behind them. "You want me to do some sailing so the happy family can continue with this line of discussion in private below deck?"

Ray looked impressed. "He can sail? You should have told me."

Jim had that self-satisfied look he got until she let the wind out of his sail. She seemed to do that a lot with that man. "For all I know, he can sail just well enough to run us aground."

That got the man's attention real fast. "Oh, come on now. I'm not that bad. Give me some credit. I tracked you down to where I first picked you up."

Like that had anything to do with sailing. She wouldn't be giving him the credit he deserved in the company of her brother. "If you know what's good for you, you better zip it."

"That's it. No more burritos for you. We're done."

Bobbie burst into tears and began sobbing, and it wasn't for effect.

Maybe Jim was right. Maybe she was acting out a reaction she'd been suppressing.

When this was over, she had to get somewhere far away.

If Jim loved her, he'd wait.

If she loved him, she had to do it for her own good before they hooked up again.

Why was her life never simple since meeting this man?

Jim Nash really tried. Maybe too hard.

He cajoled.

He begged.

When none of that worked, he told the woman he loved her.

It did no good. Bobbie wouldn't listen. She wouldn't try to understand. She threatened to throw him overboard without a life jacket, knowing he'd sink like a stone.

Finally, he had enough. "Just because you racked up a body count of one doesn't mean you're capable of adding to it. Have you had a reaction yet?"

Jim already knew the answer. He needed to know if she knew.

"What do you mean?" she asked.

"Waking up with the sweats. Talking in your sleep. Screaming. Crying. Uncontrollable trembling. Begging for forgiveness. Oh, I almost forgot. One more. Puking over the side of our car."

"I had all of that, all right. I thought it was because of my feelings for you."

Her joke fell flat.

"Hilarious. I ought to put you over my knee and spank you right here."

"Then you will end up walking the plank after I stop rubbing my ass."

A familiar image of Bobbie rubbing a pink rear end came to mind, but his mind was made up. He didn't wait to announce the decision.

"We're heading to Brownsville."

The safe house would be a good beginning. With Bobbie's problem solved and her bother found—was he ever lost?

He was ready for some me time.

It was the only way he knew to pick up the pieces of his personal war.

Bobbie and her brother went through a lot of yelling and shouting and pointing and pushing and throwing punches. He knew why she had such a devastating fist. When the shadow boxing and the dust settled, Ray and Bobbie came to an understanding.

He didn't ask.

She nodded at him and he went below.

He flipped on as many lights as he could find and began field stripping and re-assembling the weapons.

It gave him something to do as he mumbled and stumbled and tried to convince himself that having Bobbie and her brother along for the ride wouldn't drag him into the depths of Mexican water.

He completed his self-imposed exile from topside. He called to Bobbie to join him below deck.

He left the weapons out on the bunk for her to see.

Jim said, "You're getting your first lesson whether you like it or not, woman. Pay attention as if your life depends on it, because it just might."

He picked up a magazine. "This is an AK magazine. Some call it a clip. It's not. A clip is from a different war. This is a magazine. Mag for short. Across the Rio Grande, it's a cuerno de chivo—slang for goat's horn.

He handed it to her.

"Get familiar with it. Know it. Know how to load it. Start now."

He handed over the bag of ammo, and she did pretty good.

She muttered and broke nails and didn't seem bothered by it.

Overall, he was impressed. "You did good. Now here's another."

She looked at him like he was crazy but that was all right. He was becoming accustomed to those looks.

"How many of these are you going to need?" she asked.

She had part of the question right.

The you part.

No way was he going to include Bobbie once his own adventure began. He couldn't take the chance. He cared for her too much.

There was no way he was about to admit it to her, either.

Then he remembered he already had.

CHAPTER 41

Jim picked up the rifle and hefted it.

"This is the dreaded and much-maligned AK. In some parts of the world, it's known as the African credit card. The best part of it is that it just works. In the swamp. In the desert. In the jungle. Mud. Sand. Dirt. It never fails."

Bobbie reached out and he handed it to her.

She took it with both hands and hefted it. "It's heavy."

"Even heavier with a jungle mag."

"What's a jungle mag? I just loaded a magazine for you."

"A jungle mag is dos cuernos taped together. Double the action. Double the fun."

She picked up the second empty magazine and reached into the bag for more ammo.

"Wait. Don't start loading that one just yet. There's something you need to see."

She placed it on the table. Her hands went to her lap, waiting, like a patient schoolgirl—something he knew she wasn't.

Did he really want to get into this with her? Could

he put Bobbie intentionally in harm's way? He didn't consider it for long. If it was bound to happen, he wanted her prepared. Decision made. She was the only backup strategy he had.

"It goes into the underside like this."

He held the AK by the fore end, tipped it sideways, and slipped the front edge of the empty magazine into the front notch on the receiver. He rotated the mag back until it engaged the rear stop with a loud click.

"Did you see that? Did you hear it?"

She nodded. "Yes."

Jim pressed the catch in front of the finger guard and rotated the mag forward. He removed the magazine from where it slid into its front receiver.

"I'll do it again."

He repeated the motion and handed over the rifle. "Now it's your turn."

He left to go topside.

He wanted to confer with Ray. He needed to know if he was planning on staying or going. He had no need for him, and he doubted if Ray wanted to help anyway. He was relieved when he learned Ray would be leaving them in Brownsville.

Satisfied, he returned below-deck to Bobbie's side. "How's it going?"

"All right." She performed the action with the empty magazine twice for him.

"Leave the magazine in place. Hold the AK and pull back the slide."

He crooked her index finger on it and covered it with his own.

He pulled the slide back until it locked.

"Now look inside. Is it clear?"

She maneuvered the heavy rifle sideways for a good look.

"There's nothing. No bullet. It must be clear."

"And that's how we know you won't be shooting at your friends. Well, that, and don't show the muzzle to anything you don't intend to kill."

Her eyes moved to the loaded magazine on the table. She was aching to try it.

He wasn't so sure.

"Take a break. Go visit with your brother for a bit. Find out what he's going to do. I'll still be here when you get back. So will the AK."

She gave him the look and left to go topside.

The yelling started while Jim was making sandwiches.

Bits and pieces drifted past the open hatch.

He didn't venture out to investigate. The way the woman threw a punch, she'd be a match for her brother, whatever was going on.

The hatch opened wide and Ray dragged his sister, struggling and yelling, down the hatchway. "Bobbie tells me you've been showing her how to handle an AK. Is that true?"

No way was Bobbie about letting up.

He didn't get a chance to answer.

The argument went on and on, like things do between brother and sister when neither will give ground.

He waited patiently until both grew fed up with it.

"Why would I lie, Ray? You think I'm making shit up? You, who stole a car loaded with frigging cartel cocaine? Yeah, I'm the one with the problems, all right. Lying would be the least of them, wouldn't you say?"

Bobbie twisted free and sat down in front of the rifle.

She picked up a sandwich and began chewing.

"Mmm. You're a good cook, too, Nash. I might just have to marry you."

She aimed stink-eye at her brother as the words tumbled out.

Jim didn't utter word one. He knew better by now.

Instead, he opened the cooler, pulled out a Sol, cracked it, and took a swallow.

"Anyone else?"

Nobody said a word.

He leaned back and enjoyed the beer, hoping for peace and quiet.

Ray refused to give up. He wouldn't shut up, either.

"Bobbie, I'm warning you—"

"No. You're not. You're making a mountain out of a molehill. And only thinking about yourself. As usual."

She eyed him, expecting something.

Jim only sighed and shook his head and kept on with the sandwiches. He kept his ears wide open, though.

"I'm jumping ship in Brownsville," Ray told her. "You two are free to do whatever you want."

"Fine."

There was that word again. He'd heard it a few times, too. There'd be no going against her now. He wondered if her brother knew that about her.

"You won't change my mind, Ray. You can go back to the wheel," Bobbie said.

Ray climbed the stairs.

Jim gave Bobbie the once-over. "What was that about?"

"He thinks you're leading me somewhere I don't need to be. Now that he's back, he wants to return to the way things were. You know, before the cartel started looking for him."

"That's a way to certain death. Does he have any idea—"

"I know. That's what we were fighting about topside. Well, that, and having you in my life. He thinks you're a bad deal for me."

He had no idea. Perhaps he was. "Yeah. So. Am I?"

She didn't answer. "Are you going to make more sandwiches, or do I have to do it myself?"

"I take it that's a no. And take some to your brother as a peace offering. I don't want to have to force you to walk the plank."

Bobbie leaned in and kissed him. Before he could react, she grabbed the sandwiches and rushed topside.

She was turning out to be a handful, all right.

But he already knew that from the very beginning when he had crossed paths with the woman hitchhiking at a gas bar.

Sitting below deck alone with his thoughts, Jim made up his mind.

"I have to go back to the stash house."

He made the announcement to no one within hearing distance. What he didn't say out loud was he'd have to leave Bobbie behind when they docked in Brownsville. He had to. She'd object if she knew, and it wasn't something he wanted to experience after being witness to the blowup with her brother.

At that instant, as though to confirm the decision, the yacht heeled over as it changed course.

Someone topside must have read his mind.

"If there's anything left, it will be in Brownsville."

The lights flicked on.

Bobbie pursed her lips and looked at him like he was nuts.

He figured he was ahead. She wasn't glaring at him.

"Are you sure? Won't that be dangerous? Surely they'll be watching for us there," she said.

It was true. After setting fire to their cache of drugs and money in the stash house, they'd be on the lookout all right. Security would be a concern.

But why, if the house was no longer a safe house for the feds? If it was compromised, and it looked like it was, who abandoned it? Why had it been abandoned in the first place? And who turned it over to the cartel to be used as a stash house for drugs and cash?

He'd heard of them, of course. Usually, every nook and cranny in the place would be filled with plastic-wrapped bales of cash.

Sometimes a family of relatives would be left behind.

Making the place look occupied kept away neighborhood inquiring eyes and gave it that lived-in look.

CHAPTER 42

There wasn't a soul in the Brownsville marina when I crept silently off the sloop in the dark.

Ray was long gone.

He tried his best not to make a sound for fear of disturbing Bobbie. He didn't want to make excuses. He didn't want to dwell on saying goodbye.

All that was a lie. Hell, he knew he wouldn't be able to talk her out of accompanying him.

He was certain he'd succeeded, too, until Bobbie tapped his shoulder in the stash house.

"Jesus, woman. Do you want to get shot?"

"Judging by the way you so elegantly deserted ship in the dark, I figured this was where you'd be. Trying to ditch me, were you?"

She had him there. He went with the truth. "Yes. Are you satisfied now?"

"Not so much. Why?"

Damn but that woman could be annoying with the questions.

"Because I didn't want to put you in danger."

"Why not?"

She just wouldn't quit.

He shook his head and rolled his eyes and he could have done at least another couple of things to keep him from answering the obvious.

Instead, he gave in. "Because I love you. Now are you satisfied?"

"Yes."

Exasperated, he waited, but there was only silence.

"Yes? That's it? Only yes?"

"For now. We have too much to do," she said.

She explained what she wanted to do.

He took to it right away.

An hour later, with Bobbie driving, they were on the road, headed from the stash house back to the Brownsville marina and the sailboat.

It gave him plenty of time to think.

Jim was no closer to solving what happened with Kara. Maybe he never would. Maybe having Bobbie enter his life meant he needed to put the relationship behind him and move on with life. Maybe it was karma, meant to kick boot out of his search for vengeance.

For now, it would have to do. They had bigger problems in the present that could prove insurmountable. Missing cartel cash, if it was even noticeable in the mountain contained within the old stash house, was a more pressing problem.

They spent hours driving from the car to the sailboat's mooring and back.

Finally, it was time.

Bobbie fired up the engine and got underway.

She took us out of the harbor and past the breakwater.

Under sail, we headed into the Gulf.

Bobbie proved to be just as adept at sailing as her brother.

Hell, with his limited abilities in the sailing department, she could take the sloop anywhere she wanted.

Had he let himself down by allowing her to convince him they could steal the cash and make a new life for themselves?

Yes.

But not all the way.

On the final drive to the marina, he decided for the last time that everything about Kara was a lost cause. He didn't need to be letting her back into his life after the woman's death.

It was all over, finally.

Pilar, however, was another matter.

He needed closure, for her and for him.

He had no idea where that ride would end up taking him, but right now, he didn't want to know.

"Where are we headed, sailor?"

North was all he managed to get out of her.

When she stripped down to her bikini, that was enough.

For now.

"The coast guard has to think I'm out with my sugar daddy."

Where had he heard that before?

He went along with Bobbie and smiled anyway.

Her plan worked, too.

On their journey north, they came alongside a couple of times, and then waved and slipped away after a quick look.

Maybe the radio waves telegraphed a good-looking topless woman in a bikini bottom who wasn't shy in the slightest.

"Where are we going to put in?" Jim asked.

Bobbie said, "Somewhere with a bank and a dry dock, at least. A storage unit wouldn't hurt, either. We need to stash the cash we borrowed, the sooner the better."

"Yeah, well, I'm on board with that."

And he was, too, until a white, foamy wake telegraphed its arrival behind them on the distant horizon.

He didn't say anything to Bobbie. He wanted her kept busy while he went below to check the firepower.

The powerboat was holding off, matching them in the speed department.

Jim was pretty sure it would make its appearance after dark when it would come abeam. Right now, it was keeping him on edge.

It became impossible to keep it from Bobbie.

He pointed the boat out.

"He's been following us for a while. He's probably going to pace us until dark. He'll try to board then."

Jim was concerned.

He went below a second time to prep the AK and check the load.

He made sure to bring up a pistol for Bobbie. He tucked it into the seat beside her along with a second mag.

"Just in case," he said.

She only nodded.

A hard look crossed her face for an instant and disappeared in one of the fake smiles she was generating regularly.

He wondered if the sicario's death was catching up to her.

"Remember to breathe."

She had no experience with this.

"Don't do anything crazy, okay? We need to know who it is. If they try to board, that's our cue. Only then do we act. Understood?"

She nodded again.

He wasn't reassured. She had become too withdrawn since their paths crossed again in Diamondhead. The episode with the sicario was definitely catching up to her, slowly but surely.

Now wasn't the time to tell her if it was the Coast Guard, they'd be on us like flies.

No way would they hold off until dark.

CHAPTER 43

The sun dipped below the horizon and night was on them too fast.

The boat following never displayed any markers. Jim lost sight of it but for the white, foamy wake surrounded by darker water.

"You should probably switch off our markers, Bobbie."

They had no radar to monitor, but whoever was creeping up on them most likely did.

The sound of the powerful engine at full throttle grew stronger, overpowering the rush of wind in their sails.

The distance closed.

"They're coming."

Bobbie rushed below to change.

She returned dressed in long pants and a wool pea jacket. She left it unbuttoned. She pulled a watch cap down above her eyes. She looked like an old salt. She checked the automatic and returned it to the seat. The knife hung from her belt.

"Ready as we'll ever be. Now sit and keep a low profile until we know whether they're going to ram us first or shoot."

She tied off the wheel.

He placed the AK at his feet. He wanted it accessible when he hit the deck.

He joined Bobbie on the seat.

"Remember to breathe. We don't know what's going to happen. It might only be coast guard in an unmarked boat."

Jim willed himself to believe it. Could they be that lucky?

He rubbed her back and smiled. As best as he could tell in the dark, she smiled back.

"The wind is steady. That's a plus. The sail will stay trimmed."

Bobbie no sooner said the words when a single boom echoed over the water.

"Keep down. They mean business."

If they had automatics, they were holding fire.

Jim hoped they'd think they had no firearms of their own.

He waited for the powerboat to ease closer.

Bobbie fidgeted beside him.

"Wait. It's too soon. Wait for me," he told her.

The powerboat bumped against them.

Something bounced forward along the deck.

An explosion accompanied by a flash of bright light left them blinded.

The mast groaned.

A loud cracking sound split the air as the mast faltered and leaned.

It began slowly tipping over the side before disappearing into the water.

The sail caught.

They slowed and turned into the powerboat thanks to the sail dragging them in the water.

"Now, Bobbie. Now."

Jim's ears rang deaf from the explosion.

He dived to the deck and struggled to raise the AK into firing position behind the gunnel.

He raked the powerboat's cockpit with automatic fire.

Out of the corner of his eye, he saw Bobbie raising the pistol.

He waited.

Nothing.

Whoever was on board the powerboat was unprepared for the firepower.

Panicked yelling and screaming accompanied by shadowy movement subsided.

The empty mag clattered onto the deck.

Jim slammed home a second.

He made sure his aim was more discrete.

He used short, controlled bursts.

The muzzle moved fore and aft and then side to side as the second mag emptied into the powerboat.

There was no sound beyond the idling engine.

No yelling.

Nothing.

He pulled the third magazine out of the duffel and slipped it into the AK.

He called to Bobbie. "Hold your fire. I'm going aboard."

He held up a hand and looked back at her.

Still clutching the handgun, she appeared frozen in position.

"Did you hear me?"

He waited until she lowered the pistol.

He tossed a rope and climbed aboard to secure it.

Nothing moved in the darkness.

There wasn't a sound beyond the whistling wind and the waves slapping against the hull.

He tied them off and waved Bobbie aboard.

"Bring a light," he told her.

He went through pockets and bags and collected what he could.

No one had ID. Nothing.

One at a time, he illuminated the faces to give Bobbie a look.

"Do you recognize any of them?"

She shook her head. "Not a one. What are we going to do? It's going to take hours to offload our cargo."

"Losing the sail won't stop us. The sloop can power on with the engine. Where will we put in?"

She didn't hesitate. "I was planning on Lake Charles. There are plenty of places for the cargo and dry docks if we want to keep her for a while."

Jim went forward and began cutting at the collapsed mast and its rigging. It broke free of the yacht and drifted off before sinking. Bobbie turned on the fan in the engine compartment.

"There's one more thing that needs doing. Don't go away."

Jim boarded the powerboat and searched for what he knew to be there.

He tossed the grenades to Bobbie, one at a time. She blanched but caught them all.

He climbed over the rail to join her on their sloop.

"What are you going to do with them?"

Jim pulled three pins on the grenades in quick succession and hurriedly tossed each one into the powerboat.

Bobbie advanced the throttle, putting the sailboat fifty feet distant when the explosions came.

They delayed getting under way, waiting for the inevitable sinking. Twenty minutes later, only an oily slick remained.

Jim said, "Take us to Lake Charles, sailor."

He went below and grabbed a blanket and returned topside.

They huddled beneath the blanket in the cool air.

In time he dragged himself away from Bobbie to cover over the hole in the deck where the grenade exploded.

Jim said, "Do you think it will be repairable?"

Bobbie looked at him like he was crazy. "Who cares? We have enough hard cash to buy a new one if we want."

At that moment, Jim had no idea what he wanted.

CHAPTER 44

Bobbie Dawson knew the powerboat would be trouble as soon as Jim pointed it out. Her stomach started to rock and roll almost immediately. Nervous and unsteady on her feet, she held off just long enough for Jim to go below.

She rushed to get her head over the side before she gagged and threw up. Panicking, she managed to suck in air and threw up again.

Her hands shook so bad she could barely hang onto the jackline.

She didn't want Jim to know. Not now. Not ever. Especially not in the middle of whatever it was they were in the middle of.

He returned topside, but he was concentrating on the powerboat behind them, too preoccupied to notice her shortcomings. If he noticed.

The explosion took down the mast and the sail with it, and she knew they were in even worse trouble. She held the handgun the way her father showed her. She even got it pointed in the right direction.

She tried more than once to pull the trigger.

She couldn't.

Bobbie watched and listened and stood there like she knew what she was doing.

Oh, she looked good.

She held the automatic out with both hands, the way she'd been taught.

She made sure to have her feet in the correct position.

She had even dressed the part with the jacket and the watch cap.

But she wasn't prepared for anything. How was she supposed to know someone would toss grenades? At least, that's what she thought it was.

The explosion and the bright light put her in a panic. Shock, too.

Her heart beat so fast it felt like it would explode.

The light blinded her.

A cold sweat ran down her back.

It all happened in slow motion over what seemed like an eternity.

Then it was over.

She sat down, pulled her feet up and bent over her knees while Jim jumped aboard the powerboat. She guessed he was looking for survivors.

She puked over the side again. It was all she could do to climb aboard behind him. If it wasn't for Jim—

Bobbie found herself right back in the storage unit.

Except it wasn't the sicario. It wasn't Yesenia.

It was three men she didn't recognize.

"Here. Take these with you."

Jim tossed grenades at her, shocking her out of her ugly reverie.

She caught them all.

When he came aboard the yacht, he pulled the pins on three and tossed them into the powerboat.

Bobbie steered the yacht clear while the grenades were going off.

In minutes, the powerboat was taking on water and sinking with all aboard.

Jim went forward and fought with the lines on the mast and finally succeeded in cutting it free.

They waited for the rest of the powerboat to disappear in an oily foam. It sunk, she fired up the engine, and they were under way.

It wasn't long after that the uncontrollable trembling began. She couldn't stop it, no matter what she did.

She did something like this before. It was after their highway encounter and shootout with the bad guys. This time, she let Jim think it was because she was cold. She didn't dare tell him the truth. He must have figured it out when she froze at the sound of his rifle.

He brought a blanket. It covered up the obvious. So did his arm when it went around her. Even so, she felt like she'd been destroyed. When she got out of this, she was going to get far away from the gulf and boats or die trying.

Bobbie didn't dare let on to Jim. She figured he gave up on her for being a failure as his backup. He knew now he couldn't depend on her. She had no idea what she would have done if anyone had been left alive to shoot back.

In the dark she began to cry.

Jim tightened his grip and she blocked all of it out

as best she could. How long that would last—

Finally, Bobbie made up her mind to tell him the truth—or at least the part of it she wanted him to know.

Jim looked over at Bobbie, huddled beneath the blanket. It was over her shoulders as though protecting her from the gale force winds facing them on their way north.

"Jim? There's something you need to know," she called out to him. Her voice was almost lost in the wind.

There was more than one thing, he was certain. For now, he'd take them from this woman one at a time.

"Remember when you picked me up at the gas bar?" she asked.

He did. He had pulled in to take a break for gas and food. The short-lived welcome breath of cold moist air gave some respite from the broken-down air conditioner in the rental.

"Yeah. I remember. The clouds parted, the sun came out, and there you were, looking a bit like an angel the worse for wear."

She had, too.

"Like a drowned rat with a shiner looking for a place to hang out after the store manager threw you out."

"You don't have to sound so happy about it," she said.

"I felt sorry for you. I wanted to hear the story about how you got the shiner. Are you ever going to spill?"

Bobbie shifted uncomfortably in her seat.

She avoided looking at him and instead stared out across the gulf.

"Remember when I told you I crewed on a yacht? The owner refused to pay me so I jumped ship. Remember that?"

Jim nodded and wondered what was coming next.

"It was a setup."

His ears perked up. If he wasn't already, he was paying attention now.

"I agreed to take a punch in the face. On purpose. I didn't bargain on a second one. I managed a dodge but he caught me in the chest. You got to see the results of that, too."

Bobbie absent-mindedly rubbed herself through the blanket.

"I ended up booting him between the legs. I took his money for payment. That text message you showed me on Terry's phone went to his phone."

Jim said, "The man who beat you for the setup?"

"Yes. Kennedy. He forced me to search for my brother. If I didn't, he said he'd kill me."

Kennedy was using the phone to track her. Of course. That's why they ended up in a gunfight on the side of the road. Kennedy must have thought she'd found her brother.

"What about the calls you took? You wouldn't talk much past mumbling, remember?"

"That was him. Kennedy. He was asking all sorts of questions that I couldn't answer with you listening. I tried to put him off when I realized you were one of the good guys."

This was news to him. He waited for her to go on.

"Maybe that was why the car caught up to us on the highway. I don't know. But it seemed like it was. I regretted it by the time I calmed down after you emptied your gun at them and they ran off."

So that was it. He was being led on. The tracking ended when he convinced her to toss the phone.

"Do you think Yesenia thought Terry might be your brother? It wasn't very smart of her if she did, but I suppose they weren't paying her for smarts."

Bobbie said, "She could have I guess. Terry shouldn't have come back. He ended up dead because he did."

He didn't bring up Yesenia's death in the storage unit. Bobbie would discover she'd have a hard enough time without him stepping in it on her behalf. She kept looking at him, and looking away. It was as though she didn't know what might be coming next. To be honest, neither did he.

Half of his demons had been slain when he made the decision that Kara was dead and gone. That there was nothing he could do to avenge it. At least he'd gotten that smart.

"What are we doing?"

Still, there was Pilar. He'd not forgotten. Nor would he. Ever. "I don't know, Bobbie. I'm not done with what happened to my wife on board that charter flight. As far as I'm concerned, it's unsolved."

"And you're going to be the one to solve it."

"That's right. I'm going to be the one to solve it. I won't be able to do that from here. I need to be someplace else. If you want to come with me, you can."

He waited, already knowing what her answer would be.

"I can't do that."

"All right. Well, we have a pretty big task ahead of us. We have to get rid of the cash. But first we have to figure out a way to retrieve it when it's going to be needed."

Bobbie was the one to broach the subject. "How about we split it fifty-fifty?"

How could he disagree? "Sounds good. Let's get counting.

They didn't fight.

The didn't argue.

They counted.

And counted.

And then they counted some more. By the end of it, they were fed up and glad to be putting in at Lake Charles. It had the banks and the storage units. It meant multiple trips from the yacht to banks and credit unions, all with safe deposit boxes.

The picked up a rental and began the deliveries.

They followed up with small storage units, paid in advance.

By the end of it, Bobbie was having a hard time looking at him.

He had a hundred questions.

He left them unasked.

She'd left him with enough clues over the past week. He knew what was coming.

Jim said, "I guess this is it. I don't want you to go. I want you to stay with me."

"I can't. Not now. Maybe not ever. I have to figure it out on my own. I need to get away. I'm grateful for what you did for me and for Ray. I can never thank you enough."

"You don't have to keep thanking me. What's done is done. It worked out," he said.

"I guess so. Jim—" It was all she could do to look at him.

"Bobbie. Wait."

"Goodbye, Jim."

Bobbie retrieved her duffel from the rental and walked off.

Over the years he had too many goodbyes in his life.

"So long," was all he could offer.

He desperately wanted more hellos.

By the look of it, those hellos weren't going to be coming from Bobbie.

Check out all six books in the Harry Delaney Adventure series.

Find out why Harry Delaney makes his way from the North Africa desert to the Mexico Baja. Discover how he ends up having a triumphal return to the deserts of North Africa.

THE LAST GOODBYE

PX DUKE

CHAPTER 1

Bobbie Dawson knew she couldn't win with Jim. It broke her heart, but she had to leave him.

She had to leave it all behind.

She cried.

She couldn't sleep.

She couldn't eat.

She couldn't stop thinking and agonizing and dreaming and having nightmares. Night after night she woke up again and again in cold sweats, shivering and shaking and sobbing.

She couldn't think of anything else.

And so, when it was time to go, she didn't look back. She couldn't do that, either. Once they separated, she knew she'd be examining her motives.

she even considered kicking herself—if she only could. It seemed like the thing for her subconscious to do because of her stupidity.

The sicario's death was making her crazy by the time she smartened up and found a psychologist. She made up a story about a hit-and-run and he seemed to believe it. While she was going for her twice-weekly confessions, as she called them, she began working on a commercial pilot's license.

At roughly the same time, her conscience and her ability to fly met and she was the proud possessor of a shiny new pilot's license and an ability to kill herself depending on how forgiving her flying mistakes might be.

Maybe she had a death wish.

Next up, she wanted to earn a float endorsement. She promptly boarded a commercial flight to Alaska. By the time she completed the endorsement, she ended up impressing the company with her flying abilities. The company followed up with a recommendation for a flying job.

A small charter outfit showed some pity and put her on the payroll. They started her off flying out to minnow traps. She emptied the contents, re-set the traps, and flew back with the catch stored in a freshwater tank on board the Cub.

At the end of the day, she reeked of fish, but that's what showers and laundry were for.

Before long, she used some of the money she rescued from the stash house to purchase a small plane with an improved engine to increase performance. She began by building up her business among the chauvinist, macho males that populated the fishing lodges, the bars, and the restaurants in the far north.

In due time she found a capable air engineer. He was younger and a little smarter than she liked them. After Jim Nash, he was just what she needed.

Or so it seemed.

She turned herself into a damned fine pilot by listening to the wisdom of others far more experienced. She never pushed the weather. With her own plane and business, she was making money.

She even had a boyfriend.

They worked well together in the business.

Until they didn't.

He seemed to think sleeping with her entitled him to a fair share of the profits and a business and a plane in which he hadn't invested dime one. Never mind that she'd been paying him for his work.

Maybe he thought she was paying him to sleep with her while he worked on the plane for free. She let it slide. She was happy.

Until she wasn't.

She always tried to mind her own business.

She knew a couple of pilots who took the chance with their employers' planes. People were always looking to take advantage of someone else's success.

One day she found herself approached by two men, strangers both, keen to talk her into flying booze into northern communities. She said no to that.

Next it was drugs. She said no to that, too, until she caught her partner stashing what she discovered to be drugs in the float compartments.

She guessed there wasn't room for a six-pack.

Which was all the more reason she ended up jolted back into someone else's reality when she finally opened and read the email.

When it feels like it's time to go, it usually is.

Bobbie began packing—not that she had a whole lot to put away. Her boyfriend caught her out trying to slip off before daylight. The same two who offered up the opportunity to be an airborne drug runner dragged her off into the bush. They tied her to a tree while they insisted on painting pictures of how it would go.

She wasn't stupid. She suspected the boyfriend had something to do with it.

So she agreed. Why wouldn't she see the light? Why threaten her life and livelihood by refusing to fly drug runs into small, isolated communities? Many had no road access until winter set in.

When the men finished with her, she was beat, not only physically, but mentally. She struggled to make it through the deep snow back to the trailer. She collapsed on the floor. Half frozen. Disoriented.

When she came around and thawed out, she realized she needed to be gone. Far away gone.

Before the worst results of the beating set in, she struggled to pack the duffel with enough winter gear to survive in the cold if her plane went down. She threw in enough of the boyfriend's prescription pain killers to sedate a moose.

She swallowed a few, too.

The beating had convinced her it was long past time to be leaving the far north for warmer climes.

She still had some common sense, if nothing else.

Jim Nash was burned out. Worn out. Exhausted. Fed up.

He needed something. He didn't know what. Or where. Or who.

The only thing he wasn't, was broke.

It took a while.

It took mail. And courier.

Suitcases. Overnight bags.

Multiple trips. Rental cars. Motorcycle trips.

He did it all.

If he drove or rode, Jim made sure he switched out the border crossings often enough that he didn't draw suspicion. They were all linked by computer. It was a chance he took.

Rarely would he encounter the same guard twice. If he did, and if he remembered, he made a point of mentioning that he didn't learn the first time, as in bad food, bad women, and bad hombres.

He'd push the sunglasses higher on his forehead and look the border guard straight on. Right in the eyes. While he pretended to fish for his passport, he'd shake his head, all the while complaining about a bad stomach or bathroom breaks or food and water and women.

He always got a knowing grin. A head nodding in agreement.

Finally, a wave through after a cursory scan of the passport.

Never did he get pulled over.

Eventually, over time and chance and circumstance, he became a currency smuggler. He got most of the cash Kara stashed in Cabo out of the country. It made him feel like he was smuggling drugs.

He left a lot behind in case he ever needed a vacation.

At least, that was his story.

He decided to stick with it.

CHAPTER 2

Jim paid cash for another old beater. The heater barely worked. Air was a rolled-down window.

Bobbie would be proud.

He didn't stop until he hit Michigan.

He angled a job interview as a live-in estate watchman for some rich guy and his family while they were away in Europe or South America or Africa.

It didn't hurt that he was a former cop.

Following a reference check, he moved in.

Dude left behind a book bigger than a bible on how to run the place.

He settled in to walk morning, noon, and night.

He discovered a jazz bar, a coffee shop, a pastry place.

Nurses, too, from the nearby hospital.

He found a library with friendly librarians to help with research. A pretty research assistant didn't hurt. He offered to pay her, but she refused, so instead he let her sleep in his bed from time to time.

Sometimes, he ended up in her bed.

In six months, with a lot of help and a lot of

searching and reading old newspapers and studying, he found everything he needed.

He discovered a paper trail pointing toward dissidents living and working in Miami. They were the ones that brought down Pilar's plane. Some were known to harbor a serious grudge with the country they'd been living in.

None in the group was happy with the country's recently adopted position on the state of affairs with Cuba. The group's members wanted nothing to do with warming relations with the island's dictatorship. Loosening of travel restrictions after decades of forced isolation didn't help.

They demonstrated and waved flags and screamed and yelled ineffectively against the government's latest stand on Cuban relations. They stupidly condemned America for its revamped position that travel should be allowed. Local politicians went along for the ride.

How a tiny cork bobbing in the warm waters of the Gulf of Mexico could have such an effect on a nation as large as America and the Cuban refugees the country took in never ceased to amaze. For decades, America had embargoed Cuba. It continued to thrive, albeit with dependence on communist-leaning nations.

Suddenly, America had awakened to the prospect that the fifty-year-old position was outdated.

The group had blown up a few mailboxes. The guilty parties had been jailed, thanks to infiltration by one or another three-letter failures: DHS, TSA, FBI. Customs and Immigration. It was never made clear.

He read what reports he could find about what

brought down Pilar's charter aircraft en route to the resort hotel.

There wasn't a lot. Many of the proceedings were held behind closed doors with limited or no press access. Not surprising, given the political strength of the local dissidents.

And then, Bingo. He had an answer.

Pilar's killer disapproved of the latest attempts at a growing positive relationship with Cuba. It took a while for that to sink it. That a Cuban dissident had planted a bomb on board the small plane had never been investigated. The likelihood that the investigation might lead to Cuban nationals based in Florida was never investigated. Too many voters might have made erroneous conclusions about their government.

Rather than risk voter revolution, all investigations had been dead-ended and halted. On whose orders he had yet to learn.

Further still, he learned seaplane bases weren't subject to the same security scrutiny as airports. He was convinced that a dissident had planted the bomb on board Pilar's flight to force the government into delaying or canceling its developing rapport with the government of the island nation ninety miles to the south.

Finally, he had some answers.

Perhaps not all of them.

But at least he had answers that began making sense.

Had he not been so consumed, it would have happened a lot sooner. A real estate agent with a pipeline to Canada, that is.

It took her months to find the right place. That was probably because we ended up sleeping together. Neither of us turned out to be in much of a rush to not sleep together.

The relationship helped take the edge off of what he was in the process of discovering.

Eventually, he decided on an isolated cabin in the Canadian woods, mostly because it was turning out to be too easy to continue the way he had been.

That, and he discovered the realtor's growing sense of ennui with their relationship. Obviously, she started it to ensure a quick sale.

He had turned out not to be so quick off the mark.

She was fun and made him laugh, and they spent money on each other. Which, come to think of it, was probably an excellent reason to move on.

The agency made it easy to pay in cash on the U.S. side of the border.

He made it easy by declaring a bit of cash when he crossed. No problem. All signed, sealed, and stamped.

By the time he parted company with the friendly real estate agent, he was the brand new owner of a home in the middle of nowhere.

Bobcaygeon.

It wasn't even nowhere.

It was worse than that.

Cedar Lake.

A thin sliver of a shallow lake running roughly north-south.

Not much wave action.

A corduroy road over the swamps made sure only the hardy would attempt to learn where the road ended.

He outfitted the site with a generator to supplement the solar panels the previous owner installed.

He considered adding a small windmill, but nixed the idea after spending a bit of time on-site. The winds weren't so strong as he hoped.

Settled, isolated, and alone, he set out to put the facts of Pilar's death together.

During the research phase, he gathered enough material to keep busy reviewing and organizing for at least several months.

He didn't want to wear out his welcome in his new abode. Nor did he want to experience a cold and snowy Canadian winter alone in the bush.

When he tired of paperwork, he chopped wood and repaired the corduroy road. He bumped up and down on the restored trail to the main highway into a small, isolated town once or twice a month for supplies and a visit to a café with wireless.

He never lingered. He would always beat a hasty retreat to the cabin. No one asked. He didn't care. He liked it that way.

The living was easy.

Slowly, Jim began getting back into shape. The wood chopping, the runs to the main road and back, the swimming, all helped to wear away the paunch that good living encouraged.

Bobbie would be pleased with the disappearing

muffin top she had teased him about when they first met.

He tried not to think about her.

It helped that he had a homestead to build.

When night came, he fell into bed too exhausted to think of anything but what had to be done the following day.

He split his time between construction projects and working on discovering who caused Pilar's death.

By mid-summer, he had the walls covered with maps and charts and characters and rap sheets.

By mid-August, he had everything planned.

He spent another month going over it all. Checking. Verifying. Checking again.

He wasn't wrong. He couldn't be.

It was all hanging on the wall, in black and white and color.

Ready.

He was ready, too.

He took a break and, for the hell of it, drove a long way to a town with a library and a computer desk. He checked email and got caught up.

He visited web sites and checked out photos of a proud, smiling woman in winter gear standing beside a small single-engine plane on wheel-skis.

Sure enough.

Bobbie had traveled to Alaska. She had her pilot's license and a job flying for a small charter outfit. It sounded like she trapped minnows and hauled them to the bait shops in the back of the plane she'd bought for herself.

During the off season, she chartered for hunters

and loggers and ran emergency flights into isolated communities for the sick wanting to get medical attention in a major center.

He took a chance and sent her the latitude and longitude of the place. He didn't say anything else. He figured if she wanted to, she would show up on her own. His name was a part of the email address. She'd have to be blind not to figure it out.

He didn't hold out much hope for anything more than that. Why would he? At the end of it all, he and Bobbie had parted on good terms. There was nothing more than that.

He was so certain that he completely put it out of his mind. He never went back to check for more email. As much as he cared for the woman, she had her own life to live. She already made it more than plain in Lake Charles that it didn't include spending time with him.

The second thing he accomplished was a final read-through of the report he prepared on why, who, and how the destruction of Pilar's return flight to the resort was started. He called in every favor he had left in the world and some he didn't.

There weren't many.

Most of them were from people in police departments he had worked with in previous lives.

He named names.

He named acronyms.

He enclosed CCTV copies of video of a male seen placing something into a piece of luggage before loading it onto a charter flight. It was the same flight that Pillar ended up boarding.

He included the bullshit reports that deflected

attention from the group that caused the explosion.

Just for spite, he made three more copies. He debated over a cup of coffee in a small diner in the middle of the Canadian wilderness. He passed that copy on to a major paper in D.C. It had just been bought out by another hard-ass. He didn't think anything would result from that rash decision, though.

And so he prepared to move back to the southern states for the real, live Canadian winter he didn't want any part of.

CHAPTER 3

Bobbie Dawson was carrying an ace in her pocket.

It was the email she had received and printed out and carefully tucked away. She looked at it only days before. It comprised two short and lonely lines of letters and numbers. She recognized them for what they were. She didn't send a response. There was no need. Until now, and there was no computer terminal she could crawl to on her belly.

The snow dump days before and the colder weather hadn't closed the lake with ice. Her pride and joy was fueled and ready to go.

The floats had been pumped in the early morning before first flight.

She did the DI—the daily inspection—then, too.

She had charts.

She had a functioning GPS.

The biggest obstacle was going to be the snow-covered mountains to the south.

Struggling and in unbearable pain all the way, Bobbie crawled, inching her way to the dock on hands and knees. Her bag dragged behind. She grunted and made her way down the dock.

She reached the end and untied the Cub.

She climbed aboard huffing and puffing and groaning every inch of the way. She agonized over lifting and finally pulling the duffel on board.

The Cub began drifting away from the dock.

She searched through her bag for the painkillers she took from the cabin.

Not wanting to delay further, she started the Cub, dropped the water rudders, and steered with knees and feet to taxi into the breakwater.

She choked down the painkillers, adjusted the mixture and firewalled the throttle.

She waited patiently for speed to build.

She worked her magic on the stick until the floats climbed onto the step.

Moments later, she was airborne.

There was plenty of snow in the mountain passes.

At altitude, it was cold in the small Cub.

She gathered up what she could of warmer jacket and a blanket and sleeping bag and tucked each item around her.

Thankfully, the painkillers had hauled ass by then. Even so, she was aching and exhausted.

To say it was a tortured flight into the unknown of a foreign country would be the least of her problems.

She landed and slept when she felt like it.

She didn't fly at night, even with the GPS. Single-engine VFR between mountain passes on the way into northern Alberta wasn't the place to be in the dark.

Stops for fuel were the biggest problem.

By the second day, she was so stiff she could barely

move. Painkillers didn't help.

Sometimes a stray wharf rat would take pity on her and pump the floats when she asked.

He'd fuel the Cub while casting a wary eye in her direction.

She always handed over a wad of cash, hoping for silence with authorities that might come calling to ask about a beat-up woman flying cross-border without a flight plan.

Bobbie's last overnight ended up with the plane parked on a lake somewhere in Northern Ontario.

She awoke with pain like she'd never felt before in her life.

The previous days had been no picnic, but now it was so much worse.

She checked the painkillers. She had two days, max.

She popped two, made the sign of the cross for luck, and fired up the Cub. There was nowhere to go but the destination marked by the GPS.

She took off for what she hoped would be the last time.

If she was lucky, her demons would be behind her. What she needed to do was heal her physical self.

Just maybe she'd find the man she loved in the process.

The road into Jim Nash's paradise consisted of a number of corduroy sections—cut logs wide enough to drive a vehicle on top—placed over low, swampy ground.

Noise and a cloud of oily blue exhaust from the

chainsaw proved more acceptable than the manual labor he'd have to do with an axe.

He realized he couldn't do it all at once, and thus took his time. Besides, there was no rush. This year, or next. It didn't matter. He had six months at a time to make the place even more habitable than when he bought it.

He never came up in the winter.

Thus, it was one summer, toward the end of June, when the sound of a light airplane drew him out into the warmth of the early morning sun rising over the forest of trees. He shaded his eyes with a hand and squinted, scanning what little horizon he could, surrounded as he was by deep and tall Canadian bush.

Nothing.

He waited for the sound to diminish.

It didn't.

Eventually, a small, float-equipped two-seater cruised slowly into view.

The pilot throttled back the Piper Cub and made a slow pass, flying in front of the cabin in parallel with the small lake. The port wing was tipped down toward the lake to afford the pilot a better view.

He had to be checking for shoals and submerged logs and whether the craft would be able to clear the trees on departure if he chose to land.

The power came back on and the wings leveled and the aircraft turned.

The crosswind leg began and he turned onto base and then final.

Again, the throttle came off and the Cub drifted leisurely just above stall in a glassy water landing.

The craft settled slowly onto the mirror-smooth surface.

The pilot pulled back on the stick. The plane settled on the water.

The nose of the floats angled up out of the water and mushed back down, allowing speed to bleed off as the wings stalled out.

Well before the narrows, he had the craft turned and was taxiing toward his small dock.

He ambled down to see what was developing.

It turned out, not so much.

The engine stopped and he waited until the nose of the floats bumped the dock.

Whoever was doing the flying knew what they were doing.

Water rudders came up.

Jim tipped a tire off the side of the small dock and into the water, grabbed the wing strut, and turned the plane.

He secured the back of a float to the dock and waited.

The bottom half of the door swung down.

He couldn't get a good look at the pilot. A cap, dark sunglasses, and a tweed shirt over cargo pants tucked into bush boots hid him too well.

Concern mounted. He wasn't prepared for trouble.

Why would he?

No one knew he was here.

CHAPTER 4

Bobbie Dawson had no idea how long she was airborne. Too many hours, probably.

She checked her fuel indicator.

She was good.

She checked her log and read her time of takeoff.

She was good with her current fuel load.

The last of the painkillers was wearing off.

She was fast descending into a maelstrom of hurt and agony and more pain. To add insult to injury, she was nearing the end of her fuel load.

Nervous, she checked her course against the GPS.

She was still on target for a noon arrival.

She looked to port and starboard. There had been no civilization for hour after hour.

Nothing but endless lakes and swamps and rivers, all surrounded by green.

Plenty of lakes, if she needed to land.

She swiped away cold perspiration from her brow

Swatted at the tears streaming down her face.

Resigned herself to running low on fuel before she made her spot. She would be forced to land.

GPS coordinates be damned.

A wisp of white smoke rising over the trees at twelve o'clock signaled civilization.

She checked port and starboard.

Still only green trees and lakes.

Most were too small for landing.

She punched a button on the GPS. It showed she was receiving all the satellites.

The wisp of smoke grew closer.

She reduced power and came in low, the Cub's engine roaring, on a wingover with the port wing angled over the small lake.

Her inspection run said the lake looked good for a landing.

The water was clear, too.

No sandbars.

No submerged logs.

Long enough for a landing.

More important, it appeared to be just the right length for a takeoff if she had the wrong spot locked into the GPS.

Bobbie made a stab at blinking away the drug-induced, cold-sweat perspiration running down her forehead into her eyes.

She swiped one more time at the tears streaming down her face.

She lined up on final, reduced throttle just enough and powered down onto the glassy water.

She eased back on the stick to raise the nose of the floats in a braking action.

The Cub mushed onto the water with a minimum of landing run.

Fate.

Luck.

Prayer.

Whatever it was. She had arrived.

She checked the GPS a final time. According to the coordinates, she was in the right place.

She taxied toward a small clearing on the shoreline.

A dock and a log cabin set off from the lake came into view. It turned into more than a cabin as she drifted closer.

It resembled a small lodge.

She shut down and waited for the nose of the floats to bump the crude wooden dock.

She pulled on the water rudder handle and secured the rudders.

Someone grabbed the tail and positioned the Cub nose-out.

Bobbie made a stab at wiping away the tears a final time. She didn't do so good.

She popped open the door halves and stepped onto the float.

Her feet almost slipped into the water.

A voice called out.

She threw her cap and sunglasses into the plane.

She knew she was a sight for sore eyes. She only hoped the eyes she was counting on weren't so sore as hers.

Her heart could have skipped more than a few beats as she struggled through the growing pain to make her way onto the dock. It was pounding in her chest far too hard.

It was all Bobbie could do to breathe.

Jim Nash paused to take a look at the creature stepping off the plane's float onto his dock.

A huge black and bloodshot eye revealed itself.

So did a bruised cheek.

All of it was partially hidden by long, dark hair.

He couldn't begin to guess what the rest of the woman might look like beneath the baggy clothes.

"Would you like some ice to go with that?"

"If you have a tub of it, I'll climb in. You'll have to help me get to it. If you don't mind, that is."

Bobbie held out her hand and collapsed to her knees accompanied by a loud groan. She almost slipped into the lake. He made a grab for her and eased her in the cabin's direction.

At the door, he picked her up.

A loud groan warned him he shouldn't be trying so hard. He moved to set her down.

"No. Don't. Maybe I can stay for a while. I always did feel safe with you."

Obviously exhausted and weak, Bobbie aimed a feeble kick at the door.

Jim carried her the rest of the way into their cabin.

He helped her undress. Shocked by what he witnessed, Jim couldn't speak.

It was all he could do to take in what he was seeing.

There was hardly a square inch of her upper body that wasn't covered in bruises and cuts.

Her thighs were black and blue.

"You can't stay here, Bobbie."

She went even paler than she was before he got her clothes off.

Her eyes rolled up and she looked like she was

going to pass out.

"Please, Jim. You're—"

Bobbie began sobbing uncontrollably.

Jim said, "I can't let you stay here for even a single hour looking the way you do. You're too beat up. I'm getting you to a hospital."

"There is a god. I thought you were going to force me to leave."

Jim couldn't allow himself to keep her at the cabin in the condition he found her.

"I am going to make you leave. I'm going to force you into my four-by-four."

Don't ask him how, but he argued and cajoled the stubborn woman into the back seat.

He laid her back on a collection of pillows and blankets. He propped her up to prepare for the long, rough ride to the main road and the hospital.

"You only want me in the back to seduce me."

She regarded him sheepishly. Her weak smile convinced him he was doing the right thing. In fact, it was the only thing he could do once he got a look at her.

"How the hell did you get here from Alaska?"

"Illegal painkillers, mostly."

"Remind me not to fly with you for a while, all right?"

He closed the door and listened to her moaning and groaning as he proceeded not so carefully down the corduroy road.

"You should have been here when I was cutting the logs to build this road. You'd have been proud of me. I worked off that paunch you made fun of when we first met."

All she could do was groan louder.

"We're on a road? Hell of a job you did."

Same old Bobbie, even if she was damaged goods.

He managed to haul her sweet but extremely bruised ass to the hospital without doing any more damage.

Bobbie made a feeble attempt to discourage the medics from loading her onto the gurney.

"I'm not some nobody headed to the morgue. I want to walk in under my own steam."

The EMTs glanced at Jim, rolled their eyes, and told the woman to shut up and take her medicine.

That forced her onto the gurney.

She stopped talking just long enough to grin past the pain.

"I'm tired of taking my own meds. I've been doing it for three thousand miles."

Two pairs of EMT eyes locked onto him.

"Yeah. I know. She's always been that way. I knew it even before she fell in love with me."

Heads shook in amazement that she'd made it as far as she had. He didn't dare tell them she flew in.

"Jim—"

"Yes, dear?"

"Don't be telling those cute boys all our secrets, okay?"

CHAPTER 5

Jim Nash followed behind the gurney on its way to emergency. With no health card in a country with government-supported medical care, he wasn't sure how she'd be treated. Or even if they would treat her.

He needn't have worried.

Once the doctor got a look, he admitted Bobbie in a hurry.

Jim insisted her records had been delayed by the fires out west in Alberta. He told them the file was in the mail and would be along shortly. He promised to bring it in as soon as he could.

All his promises notwithstanding, they knew he was lying his ass off.

Bobbie was in such awful shape that without her self-administered meds, she was beginning to groan. That was mostly why she was admitted.

He settled in for a long wait, drinking terrible coffee and dozing fitfully off and on.

Eventually a doctor found him in the waiting room.

"She says you're a relative."

"By all means. I'm her older brother."

He didn't believe it for a minute.

"If I didn't know better, I'd say she's been tortured. You wouldn't have anything to do with that, would you?"

"Do you think I'd still be here if I did?"

The doctor said, "Probably not. She's going to be in a lot of pain. She's taken quite a beating. Part of the problem is the pain meds she's been taking on her own. We have to let her come down and dry out before we can do much more than a CAT scan and take a couple of x-rays. Fortunately, she's young. She'll recover with nary a scar. Well, no more than the ones she already has."

"Thanks, doc. I'm worried sick about her."

"She's been asking for you. I told her I needed to talk to you first. About those medical records. Don't worry about them. By the time they get here, she'll be gone. In the meantime, see if you can convince her to stay at least for four or five days. We have to know if there's any clotting to be concerned about."

"She'll be staying here if I have to set up a cot in her room," he told the doctor.

"That probably wouldn't be a bad idea. You can help her in and out of bed. From what I can tell, she'll piss off the nurses in about a day, if it takes that long. Not a good idea."

"Gotcha, doc. She's a real ball of fire."

"Yeah. And you're not her brother, either."

"Maybe not. But I'm the closest thing she has right now, and it's important to me that she knows it."

The doctor nodded, as though in agreement. "210. Down the hall and to your right. I'll check back later."

Against the white of the hospital sheets, Bobbie

looked even more a mess.

She dragged them up to cover everything but her bruised face.

"No sense hiding. I've already seen all there is to see of you. Front and back," he told her.

"Oh crap. You didn't."

"Self-prescribed painkillers are a hell of a deal, aren't they? You'd have done anything I asked. Are you going to tell me how you flew that thing from Alaska, or do I have to figure it out for myself?"

"Jim—"

He cut her off for the second time. "I can't wait to see you healed and fresh and pink and white in all the right places, back and front."

Bobbie blushed.

The nurse behind me tisked-tisked. He hadn't heard her follow me into the room.

"That's no way to speak about your sister."

It was his turn to blush.

"Jim. You didn't. Nurse, he's my lover, not my brother. Let's get at least that one thing straight right away, okay?"

Bobbie's eyes fluttered closed and she slipped into the oblivion of sleep.

He bugged out and rounded up a cot and a sleeping bag at a hardware store. He didn't want her waking up all alone in the room.

She didn't mind the flowers he brought, either.

"Who's paying the rent, partner? I escaped with nary a dime to spare."

"Don't worry about it. You can owe me. And I plan on collecting," he said with a smile.

When she felt up to it, he helped her out of bed

and walked with her around the ward.

The male patients were happy to see her passing by. They smiled and waved every time.

Bobbie smiled and waved back.

"These people are so friendly, aren't they?"

He couldn't hide the shit-eating grin, but he tried.

"What? What is it?"

"I think it's because your fine, pink little ass is in the breeze beneath the hospital gown."

She turned to make a desultory attempt at checking out her own ass. She was too stiff and sore to get a good look. Instead, she gathered the open-backed hospital gown and pulled it tight.

"You bastard. I'll get you for this."

"You made a lot of old men happy. You should be proud."

"And you should be ashamed."

"What? Why would I be ashamed of your ass? Are you?"

"Well, no."

"It's all good then. Even your ass."

She clenched a fist and drove me a good one in the shoulder and he knew she was on the way to healing just fine.

By day four, it was all he could do to convince Bobbie to stay one more night.

Come morning of day five, she was dressed and waiting for the coffee and breakfast burrito. She wolfed it down like she always did, even when she didn't need it.

"Strange, isn't it? These things are a staple the world over."

"Good to know, sunshine. You won't be

complaining about my cooking then, will you? I think the nurses are lined up at the exit. They're waiting to shower you with confetti and rocks."

Somehow, he convinced her to climb into the wheelchair for the ride in the elevator.

The hospital wasn't so big that a couple of the nurses weren't waiting. They joined two of the old men from Bobbie's floor who were more than a little sad and wistful to see her ass departing.

"See what I mean? You've still got it," he told her.

"You say that to all the girls."

"No, I don't. Only to this one girl I know."

CHAPTER 6

Bobbie Dawson's badly beaten and bruised body repaired itself, no thanks to the woman's stubborn resilience and a foreign country's medical care.

Jim knew she was well on her way to recovery when she gave him a good one in the shoulder for allowing her to walk around the small local hospital with her ass hanging out of the back of her hospital gown.

He only considered it his daily good deed. After all, it helped raise the spirits of the men on the ward to a new level. Every time she walked past an open door, she was greeted enthusiastically.

All the smiles and waves made her feel good, too.

It was definitely a win-win for everyone.

The honeymoon had to come to an end, of course. Following the warm, welcoming summer, a cold, snowy Canadian winter was about to descend with a vengeance. He started making preparations to shut down the cabin.

Bobbie prepped her small plane to spend another winter in a cold climate.

She gave directions on how to construct a tripod

using rope and trees.

He helped her dig a ditch for the floats.

They used a block and tackle to lift the plane.

They ended up lowering it on logs laid across the ditches.

They spent a lot of time talking about how they'd handle the questioning at the land border. When that went without incident for both of them, he made certain she took a taxi to the airport well in advance of his arrival at Detroit Metropolitan.

He dispatched more packages filled with research to the newspapers. He hoped they'd get approval to do a story since nothing happened the first time.

Like I said, I hoped, but I doubted, too.

More than likely, the packages had been sent on. Once the conclusions had been read, if nothing else, he would be put on watch lists. Not enough to get him banned from flying. Just enough to let him know they were tracking him.

In any case, he had to have struck a chord when the TSA handler at Metro insisted he proceed to a room for further inspection.

He requested a supervisor.

Two showed up, with the FBI suits in tow.

The only thing missing was Mulder's dark glasses.

That, and the fact that he had nothing to do with UFOs.

The FBI had a lot of questions. Most were related to information contained in the reports he had submitted to newspapers, where he hoped to get some appreciation and follow-up. His report into the plane crash was meticulously detailed, and he had ended by naming the perpetrator.

Alas, Jim was finding out first-hand that nothing would happen.

So much for a free and unencumbered press post-9/11. The press had turned into toadies, note-takers told by unnamed or anonymous sources what to write.

With that in mind, he couched his responses as delicately as he could.

It was good enough. He made the flight, but only barely.

If nothing else, he learned he wouldn't be able to travel freely and anonymously by staying on the grid.

Call me stupid, but I try not to make the same mistakes more than a few times before I learn.

Jim's flight arrived in Miami on time.

In arrivals he picked up a hotel house phone and pretended to talk while he looked around. There were too many people to begin to get a handle on whether he was being tailed.

At the last minute, he jumped aboard a random hotel bus headed downtown. He made sure the door closed behind him.

It halted and he got off and walked into the high-class hotel. Just as fast, he hurried through the lobby on the way to the back door.

Down the street, he hailed a cab. He checked for vehicles that might be tailing him. There were too many cars to know for certain.

He asked the taxi driver about fleabag hotels, and the driver came up with a couple.

He made sure he dropped me in between and

waited until he left before making his way.

He looked up some old contacts in Miami and discussed the need for counterfeit IDs for two and a sense of accomplishment.

He had agreement from one, and handed over his and Bobbie's photos.

The new IDs took a week. The feeling of accomplishment took over when he ended up a new man with a new name.

He made up some back-story history to go with it, and then checked out of the fleabag.

Jim Nash disappeared—but only temporarily.

Next on Jim's agenda was a couple of burn phones. He tossed them into his bag and went in search of used car lots with a love of cash and a beater with air.

Bobbie would be proud.

If you're going to play the game, sometimes you have to jump in with arms and feet flailing. Perhaps he should have used the time up north to teach himself to swim in his own private hell after all.

A full gas tank and a gas-station burrito later, Jim headed out to hook up with Bobbie at their prearranged no-tell motel.

CHAPTER 7

The retro motel where Bobbie had holed up didn't look so seedy after all. The older building had been renovated by the owners intent on capturing the look as it was constructed back in the 60s. A colorful exterior and flashing neon must have been meticulously matched to an early postcard picture.

Jim didn't bother checking in. Instead, he left his bags in the car. He knew Bobbie too well. He followed the arrow pointing to the pool out back. He paused at the building's edge and squinted into the sun.

Evidence of the beating Bobbie took was long gone. She looked pretty good in the bikini and sarong she had to have paid top dollar for. If he knew her at all, he figured her for two or three more swim suits tucked neatly into her bag.

The audience of laughing teenage boys scattered when he approached. All but one ended up belly-flopping into the pool on purpose. Water splashed onto his shoes and pants. The one holding back was older. More sure of himself.

He gave off an aura of one who was accustomed

to women coming out of his ass. There was one woman by the pool. She didn't look like she was coming out of his ass, but she was definitely interested. It wasn't his first day poolside to recognize that.

Whatever it was Bobbie said to get them laughing was lost to the sound of splashing. She must have wondered why the laughing and flirting stopped so suddenly.

She turned and looked up behind dark glasses. Her forehead wrinkled under the beach hat's floppy brim when she recognized him.

"You know how to ruin a good party. You'll be the talk of the crowd as soon as you turn your back."

Jim looked out over the pool at the youngsters in the water. There couldn't have been one over twenty. And they weren't waiting until he turned his back. Dirty looks were definitely floating his way.

"It can't be spring break. Your college boys are sober."

Bobbie collected her bag and joined him on the walk past the ice machine to the small office.

"It's nice not to have to reach in and load up for you."

She ignored him. Nothing new there.

Bobbie said, "I spent the last week fending off boys who wanted me to buy beer. Once they figured out I wouldn't be doing that, they started showing off. At first, I kind of liked it. Now it's tiring. Get me the hell out of here, please."

He pretended he was interested and nodded his head.

"Then this older one shows up. It looks like he's

the one buying the beer for them. Jim—"

This was no time for poolside gossip. He got right to the point.

"I got pulled out of the line in Detroit. They knew I was coming. I ended up with a personal interview room courtesy of the TSA and the FBI. As far as I know, they followed me on the flight into Miami."

"What are we going to do now?" Bobbie asked.

"I'm late because I stopped off for a week while I waited for a shady acquaintance to prepare a package. I got one for you, too, thanks to the head shots."

"So what you're telling me is that we're strangers to one another all over again. I'm going to have to think about this. When it starts raining can you drop me at a gas bar?"

"Very funny. I'm not checking in. I think we need to find another no-tell and shack up under the new names."

Bobbie said, "Damn you and your friends. I was just getting used to my pool buddies."

"Don't be such a Miss Negative. I picked up a car with air this time."

"Yeah, but does it do the job? I remember how you like to work your budget."

He handed Bobbie her half of the burn phones, already programmed with numbers. She was such an old hand by now that she didn't even ask.

They dumped her car at a hospital lot and headed for the strip. By now they were so accustomed to one another that it was more like old home week than a search for a killer.

Jim said, "While I waited, I was able to track

down a couple of swamp boat operators. I don't know if they'll be any good. The kids at the pool wanted to take me out on a tour of the swamps."

"It was the bikini, wasn't it?"

"Maybe. But there's this one—"

Jim sent her some of the side eye he was so accustomed to getting from her. "It's none of my business. I don't want to know."

"Jim. Don't be an ass."

She slammed him in the shoulder with a good one. He figured he deserved it.

"Remember the older boy clinging to me?"

"You mean the one you were all google-eyed over?"

He got the look anyway, even though he didn't deserve it. She was definitely all eyes for him when she didn't see him looking.

"Yeah. That one. You'll never guess what his name is."

Jim waited, wondering how many ways he'd be disappointed.

"Yup. Nicholas junior."

The woman had horseshoes falling out of her ass. Fortunately, it was an ass so fresh and firm the horseshoes didn't leave any lumps. It was going to take time to digest this new information. A lot of time. Because it couldn't be. Could it?

"While I was waiting in Miami, I had plenty of time to scope out the seaplane base. It has a flight school. There's a glider training facility as well. I didn't spot the old man, but I wasn't really looking for him. I only looked around the facilities."

"It sounds like we can find reasons to be there,

don't you think?" she asked.

"I do. And we do. Now let's get the shit-show on the road before your pool buddies out back decide they want to take me out of your life. And by the way—"

"Yes?"

"You look pretty good in that bikini."

A warm smile was his reward.

Bobbie said, "I missed you. And I should look good. You helped me pick out three of them, remember?"

Women and clothes.

He didn't remember. But then, what man would?

"Of course I remember," he insisted.

CHAPTER 8

Jim needed to be sure Bobbie understood why he was late for the meet up.

"I called in a favor and asked an old friend to find out anything he could about this Nicholas character. It seems he has quite a rap sheet. He's not only involved in the anti-Cuba movement. He's a petty thief and a con man, too."

And Bobbie was right. He did have a son.

"Were you able to come up with an address?"

"That I did. In fact, he's not so far from here. What do you say to a drive-by?"

He tossed her the keys.

"I might be too noticeable if the house is under surveillance. They could be keeping an eye out for me."

She looked at him warily. "Do you think?"

"I think anything is possible. Since they don't seem to have identified you so far, you're it."

It took fifteen minutes to get to the house. Jim used the time to talk to Bobbie about an empty office space he had walked by while killing time in Miami.

"It's in a great location. Retro building.

Refurbished on the outside. Second and third floors. I only checked from the boardwalk, but it looks like it has windows on both corners. Lots of daylight in that case."

She might have been pretending to ignore him. He couldn't tell.

"I talked to someone who lives in the building. It's well kept up. Refurbished on the inside, too. No shady characters hanging out. The landlord takes good care of it. The girl said—"

Bobbie's ears perked up, and he knew right away it was the wrong thing to say. It was always over the last thing he said.

"Girl? What girl?"

Why did this woman have to choose just that moment to begin paying attention? She had all the boys hanging off of her by the pool, but he couldn't talk to a woman in the middle of the street.

"Her name is Andrea. She lives in the building. Or next door. I don't remember. I bumped into her while I was taking a look. I asked the woman about the place."

He was saved by their arrival at the house. He ducked down to allow Bobbie to do her thing.

"Do you see anyone that looks like they're keeping an eye out?"

Bobbie's head swiveled.

"No. The house has a for sale sign on the lawn. What do you say I get out and take a picture for old time's sake? It could be useful if we need to have a look. All it would take would be a call to the realtor."

"That's a good idea."

She gave me the look. "And maybe you know her."

Damn the woman. She had to get back at me.

When we were up north, he had told her about how he searched for the cabin in the Canadian wilderness. He figured it was her way of getting even for his comments about the teenagers crowding her at the pool.

"Are you sure it's a woman?"

She looked at him like he was some kind of dimwit. The woman's picture was plain as day on the sign. He was going to have to start paying attention.

"Well then, what are you waiting for? I can't take the picture from back here."

She tossed her phone at him.

"Why don't you call while I'm checking the place out? If we can get a tour, we might learn something. If Nicholas senior finds out about us and decides to move out of state while we're still positioning, it could mean a much longer time line."

Bobbie was right. He got on the phone intending to make an appointment.

"You're coming with me."

"You're darned right I am. I heard all about how you treat real estate people."

The agent turned out to be talkative. She told him the family was going through a breakup. The husband worked at the local airport and would be moving to a small apartment nearby. He was hoping for a quick sale.

Bobbie looked over the seatback.

"No. We are not buying it. When I'm done with this, I don't plan on returning. Neither of us will want to live anywhere near here."

Was she talking about Nick's place, or the office

space in Miami he told her about? He liked the Miami area after only seeing a little of it. If he was going to start a business, it would be the place."

"I think you're going to have to take that tour after all. I need to know if there's an alarm system in the house."

"I didn't see anything. What do the photos show? Sometimes they have signs."

Jim flipped through the pics and zoomed. He couldn't see anything resembling an alarm sign in any of the windows.

"Even so. You need to do it," he insisted.

CHAPTER 9

Jim waited, impatient for Bobbie's return after she dropped him at the motel before proceeding to the house and the inspection.

It was a simple job, and one she needed to do on her own. He didn't want to give himself away by having Nicholas senior recognize him in any future dealings they might have. It would warn him and most likely scare the man off.

Besides, Bobbie was getting antsy. It gave her a chance to play dress-up.

The woman returned from her mission so high on life he offered to take her to a fancy restaurant as a reward. He didn't use the word reward, though.

She showered and dressed and slapped his hands away about a dozen times.

At the restaurant, he plied her with wine and made her laugh and by the time they were ready to head back to the room, she was sitting so close in the circular booth that her head was on his shoulder.

They strolled to the room, holding hands and bumping hips and stopping to kiss.

He ended the evening by picking her up and

carrying her through the door to their room.

"Have you put on weight?"

Too late, Jim realized his mistake. As penance, he bit his tongue so hard he almost tasted blood.

Bobbie said, "Way to ruin a nice romantic evening, Nash. Now come to bed before you ruin that, too."

He set Bobbie down and took a rap on the back of the head for good measure.

She screamed.

He went down as far as his knees. A second blow sent him to sleep on the floor.

When he came around, the room was dark.

Bobbie was gone.

It was turning out to be just like old times.

Jim worked himself into a standing position before sinking into a chair and collapsing. When the dizzy spells stopped, he headed for the front desk and the clerk.

According to the clerk, no one made any inquiries. The man working the desk had come on less than an hour ago. He wasn't there long enough to register anything.

Should he go to the police, or keep it in the family?

For sure he was at a disadvantage.

He knew no one but for where Nicholas lived. It couldn't be possible that someone had taken Bobbie to his place.

Surely the feds weren't so stupid as to tell Nicholas about them. They weren't even aware of Bobbie's relationship with him.

He made for the car while rubbing the lump on

the back of his head.

Bobbie could learn a thing or two from whoever had sucker-punched him.

He drove to the motel and the pool where he first encountered a bikini-clad Bobbie and the friends she collected.

Loud music greeted him from the back of the motel.

Bodies dived and splashed and women screamed in false alarm.

Through the fence he recognized the older boy at Bobbie's earlier party.

It was Nicholas junior, and he and Bobbie appeared to have kissed and made up.

It couldn't be. Could it?

Jim looked again. Kids, mostly, but for the older Nick. No one else.

He hopped the fence and approached the boy.

Bobbie screamed.

"Don't hurt him, Jim."

He grabbed Nicholas by the scruff of the neck and shoved him into the pool house.

Bobbie got another scream out before he closed the door. She grabbed his arm and dragged him away.

It gave her just enough time to explain that she had told him he was beating her.

"Damn you, woman. Why didn't you tell me?"

"I thought it would go better if you didn't know."

Well, that was sure as hell true. Or so it seemed now that he knew. Judging by the lump on the back of his head, she had sold Nicholas junior lock, stock and barrel.

"What the hell? You've got to stop it with these

impromptu pool parties, dear. I'm starting to wonder about your true intentions."

"Yes, well, if you know what's good for you, you'll get me back to our motel and pick up from where you left off before we were so rudely interrupted."

The situation Jim found himself in was getting stranger and stranger.

Bobbie had accidentally rubbed elbows with Nicholas senior's son at the motel pool. She told him they weren't happy as a couple despite appearances.

Somehow, Nicholas had managed to find out where he was staying. He cold-cocked him in order to haul Bobbie back to his motel.

"How can we use this to our advantage?" he asked.

They had to find a way. The kid had obviously taken a liking to Bobbie, although his methods of seduction left something to be desired.

"Do you think you can get lover-boy to forgive me for beating you up? Maybe you could convince him we're breaking up because I'm an abusive male who won't let you go."

Bobbie said, "Are you telling me you have a plan?"

"Well, since you put it that way—"

Bobbie appeared convinced.

"All right. I might as well let you in on something else. While I was eye candy in back of the motel, I kind of let it slip you laid your hands on me from time to time, and not in a good way."

"Was that before, or after you found out who the boy was?"

She looked at Jim like he was a fool. It was a convincing look. "What do you think?"

He held up his hands.

"Okay. I surrender. But this is all new information. I need time to process it, Bobbie."

It might not be a plan yet, but whatever it was, it was taking form.

Would it work?

He knew for sure the plan needed a lot more thought. And they'd both have to agree to go along for the ride.

Judging by the way Bobbie was enjoying Nick junior's eyes glued to her, it should be a walk in the park.

CHAPTER 10

Jim happened across a diner close to the motel. They walked for breakfast in the cool Florida morning. It was humid, though, and they were grateful for the relaxed comfort of the air-conditioning and relief from the humidity the diner provided.

An older woman with a name tag that said Mabel promptly dropped off coffee and waited while they ordered. Through it all she didn't appear impatient when they couldn't decide on tomato or potatoes.

Mabel hurried off to grab the coffee pot.

"Did you get a look at her name tag? Where else but in an old diner would you get a kindly, gray-haired server with a name like that?"

Bobbie slid the old-style coffee mug around on the table. The fat round handle had room for a single finger.

"Where do they come up with these mugs? I've never seen anything like it, have you?"

Mabel dropped off our orders and went back for the coffee pot. "If you need anything else, just wave or holler. I'm not far."

He waited until the woman left.

"Bobbie—" He hesitated. "I need your help."

Already he could see the wheels turn.

There was an uncomfortable silence while she waited for him to go on.

She toyed with the food left on her plate.

She waved for more coffee.

She got up and left for the washroom, and for an instant he wondered if she'd come back.

He almost sighed with gratitude when she returned, looking wonderfully refreshed with a bit of lip gloss and the slight scent of a perfume he recognized from their past.

Bobbie said, "On one condition and one only."

He didn't even stop to think. "Of course. Just name it and it's yours."

"If I'm pregnant, we're getting married."

She didn't take her eyes off of him for an instant.

He blinked. He was pretty sure he went pale as a ghost.

"What?"

His hands shook enough to cause ripples to form on the coffee. He set the mug down and hoped Bobbie didn't notice.

"You heard me. When I was going through your bag back in Texas, I noticed a private eye license in your wallet. That's one of the reasons I never deserted you when I discovered the knives and the handgun. I figured you for a good guy who knew what you were doing. Tell me I was right about that."

The Private Detective license wasn't good in Florida, but she wouldn't know that.

He figured one word would do it for her. After all,

she'd used one word to answer him more than a time or two and he'd accepted it. Grudgingly. "Yes."

"Yes what?" she asked.

"Yes what? What do you mean, yes what?"

Then the light went on in his thick male brain.

"Yes, I'll marry you. I'll marry you even if you're not pregnant."

A shocked expression briefly crossed her face. When it turned into a smug grin, she was forced to look away.

"I only asked for a yes on the good guy thing, remember?"

Jim opened his mouth and shut it instantly. He knew when he was beat.

Bobbie said, "But we're going to work on that second one. If I'm not pregnant, I might not want to marry you when I find out how much money Nicholas junior is worth."

Jim wasn't sure if she meant it.

"He's the son of a Cuban airport worker. How much can he possibly be worth?"

And then he added an afterthought, knowing it had to be impossible.

"Did you run through all that cash already?"

He looked at her, waiting, while she cast her gaze out the window.

"That's for me to know and you to find out."

Bobbie's admission shocked him. He never considered for a minute she'd want anything more to do with him beyond helping him out after he helped locate her brother. Who, it turned out, wasn't really lost when he showed up on board the sloop with her.

Of course she could be pregnant. They hadn't

been counting days or using birth control. In fact, they never discussed it. Typical male that he was, he held the expectation she was on something.

After her admission, he knew she wasn't.

He had a lot to think about. He'd convinced Bobbie to help with Nicholas junior to get to the old man. He hoped through his ignorance and stupidity that he wasn't about to place her in a situation that neither of them was capable of handling.

He had to reconsider. His problem now became one of how to talk her out of what he had already convinced her to do.

Jim waited until he had her back in the room.

Learning Bobbie was pregnant—was she, or wasn't she? She hadn't confirmed it as far as he was concerned—came as quite a shock.

He asked her not to go through with the plan. It was a simple enough request. He was nice about it, too, or so he thought.

Bobbie said, "I'm going through with it. You're not going to talk me out of it. I owe you and I'm going to pay up."

How could he possibly put her in harm's way now? "I won't allow it. I refuse. No way. Never."

She held up a hand and looked at him like he was a fool. "Are you finished? For your own good, you better be. Now here's how it's going to go."

Jim listened. He wasn't happy. When she finished, he stormed out of the room without saying a word. In case there was any doubt, he slammed the door and headed off in the car. He only wanted to know if she was really pregnant. He didn't think it would be a big deal. When he came back, he handed her the bag.

"What's this?" Bobbie opened the bag and looked inside. "You shit. No damned way."

Apparently, it was entirely the wrong thing to do. "Why not?"

"You don't trust me."

It wasn't even a question.

"Of course I trust you," Jim said.

Why wouldn't he trust her?

"You don't believe me."

Jim said, "I believe you enough that I want to know if you're pregnant. If you are, I refuse to let you do what I asked you to. It's not right. Besides, you need to know, too."

"You're not telling me what to do, Jim Nash. I refuse to allow it. And one more thing. Nicholas will be here shortly to pick me up. When you were out, I called and told him I was leaving you. I have to finish packing my bag."

So she was going through with it after all. Damn the woman to hell.

"Bobbie—"

"Don't even try," she said.

"But—"

Exasperated, her hands went to her hips. She looked like she was about to fly off. In truth, she was. With Nicholas, thanks to the plan they had hatched together. Before she told him she might be pregnant.

"I won't be able to protect you. If you're pregnant you can't—"

"I can't what? Stop trying to baby me. I'm an

adult, dammit. I'm a bush pilot. I'm I'm—" Sobs wracked her body.

He wrapped his arms around her and they rocked back and forth.

"All right. I'll let you go. But you'd better know—"

"Speaking of knowing—maybe I already know."

There was no time.

A knock on the door halted all discussion.

Bobbie opened it and grinned like the sun had just come out. Actor that she was, she wiped the tears away for effect.

"I'm ready," she announced to Nicholas.

She picked up her bag, winked at Jim, and walked out of the room behind Nick.

Jim stood in the doorway, watching, as the woman he loved headed off with another man.

She threw her bag into the back and opened the door. She climbed into Nicholas junior's convertible, slid across the seat, and pasted herself to his side.

If she got any closer, Nicholas would have to open the door and drive from the outside.

She looked to be awfully chummy with the son of the man who killed his pregnant wife, Pilar, with a bomb in her luggage.

What could possibly go wrong?

CHAPTER 11

Still in its infancy, the plan they had come up with appeared to be working. Even so, he wasn't pleased with the affection demonstrated between Bobbie and Nicholas junior. He had to go along. He had agreed to it, after all.

So why did he want to kick himself in the ass, hard?

in my room and unpacking I'll be fine don't worry

Bobbie's text didn't ease his concerns. He worried. And then worried some more.

If he was going to play the aggrieved lover, he figured he might as well put himself in the proper frame of mind.

He walked to a bar down the street and bellied up.

The antsy from the Diamondhead yacht club greeted him from the opposite side of the bar.

Diana.

What were the chances?

The familiar face with the leggy body attached remembered him with a wide smile.

"Hello, stranger. It's been a while."

After he was mauled by three of Bobbie's tormentors, Diana made sure he got home safe and sound. He ended up in her bathtub, soothing his aches from the beating.

She managed to soothe just about everything else, too. Twice. And then she threw him out.

Her house, her rules, she had said.

The legs were still long. And the too-tight blouse hadn't been replaced.

He smiled back. "Small world. Been here long?"

Diana came around the edge of the bar to stand beside him.

He couldn't resist casting his eyes downward to hell while enjoying the legs all over again.

"A while. And you're still looking at me like you want to take me home."

"Can I get to know you first? I'm a little old-fashioned that way," I said.

Diana said, "I get off at three."

Jim showed up early and re-introduced himself to Diana. He didn't want to take a chance that her legs would go short on him.

At quitting time, they headed off.

Diana said, "I have a place just around the corner. I smell like beer and cigarettes. I need to get out of these clothes. You can come up and wait. I trust you."

Jim wondered who she trusted to get her out of Diamondhead and into Miami, but he knew better than to ask.

He knew better than to look, too, when she left

the door to her bedroom open.

Diana came out wearing a short robe and not much else from what he could tell. His eyes wandered but his mind didn't.

Diana said, "I need a shower. Smoke and all. Don't go anywhere."

Jim busied himself wondering how he could fit Diana into the plan Bobbie and he had hatched. Could he be so stupid as to haul Diana off to the pool behind Nicholas' house and hope for a party? Bobbie would be certain to be pissed off if she saw him with the likes of that one.

He wondered how she'd look in a bathing suit— Diana, that is, not Bobbie.

He already knew what Bobbie looked like. They'd already spent more time naked and sweaty than clothed when they were on the run.

"How do you feel about a pool party?" he asked Diana when she got out of the shower.

"I'm already changed. Now you want me to pack a bag? Who are you and where have you been lately?"

Something was nagging at him, and it concerned his last encounter with this woman. It was in Diamondhead, where she ended up taking him home from that bar, too, after he suffered through a beating at the hands of Bobbie's friend, Kennedy. It was the comment Diana made when he left her place. It was something about blowing something up.

"You don't want to know where I've been, but I'm here now. Are you coming or not?"

Jim drove them to a restaurant with small tables and huge tablecloths.

Diana rubbed her foot along his leg for most of

the meal.

By the time dinner was done, he was ready for Bobbie. Unfortunately, she couldn't be here, but he'd be seeing her soon enough.

He opened the car door for Diana and she slithered across the seat, mirroring the position Bobbie took up next to Nicholas junior. Her hand wandered his thigh until he was able to get parked beside Nick's convertible in the circular driveway.

They walked arm in arm past the side of the house into the back.

He recognized Bobbie's laughter. She wasn't too busy frolicking in the pool with junior to give his date the look. He only winked and asked about the change room.

The look started all over again when Diana walked out of the cabana at his side.

The woman was taller than Bobbie by a couple of inches. She knew how to fill out a not-so-simple one-piece bathing suit to make it look like skin. If it was any more sheer, she'd get arrested just for being here, and she wasn't even in the water yet.

"Bobbie, this is Diana. We met back in Diamondhead. She bartended in the clubhouse."

He figured that was all she should know. The women traded looks and he was thinking world war three would begin if the lights ever went out.

Diana sensed something was going on. She just didn't know what.

Poor junior had a look on his face like he thought he might beat him up, but he shook his hand and thanked him for inviting them.

The questioning look disappeared and Nicholas

went to nodding and grinning like a baboon with a rock to throw. He must have thought he might get a chance at Diana, too.

If he remembered anything about her, Nicholas just might if he played his cards right.

The party ended too soon.

Bobbie made excuses it was getting late.

Diana agreed, and they headed back to town. He was stuck to come up with an excuse to dump Diana at her apartment.

She solved the problem by letting him know she had a date for later.

"That's too bad," he said. "I was looking forward to spending more time with you."

It was a lie. He did his job. If Bobbie didn't kick him the next time she saw him, he'd be happy.

Diana said, "You know where I am. Don't be a stranger, stranger."

She didn't offer her number. He took that to mean he was delegated to be a drop-in at the bar. It was fine by him.

She squeezed his thigh and got out of the car.

Jim pinched himself and headed back to the hotel to wait for a text from Bobbie. While I waited, he rehashed what Diana said to him in her apartment back in Diamondhead.

At least, as best as I could remember it.

Perhaps it should have registered at the time, but the woman was playing hell on his eyes and his beat-up body.

He had been too enthralled to notice.

CHAPTER 12

Jim Nash knew his partner, Bobbie Dawson, would be all about the damned plan.

If he'd known Bobbie thought she was pregnant, he'd never have allowed her to do it.

Worried as he was now, he couldn't spend another minute in the motel room. It was too small. Too hot. Too lonely. There was no room to pace.

He used the walk to the diner to solve the problem.

He strolled past the empty booths and settled at the end of the counter. He put his back to the wall and looked out over the street.

The server dropped a menu and a napkin surrounding the tools of the trade.

He looked over the pie menu.

She returned with coffee.

"The Key Lime pie. What color is it?"

She harrumphed, frowned, turned on her heel, and stopped at the pie cooler. She slid a slice in his direction, half-way down the long counter. It had to be a practiced move. The pie halted in front of him and he heartily dug in with a bent fork.

Before he finished taking up the crumbs, she ambled back with the coffee pot.

"I don't think I need to ask if the color was the one you were looking for."

"Then you know why I asked."

"We don't get a lot of questions like that. You're new here."

He took another look. She was pushing forty. No wrinkles at the corner of her eyes. Blonde. Blue eyes. Pretty, though.

His eyes flicked to her left hand.

"No. I'm single. Got rid of the bum two years ago. All my stress and wrinkles disappeared almost overnight."

"Almost?" I asked.

"Yeah, well, that's what I say. It took longer than that, actually. You married?"

"No. Never had time to make it fit with my job. Ex-cop. I know you're going to ask."

"Good ex, or bad?"

"Probably somewhere on the high end of in-between," he told her.

She smiled and didn't ask which end to measure against.

He didn't mind.

She had a nice smile.

"What do you do now?" she asked.

What's to tell?

He thought about it for too long. "Contract work with the government, mostly."

His phone pinged, and the name tag that said Rhonda wandered off to talk to the cook.

He checked the time.

Past one a.m.

where are you?

i'm sitting in an all-night diner pining away

you'd better be pining alone and it better be for me, mister

just because I love you doesn't mean you can pick on me. how did it go with junior

senior owns a tour boat outfit in the swamps

The new information gave him pause. He wasn't expecting anything like that.

it's where he spends his weekends

you didn't answer my question

if I see you with that woman again you'll never get an answer. you're grinning aren't you

pretty much. I need to think about the swamp boat info. could mean a change in the plan

in that case keep me posted. I have to go now and wash the wine glasses

Damn the woman to hell. It seemed she was having too much of a good time as far as he was concerned.

He turned down a coffee refill and stopped at the till.

Rhonda kept talking and he kept listening.

Finally, he paid.

"Come back again," she said.

Jim hit the sheets and slept on what Bobbie had told him about the swamp boat.

Nicholas senior's business in the everglades could be a definite bonus. It might mean changing the plan he'd spent so much time working out these past months. It could also mean the changes might be a lot easier to implement than the original.

Knowing he didn't have anything remotely resembling a new plan, he got out of bed and headed for the diner.

The shift had changed.

Mabel brought breakfast and he ate his two eggs-over, toast, and bacon like it was his last meal.

He considered how he could fit Diana into this thing.

Bobbie warned him not to see her again. Maybe she wouldn't be so stuffy if he came up with a valid reason for using the woman.

Suddenly it dawned on him. He remembered how Diana impressed him as being a social climber back in Diamondhead. He was almost certain she'd clawed her way on top of, or possibly through, someone to get to Miami. Perhaps she'd like to meet Nicholas senior, newly separated and a business owner.

If only he could convince Diana to come out to the everglades and introduce her.

Surely Bobbie wouldn't mind he was still seeing her if that was the case. He was sure of it.

His phone pinged and Bobbie's text appeared.

just out of the shower how are you doing

i miss you

He did, too. He missed her a lot.

even with Diana for company

Damn the woman. She never missed taking a shot.

you told me I couldn't see her any more

I regretted the text as soon as I pressed send.

and you listened must be a first

well

Here we go. He stepped in it again.

don't well me SPILL

He almost waited too long.

i figure we can use her now that i know senior has a business

you'd better not use her any other way or there'll be BIG trouble when i get out of here

It was his turn to twist the screw.

so then you are coming back

Jim closed the burn phone. He knew Bobbie wouldn't respond.

They traded texts for another day. The time allowed him to think through the revised plan. Bobbie grudgingly agreed he should go out to look at senior's business. She didn't think it would be a problem convincing junior to take them for a boat ride. He was that eager to show her off to his father.

She started to tell him she should have brought more clothes.

He was tempted to ask why, and then he threw caution to the winds.

you're spending all your time in the bikinis I helped you pick out. why would you want more clothes? maybe you can find someone to do laundry

It was the end of that conversation. He knew before he pressed send. Obviously, he'd been misinformed. Bobbie chose the bathing suits for some unforeseen event in their lives that included Nicholas junior and his father.

He knew he had to let that part of it go.

Bobbie was in the position thanks to the plan. The woman would end up killing him when this was over.

Okay, so maybe she wouldn't kill him right off. She'd stick the knife in from the front, rather than the back.

She would want him to see it coming.

CHAPTER 13

Jim Nash discovered it wasn't difficult to talk Diana into coming along for a drive to the everglades. She appeared almost too happy he had asked.

She made arrangements to take the time off, and the next day he picked her up at her small apartment.

She was ready when he arrived.

"How do I look?" Diana asked.

There was no replay of the open bedroom door.

Diana looked stunning in her white blouse and tan shorts.

The straw hat was cute, but he didn't say anything. She'd only toss it.

"Well, your legs are still looking pretty fine. And I think you made every woman jealous the other day."

She couldn't possibly toss her legs, unlike the hat.

"Yes. I remember how much you enjoyed the view in Diamondhead. And that wasn't all. Who was that woman at the pool again?"

With a woman it was always the question at the end of things that needed answering. He ignored it.

"How could I not? You were showing off, if I remember."

He remembered all too well. Diana wanted out of that place so bad he could taste it, too. He wanted to ask how she did it, but he thought better. Besides, he figured he already knew.

Diana slipped across the seat and put her hand back where it was on their first ride to the glades.

He couldn't get to junior's place and Bobbie fast enough. The love of his life would kill him by the time he dragged her out of the everglades if this was how it was going to go with this one.

He was right, too.

The crowd greeted him as he parked.

We traded cars for junior's convertible.

Jim opened the door and shifted the split-back. Diana climbed in and dragged him into the back beside her.

Immediately he found her feet in his lap. She handed out a bottle of oil and he had his unspoken orders. He had already made it more than plain he was a leg man.

He didn't feel so bad when he finished with the exercise.

Then Diana shifted her shoulders to allow her to do her back.

He sensed reluctance by Bobbie to cut him any slack, even though the new plan was coming together. Of course, he couldn't tell her that. His hands were too full of Diana.

She leaned back and crossed her ankles on his lap. He took his mind off things by tickling her toes. It managed to get her giggling.

Bobbie, not so much. She didn't seem to think it was amusing in the slightest.

It was better than he hoped.

Following introductions, Nick senior and Diana began their slow dance. They started with furtive glances, morphed into outright stares, and progressed to unsubtle touching.

Jim had set a hook he wouldn't be able to remove. Before long they were throwing subtlety to the winds as their mutual seduction continued.

Diana happily submitted to senior's fawning compliments with smiles and touching and doe-eyed looks that left nothing to anyone's imagination.

Bobbie went for Nick junior like she used to go after me. She was only pretending, but even so—

It didn't seem to bother the old man that Diana came with him.

It didn't bother Diana, either.

Bobbie appeared more than happy when she witnessed how well the duo was getting along. If Bobbie was happy about it, who was he to complain?

The old man was only too eager to show them all around, knowing it would give him more time with Diana close by. He took her arm, leaving Bobbie and junior to do the same.

It seemed the odd man out vibe was becoming a permanent part of his life.

Bobbie didn't mind.

On their drive from the city, she had suffered through the indignity of his hands wandering over Diana's legs. Listening to the mindless giggling, he figured he deserved what she was dishing.

Nicholas senior led them to the souvenir shack and the dock.

Living quarters for the staff of two comprised

small trailers, separated by about a hundred feet.

Palms and mangoes towered over the property, creating plenty of shade.

There were plenty of flies, too.

Frogs croaked like there was no tomorrow.

Birds screeched and called.

The odor of decay and rot permeated throughout, thanks in no small measure to the humidity.

An expanse of shallow swampland covered in tall, thick green grasses stretched out from the dock. The occasional clump of trees rose over the endless horizon. It didn't appear as though any of it was high enough to be dry land. He'd have to wait for the swamp boat tour he suspected would be forthcoming before long.

Senior directed them to a pair of tables shaded by low, stubby palms. The liquor cart was already waiting. He expertly prepared Cuba Libres in sweaty glasses for the women.

The rest of them settled for beer with a breath of humidity running down the sides.

Noisy air boats left on schedule for their fifty-minute runs through the swamp. They were filled with adults and children and grandchildren, eager to experience the swamp while discovering alligators and manatees and birds in the everglades. All returned with happy faces.

Excited kids tugged adults toward the souvenir shack to drop money on items that would end up tossed out in six months or a year, if it took that long.

Following a run, Jim excused himself to check out the souvenir shop.

Customers audibly tisk-tisked over the alligator parts on display in the small store. Some wondered how they had been harvested. Some picked them up only to replace them. Only a child's demands caused shrugs before heading to the cash register, alligator part in hand. A souvenir is a souvenir.

They talked and drank and laughed and enjoyed the warm and humid afternoon in the shade.

Diana hovered over senior, but she didn't ignore junior.

Perhaps junior was beginning to realize Bobbie might be out of his league.

It was subtle at first, but he was transferring his affections.

Bobbie appeared happy with the switch now that Junior's inclinations toward her were turning to another woman.

Jim was sure Bobbie wasn't displeased Diana was ignoring him.

He know he sure as hell wasn't disappointed Nick junior was giving Diana the once-over with a fresh set of eyes.

The women left for a bathroom break, one following the other.

The sound of an argument between familiar voices floated by.

Thankfully, they were drowned out by a noisy engine idling at the dock, waiting for passengers to board.

Things settled down and Bobbie took the seat between Jim and junior.

Diana's oily legs graced the view of the old man. She made sure to take a seat directly opposite. Old

Nick's eyes roamed over her shapely legs exposed by the open slit in the sarong.

Jim had no right to be jealous. As close as Bobbie was in the chair next to him, he knew she could do nothing to ease his apprehension. This was what they had agreed to. Anything to cause alarm or doubt had to be ignored.

And he was jealous as hell, not only of Bobbie. While he trusted her, he was physically drawn to Diana.

Old habits die hard when the woman you love is so immersed in the plan that she's blind to the dual temptations of lust and love. Even that was gone since Diana became obsessed with the old man.

Jim drowned his sorrows in beer and turned a blind eye to both women.

He concentrated on old Nick.

The man was a drinker. He bullied his son into bringing him drinks and preparing food. He belittled him in front of them all.

Bobbie took it upon herself to referee between junior and senior.

He sensed an understanding develop between the old man and Diana. She moved to sit on the arm of his chair, waving a leg, her foot brushing against his.

It became even more than obvious she was done with him.

Jim couldn't ignore Bobbie, although she was gone, too, deep into their plan as it was working so far. He excused himself a second time and jumped on one of the tour boats. The operator handed over ear protectors and they headed off, two or three short of a full load of passengers.

They zipped and zagged along the watercourse.

Grasses and swamp surrounded the well-worn, open water trail through the expanse. It had to have been used hundreds—maybe thousands—of times.

The trail had to be kept clear by the constant back and forth of the flat-bottomed boats and their powerful and noisy converted aircraft engines.

CHAPTER 14

Eventually, the swamp boat driver returned to the dock and Jim headed for the party.

It had moved to the cool interior of the chickee. It alone was an impressive sight. Huge logs of cypress supported palmetto thatch. The interior was open. A fresh breeze floated through the window openings, keeping the house cool in the humid late-afternoon heat.

Diana was curled up on the sofa beside Nicholas senior. Her long legs stretched out for what seemed like miles.

Junior was relaxed and draped in a huge chair.

Bobbie sat at his feet, looking attentive and too friendly.

Jim took another glance and knew he was the fifth wheel.

"Nick. I'm taking your car into town. I'll bring it back tomorrow."

He caught Bobbie's panicked glance. Immediately it was replaced with a weak smile.

Well, woman, you asked for it. Now you're going to have to decide whether it's worth it to keep fighting him off.

Diana appeared happy at the prospect of spending the night. She was so pleased with herself she didn't bother asking for a ride to the city. With Jim happily out of the way, she'd be able to consummate the deal—no matter what the deal was that she worked out with herself.

Nick junior tossed Jim the keys.

He thanked senior for his hospitality and headed off. He didn't waste time, since he was burning junior's gas.

He parked and walked to a second small deco bar he passed on the way to the hotel. It looked quaint from the outside.

Hipster interior, probably.

He was mildly surprised when the air conditioning wasn't freezing out the customers by blasting from the ceiling. Maybe they only switched on when they wanted to trade the senior citizens for the younger crowd in the evenings.

Jim bellied up to the bar and faced the day's first major decision. He went with Crown Royal, his old favorite.

He lost track of time by the fifth shot.

The pretty bartender's attempts at getting me to cut it with a beer back went for naught.

It was Andrea who recognized me. She went on break and sat and reminded me that they had met while he was admiring the second-story office in the building she lived in.

He began paying attention.

Andrea liked to talk.

he liked to listen.

She was about Bobbie's age. Maybe a little younger.

Working the bar to pay off her college loans.

In between customers and regulars, he got the woman's family history, her story, and the story of every one of her favorite customers.

At closing time, he dutifully slipped off the barstool and headed for the door.

Miss Tenderbar helped me stumble along until he bumped into two lugs trying to get past the door at the same time.

They took him off Miss Tenderbar's hands until she figured out they planned on laying a beating on him.

All by herself she managed to drag him back inside, lock the door, and sit him down on the floor while she closed.

The woman slapping his face was pretty. He could tell, because she was as close as she could get to me, generously sharing the floor. She was struggling to help him come around and get him up on his feet.

She patient person, too, if he knew anything about women.

"All right, big guy. It's time for you to go."

"Just help me to my car. I'm capable of driving the rest of the way."

"Fine."

A word he was familiar with. He'd heard it more than a time or two from another attractive woman he was acquainted with.

"Give me your keys and I'll unlock the door for you."

Fat chance.

She packed them away in her back pocket and half carried me down the street.

Grateful for the assist, Jim leaned heavily on her all the way.

"You know, those keys in your back pocket make it look all lumpy."

"Make what look all lumpy?" she asked.

Already he was ahead of the game. he knew what to say.

"Your ass."

Andrea sighed and ignored him.

He was used to that, too.

"I'm up on the third floor. Think you can make it, Jimbo?"

Jimbo.

He hadn't heard that for a good while. Which was probably why he meekly followed the woman up the stairs.

Three stories wasn't all that difficult.

Except he was shitfaced drunk times three.

"Andrea."

"Yes, Jimbo?"

"Just leave me."

It was the second level and he figured he was done. He didn't have it in him to climb to a third.

"You have a way with women and words, don't you, Jimbo?"

How difficult would it be to travel back down a landing or two?

"All right. We're here. Welcome home."

Andrea led him to her sofa and dropped him.

The last thing he remembered was collapsing on it.

CHAPTER 15

Jim Nash woke up on a strange sofa in a strange room with daylight flooding in through open windows.

He squinted past a hangover and a headache like none he'd ever known.

Someone had thoughtfully placed a bucket near his head.

He groaned and looked into it.

The bucket was empty.

He mumbled incoherently.

So far, so good.

Footsteps. Who could it be?

"You're awake. What took you so long?"

A pale-skinned vision of a woman appeared with soaking wet hair and long legs tucked beneath a short bathrobe.

Hung over as he was, he had to admit he noticed what was falling out of the short robe all the way to the ground she walked on.

Small feet.

Great legs.

He had an overabundance.

Jim looked up at her. "Did you fall into the pool?"

"No, goofy. I'm fresh out of the shower. How are you feeling?"

"Don't take the bucket away just yet."

Jim rolled onto his back. In seconds he returned to his side, just in case.

The move made the bucket closer, too.

Andrea said, "That good, huh? You wanted to drive home last night. I wouldn't let you. Well, okay, there's that, and you got in a fight with two of my regulars. To get them off you I had to tell them you were my father and that my mom just died."

He regarded Andrea in wonderment.

"Yes. Really. The only thing that saved your drunken ass was that we chatted all night. You told me stories that made me laugh, and you didn't make a single pass. I was wondering how unlucky a girl could get until you ended up shitfaced. Still, I got the feeling you don't do that often."

Jim sat up and groaned. "About that father thing. We need to talk. So you're saying I should have asked you out. I'll remember for next time."

"I have to get to work. You can crawl into my bed for the day. It's obvious you're in no shape to go anywhere. I hope it's obvious to you, too. I'm not comfortable giving you your keys. Come on."

He followed Andrea into the bedroom and fell back on the bed.

"Sorry about that lumpy ass thing. It's perfect. I can see that now."

It was, too.

She turned away, giving me a good look when her robe crept up above her rear. She looked over her shoulder with an impish grin.

"What's that you say? Perfectly lumpy?"

She opened her dresser.

"Don't you know the way to a girl's heart and mind. You must be a real charmer with the ladies. Take off your shoes. Your shirt and pants, too. I'm not letting you sleep in my bed in that mess you're wearing."

She began digging into drawers and moved into the closet before closing the door.

"What are you doing?"

"You're a complete stranger. I'm not getting dressed in front of you just because I let you into my bed. Perhaps later when I get to know you better."

Jim didn't hear the last part.

He pulled the sheets up and died in some strange woman's sweet-smelling bed.

By late afternoon he was feeling pretty good.

He got out of bed and dragged his hung-over ass into the kitchen and checked the fridge. A six-pack of water and a pregnancy test kit stared back at him.

He guessed a bottle or two of the former would be necessary before accomplishing the latter.

He checked his pockets and still couldn't find his keys.

He made a grab for a water and hot-footed it down the stairs in search of a market.

He found one and stocked up on eggs, bacon, bread, and orange juice. He added a tomato for luck and stopped to pick up flowers to dress the place up.

On his way into the lobby using the key he pilfered from Andrea's apartment he noticed the office for rent sign hanging on a door.

He twisted the knob and the unlocked door opened. He pushed it open and looked in. It looked even better than it did from the street.

He carried on up the stairs, dropped off the goodies, and retraced his steps to Andrea's place of employment.

A bit of the hair of the dog that bit him definitely couldn't hurt. He sidled up to the bar with a sheepish look.

"Well hello, stranger. I see you survived. How are you doing?" Andrea asked.

"Thanks to you, I'm doing just fine. By the way, I borrowed the spare key for your place."

He pushed it across the bar.

She didn't look at it.

"What time do you finish?"

Andrea raised her eyebrows. She must have thought he was a stalker. Even though she was the one who let him into her apartment.

"Why? What are you planning? Should I be worried? You're not a stalker, are you?"

There it was.

Andrea smiled warmly.

"On the prowl for something to eat I took a look inside your fridge. Imagine that. I can tell you don't have a lot of company staying over by the water six-pack. On the other hand, there's the pee stick. You planning on taking the test when you get home?"

She blushed.

He grinned. "You're down a water."

He held up his hands.

"All right. I'll stop now. I'm inviting you over for dinner at your place. Don't expect much. It's only my way of thanking you.”

Andrea pushed the key toward him.

“Take it. I’ll be home at nine.”

She stayed busy before surrendering and pushing a drink in his direction.

Jim shook his head and thanked her before sliding it back.

She looked at me and grinned. “Don’t go all pouty on me. It’s a Virgin Mary.”

He made the sign of the cross. It got a laugh, and he retreated out the door carrying the drink all the way to Andrea’s.

He phoned the number for the rental office scrawled on the sign taped in the window.

He chased down the building manager and talked him into showing the space.

It was even better than he remembered. It overlooked the street in both directions. Corner windows on both sides allowed plenty of light. Inside, a fresh coat of paint wouldn’t hurt.

Jim took it on the spot.

Bobbie would have to be happy with choosing the furniture.

It was a good place for the P.I. business he thought he should start with her.

He silently thanked her for reminding him about the license he forgot about.

The key would show up in a couple of hours.

He gave out Andrea’s address and settled in to wait.

CHAPTER 16

Before Jim realized words were coming out of his mouth, he had invited Andrea to tour the everglades.

Small-town girl that she was, she must have been feeling magnanimous when she agreed. Why else would she accompany a too-drunk customer she felt obligated to rescue from her bar patrons as well as himself?

While he waited in her small apartment, she reappeared in a short, filmy skirt that came halfway up tanned thighs.

High-heeled sandals put shapely legs to work.

Intriguing bare thighs peeked out from beneath the hem of the short dress.

He followed her lead on the walk down the stairs and into the street.

"I don't mind if you look forever," Andrea said. "In fact, I'm flattered. When you've had enough you can catch up and walk beside me."

Could she read me or what?

"You're blushing, aren't you?"

Jim said, "No. Well. Maybe. Yeah. But—"

"Never mind my butt. All you get for now is legs."

"Promises," he said.

"Perhaps. We'll see what happens when we get back."

She gently refused to accompany me into the hotel and instead insisted on staying in the car to wait for him to change.

Jim said, "I'm not trying to get you up to my room."

"You're darned right you aren't. It's too soon for that," Andrea chastised him.

Jim said, "You'll like the lobby. Plenty of people-watching."

Convinced, she accompanied him into the hotel.

She picked out a chair in full view of everyone, sat, and crossed her shapely legs before smiling up at him.

"There. You've seen them from both sides. Are you happy now?"

In twenty minutes he reappeared downstairs hoping he looked like a new man.

"You clean up pretty good for a stranger. You shaved, too."

Her eyes wandered over him. To his credit, he showered and shaved and changed wrinkled clothes for fresh and pressed.

His eyes wandered as well, down and then back up. Slowly.

"You're not so bad yourself."

The back of her hand brushed softly against his face and hesitated for an instant before withdrawing.

"Good job shaving. I wondered if you would."

Jim opened the car door and she slid into the seat, all the while adjusting her skirt as best she could.

He was enjoying Andrea's company far too much already.

"Eyes on the road, Jimbo."

She was smiling. It was a smile he liked.

Andrea slipped closer.

She took his hand in hers and allowed it to rest beneath her own on a warm, lovely thigh showing no tan line.

"I can tell you never wear shorts. Perhaps you should—"

"We're not going back to my place or yours. We're in enough trouble already," she admitted.

He ignored her comment and managed to keep an eye on the road for a mile or two. And admitted silently that she was right.

"Are you going to tell me what this is about? Or do I have to imagine it as we get closer to wherever it is we're going?" she asked.

He told her about his partner, Bobbie, and how she became trapped in the everglades through no fault of her own.

He even told her about Diana.

The car might have come up, too, so he explained it wasn't his.

"So basically, you brought me along to get your business partner—who you're romantically involved with—away from the clutches of some random guy?"

She removed his hand from her thigh and placed

it on his own before releasing it.

"Guys. Plural. But I'd say you pretty much nailed it. Would you like a part-time job?"

"You rented the office space below my place, didn't you? You brought me flowers. You cooked me breakfast at nine at night. Are you nuts? I'm this far from sleeping with you and you're bringing me along to rescue a woman who loves you. What could possibly go wrong?"

Andrea sighed and took his hand in hers again and kept it there. She appeared resigned to the outcome, whatever it might be.

"Yeah, but are you pregnant, and do you have any sisters?"

Andrea sighed again and shook her head and settled back in the seat. She even started to relax.

He was pretty sure she thought he was nuts. Maybe she was just a bit, too.

His phone rang.

He handed it to Andrea. "Answer that for me, would you? You can listen if you want."

She put it on speaker and held it between them.

Her head rested on his shoulder.

He had to admit, he liked the way she answered a phone.

He thanked the other party and Andrea hung up.

Her head stayed on his shoulder.

He liked that, too.

"I made some calls to a couple of connections while I was upstairs. That's why I took so long. As you heard, Diana has a rap sheet and a penchant for older men. She likes to empty their bank accounts. I'm counting on us to get Bobbie out of there."

"Diana? Who the hell is this Diana? Tell me again. How many women have you got stacked up out there? Now I know why you didn't tell me what I'd be letting myself in for."

Jim wasn't surprised by Andrea's reluctance to get involved now that she knew more.

"Promise me you won't change your mind after I explain everything."

"Yeah. No. Maybe. Promises are hard to keep," she admitted.

"So then, you'll be staying. I met Diana when I rescued Bobbie and her brother from a drug cartel."

"Wait. What? A drug cartel?"

"It's a long story. Short version. Bobbie badly beat up and hitchhiking by the side of the road. Rain. Thunder. More rain. Sketchy motel room. Plenty of humidity. Sweaty sex. Missing cartel drugs. Crooked border guards. A rescue aboard a yacht. Brother found. Case solved and case closed."

"Okay then, so why do you need me again?"

"Well, since you asked. I need someone to answer phones and take messages."

She looked skeptical.

He couldn't blame her.

"That isn't what I meant, but I'll run with it for now. That's what cell phones are for. And texting. Before I forget, and in case Bobbie checks your phone, I'm in it."

"Perfect. You can text both of us when you take a call from someone with a case that needs solving. Bonus points for you if you get a deposit before accepting the case."

Jim separated his hand from hers and reluctantly

withdrew it from her warm, wonderful thigh.

She ruffled her skirt and smoothed it.

"You were right about the humidity."

He turned off the highway onto a smooth dirt road surrounded on both sides by tall trees. The odor of swampy marshland surrounded them, replacing the fresh air of the clear blue sky in the open convertible.

"We're here," he announced. "Follow my lead."

"If I was following your lead, right now we'd be parked on the side of a road somewhere. The top on this convertible wouldn't be the only thing that was going down.

It was hardly noon, but Andrea had pretty much made his day.

CHAPTER 17

The fog left over from last night's rain began to lift, chased by the slight breeze. Water dripped from overhanging trees and splashed onto the ground. The stench of decay coming off of the fetid swamp water was overpowering.

Jim held the door open.

Andrea slipped across the seat, obviously not worrying any longer about the skirt that so wonderfully revealed her tanned thighs.

She almost fell into his arms.

She caught herself at the last second.

He smiled.

She blushed. "For some reason, I can't help doing things like that around you."

That was all right with him.

She turned her attention to the laughter coming from the patio.

"Which one is your girl?"

Jim didn't get a chance to reply.

The four were gathered on the patio.

Loud voices and laughter drifted across the parking lot.

Senior had to be mixing the drinks on the strong side.

His words slurred as he called out. "It's about time you made it. You had good reason to be a day late, though. The woman is beautiful."

The old man slumped in his chair.

Andrea almost began pawing the ground in her haste. She blushed brighter than a teenager in a too-short prom dress.

Bobbie looked from the woman to him and back. She didn't appear to be so happy.

"Who's your company, Jim?"

"Everyone? Meet Andrea. She's my new secretary."

It was beyond him how she knew, but Andrea was already striding purposefully in Bobbie's direction.

She held out her hand and the women shook.

They stood, toe to toe, each eying the other.

He wasn't certain he liked that, unsure as he was of what might come next.

"And that's Diana. Meet Andrea."

Andrea turned to face him.

"You know the most beautiful women. How long have you been in town?"

Bobbie smiled regretfully. "Far too long, I'm beginning to think."

Andrea's wide smile totally disarmed Bobbie. "Would you show me the lady's, please, Bobbie? It was a long ride."

Bobbie took her arm and they headed off toward the bathroom.

Voices muffled by laughter spelled trouble.

The two women he absolutely didn't want to get

together right this instant were on their way to the restroom. Together. Trouble was sure to follow if he knew anything about women.

Most of the time, he was forced to admit, he didn't.

Sometimes, he only pretended.

His troubled heart wasn't becalmed by the sight of Andrea's long, slender legs in step with Bobbie's, just as long and perfectly matched.

He hated getting down to business, but sometimes it was necessary.

He tore his eyes away and concentrated on the old man.

"So. Nicholas."

Senior and junior turned.

"When are you taking us out on the swamp? I think we'd enjoy seeing the everglades with an expert guide."

An obviously inebriated Diana leaned on Nicholas senior, hoping for a helping hand. Unbalanced, either by lust or plain old alcohol or a combination of both, she stumbled against him.

Her words slurred. "Yes. I'd like to go, too."

Nick caught her and eased her down into the lounge chair. "Behave or you'll be staying by yourself."

Nicholas' eyes roamed over the reclining Diana. It didn't help that her half-open blouse exposed an ample portion of a tanned breast.

Somehow, she managed to keep what was left together.

"I'll stay with her, dad. We don't want her falling into the swamp with the gators."

And pigs could fly.

If he knew anything, it wasn't the swamp gators Diana needed to watch out for.

Right then he'd have given his eye teeth to be a fly on the wall in the restroom where Bobbie and Andrea disappeared. It seemed like it was taking them an especially long time to return.

How much longer could they be?

What could Bobbie and Andrea possibly have to talk about?

CHAPTER 18

Nick senior stood up and made his way to the dock.

Jim used the distraction to knock on the bathroom door.

Unsure what to expect, he waited.

Andrea poked her head out.

"Oh. It's Jim. Yes? What would you like?"

The sweet, innocent look said he shouldn't dally. He took a chance anyway.

"Nick is going to start the tour in a minute. Are you two coming or are you going to stay behind to compare notes while I'm gone?"

Jim closed the door and beat a hasty retreat toward the dock. The noisy air-cooled aircraft engine fired up, emitting a cloud of blue smoke from the exhaust. It blew away in the light breeze and the engine settled into a steady, ticking idle.

Bobbie and Andrea hurried to join them.

At the last minute, Nick junior and Diana announced they would be staying behind.

Bobbie took it in stride. She answered Andrea's puzzled look with an explanation of her own.

"She's doing both of them. After she puts the old man to sleep, she tiptoes down the hall and literally bangs on junior's door. I think he keeps it locked just for spite. He always seems to open it wide, though. Just as wide as she does."

It became obvious Bobbie and Andrea had come to some sort of an understanding during their extended time in the bathroom. He wondered what they might have concluded, but he knew better than to ask.

It was time to climb aboard for the grand tour.

Jim said, "Andrea, you might want to put on a pair of shorts. You look to be about the same size as Bobbie."

Bobbie threw him the look.

He wasn't certain whether it was the one approving of his choice, or the I'll kill you later look that he seemed to be getting more and more lately.

She gave in, though.

Bobbie said, "He's right. I have another pair. The wind on the boat will make short work of what you're wearing."

"She's right, Andrea. I'll get Nicholas to wait."

The women hurried off together.

More time to tell stories, he feared. He was beginning to think it might have been a lot smarter to have left Andrea in the city. Presupposing he had any smarts about things like that—which apparently, he didn't.

Four departed in the boat.

Nicholas senior drove.

It was a perfect day.

Not too hot.

They passed through wisps of fog to be scattered in the wind created by the huge propeller.

Light cloud cover kept the sun from frying them.

The old man expertly guided the boat through the swamp, slowing here and there and shutting down occasionally to coast in silence.

He pointed out birds and snakes and the overgrown mango trees housing them.

Occasionally an alligator made its presence known, all eyes and bumpy snout moving silently in the water.

Finally, Nicholas senior slowed and pointed the boat toward a point of dry land. Then he accelerated quickly and the flat-bottomed boat bumped against the shore.

The nose halted on dry ground surrounded by tall green grass. The much heavier stern remained over the water.

Satisfied, the old man's expert touch silenced the powerful aircraft engine.

They all clambered ashore, happy the noisy engine was silent, even if only for a short time.

Trees on three sides surrounded the watery island. Water dripped from the overhanging branches.

In the overwhelming humidity, perspiration streamed down faces. In minutes, clothes were soaked by the uncomfortable humidity.

"Here's the land you wanted to see, Jim. There should be alligators close by. Be careful. Don't get too close. Despite appearances, alligators are capable of traveling fast for short distances on dry land."

The women wandered off, carefully checking

every step. Out of the relative safety of the boat, they weren't so eager to see a live alligator.

He stepped out behind them.

The old man stayed behind.

Bobbie called out. "There's an old cabin beneath the trees. We're going to take a look."

Nick said, "Jim. Wait a minute. I want to talk to you."

He eased a concealed pistol from behind his back. He leveled it at him with a drunken man's trembling hand.

Even so, he felt fairly certain he wouldn't be able to dodge whatever he was about to throw at him. Given a drunk's propensity to act in an alcoholic fog, he didn't chance moving even so much as a muscle.

"I have many friends. One told me you submitted your report to the government. Did you think you'd get away with it?"

So he knew. Someone sold him out. Who could it have been?

"Someone in the press?"

His eyes narrowed. "I can't tell you who it was."

Something told him Nicholas never considered he might send the press copies of the report, too. It had to be the feds.

Jim said, "What are you going to do, kill us all out here in the middle of nowhere?"

It would be easy. He'd leave them with the gators and they'd end up nothing but bad-smelling meat until they had their fill.

What the hell had he done?

He'd gotten two innocent women involved in his

business and now they were all going to pay the price.

It would never end.

Bobbie and Andrea appeared out of nowhere, giggling.

"I think we made our day. We managed to pee without getting chewed up by alligators. We're ready to go now."

Nick's handgun wavered between Jim and the women.

"Not quite," he told them. "Get over by Jim."

Radiant smiles turned instantly to looks of surprise and fear.

Bobbie, realizing what was up, was more restrained.

Andrea was shocked. A look of terror appeared on her face. "What's going on? Why the gun? What the hell? Jim?"

Old Nick looked at them like he wanted to shoot sooner rather than later.

Jim's mind raced, trying to figure a way out.

Old Nick said, "I found out all about your cop friend and his vendetta. He wants to put me in jail. He thinks I'm responsible for killing his wife."

A smug look crossed Nick's face. He'd figured it out all by himself. More likely, his informant told him.

Jim said, "I saw the CCTV footage, Nick. You're the one who placed the bomb in Pilar's luggage. It was plain as day. Why you're not rotting away in a federal prison is something I haven't been able to figure out. But I will."

"You don't have time to figure anything out. You

dragged two women into your scheme. They'll die along with you. How does it feel? From what I've seen, I'd say they've taken quite a liking to you. You'll never live to reap the rewards."

Bobbie and Andrea began slowly backing away from the flat-bottomed boat beached on the small point.

"Not so fast, ladies," Nick said. "You're not going anywhere. Get back here."

He waved the muzzle at Jim.

The women halted beside him.

He had to find a way to delay the inevitable.

"So who kept you in the loop? It wasn't the press. I could tell by the look on your face when I told you I sent them a copy. Who is it, Nick?"

He appeared to be considering.

Jim said, "If we're going to die, don't you think we deserve to know who's responsible? We'll take it to our graves. I promise."

That wasn't a stretch. Nor was it imagination. If Nicholas got his way, they'd be dead in a heartbeat. If that didn't scare the shit out of the women, it scared it out of him.

He'd gone and done a foolish thing.

He'd placed Bobbie in the lion's den, and then added Andrea into the mix for good measure.

Jim had to admit, he didn't think it would come to this, or he'd never have done any of it.

CHAPTER 19

Bobbie and Andrea were getting more than antsy.

Behind Jim, feet shifted nervously and worried whispering and gasps filled the thick, humidity-laden air.

Bobbie moved closer and lowered her voice even more.

"Jim. Don't look. You have to get us away from the water and close to the trees."

He didn't know what the pair had worked out. He was certain they were trying to stay alive as long as they could.

"Nick. Let's all get in the shade and talk about this some more," Jim said. "All right? The women are getting sunburned, and you know how a girl feels about that when she wants to go shopping and try things on."

"It's no use. But all right. They can have that for now."

Nick kept the gun leveled, herding them toward the trees. By the time he had them beneath the canopy of thick branches, the old man's back was to the water.

"Stop whispering or I'll shoot all of you right now."

Jim couldn't halt their scared shaking. They knew how it was going to go.

It was his fault for dragging them into the swamp. Although Bobbie had come willingly, Andrea was something else. All she did was allow him to spend a drunken, hungover night in her apartment. He'd taken it upon himself to bring her along because she was so likable.

Well, they were all in a swamp with no paddle now, thanks to yours truly.

Suddenly there was more whispering. "Holy shit. Look."

A huge dark shape crawled quietly out of the swamp and made its way silently toward Nick.

Jaws opened wide, displaying rows of razor-sharp teeth.

They closed on Nick's leg with a satisfying snap.

Part of the sound had to be Nick's breaking leg.

He toppled to the ground with a blood-curdling yell.

Nick's yell turned into a scream.

The handgun went off.

A bullet grazed Jim's arm.

In agony, the old man struggled to get the muzzle pointed toward the razorblades clamped on his leg.

The huge alligator began backing toward the water's edge with Nick in tow.

Arms flailed.

Nick's good leg kicked.

His torso bucked.

He tried to hang onto handfuls of long grass that

pulled out of the ground. It was to no avail.

The gator's jaws opened and snapped shut a second time.

The alligator doubled down on his grip, knowing he had a tasty morsel once he got it into the water where he could really go to work.

The gun went off again.

Nick thrashed and yelled in agony.

He released the gun and it flew into the grass as his arms flailed.

He clawed the ground and discarded more clumps of grass to dig up fresh as the huge alligator inexorably made its way toward its natural habitat.

The gator made good progress forcing its prey into the water. In seconds it would have Nicholas where it wanted him.

Nick continued to flail.

His body contorted.

His struggles continued in vain.

He yelled and screamed and begged for help.

It was to no avail.

Unlike the alligator who had Nick in its death grip, they were relegated to observers. They were frozen by shock and fear.

The terrifying jaws opened and closed in a flash of teeth.

Both Nick's legs were trapped by the powerful jaws.

"Get into the boat," Jim commanded. "Give those two a wide berth. Hurry."

He picked up Nick's gun. He didn't offer help. It was too late for that.

If he shot, he'd hit him, and he didn't want to

answer for that.

It would be useless anyway.

The alligator had Nick at water's edge and was wrestling and thrashing and rolling and chomping in a feeding frenzy of blood-red, watery foam.

"Jim—"

He looked up.

"Can you start it?"

Both women looked at him. There appeared to be some doubt.

"All right. I'll be there in a minute. I have to make sure of this."

He made his way cautiously to the boat, careful not to disturb the alligator intent on its meal.

He was even more shaken by the animal's base instincts.

His arm ached. Blood covered his sleeve and streamed down his hand from the errant bullet. Still, he wanted to keep an eye on the deadly progress the gator was making.

He wanted to see Nick dead.

Satisfied and horrified by what he was witnessing, he made his way to the swamp boat and came came up with a story.

"Here's the way you're going to see it."

He pointed. "Look over there. See the flamingos? You're watching them. Waiting for them to take off and fly low over the water. You've never seen it before. Maybe on TV. But not in real life."

They looked at him like he was crazy.

"I'm going to have to report Nick's disappearance. Trust me on this. You don't want to be involved. Understand?"

Bobbie said, "He's right, Andrea. I'll explain later."

Andrea picked it up and ran with it. "Bobbie, look over there. Flamingos. I've never seen anything like it. Have you?"

"I think Andrea is going to make it after all, Jim," Bobbie said.

He put his arms around them and hugged. "That's my girls."

Andrea cried out. "Jim. You're bleeding."

"Who's got a shirt to loan me?"

Andrea immediately began unbuttoning.

She had her blouse wide open before Bobbie caught her.

"Wait just a minute, girl. That's my job around these parts. And don't you forget it."

Andrea ignored Bobbie and passed her shirt over.

He wiped prints off the gun and then wrapped the blouse around his upper arm.

"I'll break up the gun and toss it on the way back to the dock. Sorry, girl, but you don't get your shirt back just yet."

Bobbie gave me the look he was so accustomed to by now.

"Wounded or not, I'm telling you two. If I ever—"

"You don't have to worry, Bobbie. Now that I know you, I'd never do anything with Jim. Just don't die."

Their eyes wandered in his direction.

He grinned and shrugged. "It's only a flesh wound. I'll be fine. It's time to get out of here."

"We weren't talking about you," Bobbie said.

He turned his attention to the swamp boat's controls. They didn't appear so different from a powerboat. The small panel was clearly labeled.

He pushed the starter on the warm engine and allowed it to settle into an easy idle.

He played with the throttle handle, moving it forward slightly to familiarize himself. The engine speed increased, along with the wind through the blades. He allowed it to ease back to idle.

Next, he tested the left-side steering handle. Easing it forward directed the fins to move for a right-hand turn. Pulling back positioned the fins to turn the boat to the left.

Twin arrows pointing forward and backward on the panel clearly indicated propeller pitch.

Still at idle, he moved the lever from neutral to reverse. The engine faltered momentarily while the blades grabbed for air.

He called out to warn the girls. "Brace yourselves. Better yet, sit down. I'm going to try backing us off this island."

He slowly advanced the throttle. The engine screamed on its way to full power. The flat-bottomed boat bumped and jerked and reversed off the island, floating free in a giant rush of air.

Immediately he released the spring-loaded throttle handle and the engine went to idle.

He moved the propeller selector through neutral to forward pitch. The propeller engaged, and they idled forward, inching over the water.

He wrestled the boat into position and slowly eased the throttle forward.

He tested the steering handle on the left side.

Forward, go right; backward, go left.

He increased throttle and went through the motions again. He was no expert, but reassured, he figured he could get them home.

At half-throttle it wouldn't be fast, and it wouldn't be smooth, but it would be safe. They'd get there eventually.

The GPS would help.

He struggled to keep the flat-bottomed boat with its square bow straight and level. Every turn at half-throttle felt like they'd all fall out as the boat tipped precipitously.

He wasn't confident enough to go any faster. Thus they mushed along.

He slowed even more in the tight corners.

Occasionally he'd dodge what looked to be logs in the water. Or alligators. He couldn't tell the difference.

Sometimes, the swamp grass would whack the aluminum, but it was a familiar sound he'd heard on the ride to the island. It didn't cause any panic now.

Following a couple of wrong turns, he made sure to consult with the women and caught flak in spite of it.

He shrugged and carried on, glad they were making headway back to Nick's.

He remembered to toss the handgun after wiping it again.

He returned Andrea's blood-stained shirt when the bleeding halted.

She looked at him with a What the hell am I supposed to do with this? expression.

Bobbie shook her head and shrugged.

The women stayed silent until he shut down and bumped hard into the dock.

He'd never make it as a tour boat operator.

He helped the women ashore and tied the boat off.

Andrea donned her bloodstained shirt.

There was no time for further discussion about how Nick senior met his end.

CHAPTER 20

No one rushed to greet them. Surely the sound of the powerful engine arriving had to have alerted someone.

After tying off, Jim hurried to join the women on their way to the chickee. Part-way there an outcry alerted them.

Unsure of what was happening, they walked into the living room and discovered Nick junior making his way between Diana's long legs. Both of them were bare and sweaty and aimed at the ceiling.

"I don't know about anyone else, but I'm not sitting on that thing ever again," Bobbie announced.

"You two get your asses out to the car. I'll get your things. Go."

Jim pulled Nick off of Diana.

A disappointed grunt and a squeal from Diana echoed through the chickee when she realized what was happening.

For some reason it gave him great pleasure to disturb the happy couple.

Nick huffed and puffed and put his pants on while listening to Jim's tale of woe on the island.

"The women were off in the bushes. I was standing guard. When we returned, your father was wrestling with a huge gator. He screamed and pulled a handgun from somewhere and started shooting. He got off a wild shot at me by mistake.

Nick didn't say anything. He could only listen.

"There was nothing I could do. I wasn't about to wrestle with an alligator. Your dad managed to get off a couple more shots, but he didn't hit anything. It was too late. He was already in the water with the gator."

It looked like Nick junior believed the story.

Hell, he believed it.

"I managed to get the boat home, thanks to the GPS. The girls are all right. Shocked, but they're fine. We need to call the police."

Diana was eagerly comforting Nick. She had her clothes back on and was fluffing up her bed-head hair.

She directed a smirk his way, but he couldn't tell if she believed him. He was almost certain she had to be busy imagining life insurance and dollar signs falling off of young Nick. He'd probably slip and fall any number of times. There was no doubt that Diana would be only too eager to catch him between her legs in the coming days and weeks.

"Call the cops. I'll do damage control. Bobbie and Andrea are in shock. I sent them back to town."

The last he heard was the convertible's tires spinning on the gravel drive.

They'd get a few hours respite before the police tracked them down.

If they were smart, they'd rehearse their stories.

CHAPTER 21

Jim Nash dragged Bobbie and Andrea downstairs and chased them across the street.

He looked up at their office window.

Fresh neon glowed.

"Dawson & Nash Investigators. It has a nice ring to it. What do my two favorite girls think?"

Bobbie and Andrea looked up and regarded the sign in the main window. "I don't know about you, Bobbie, but I'm keeping my job in the bar. I figure all I need to answer the phone is a pen and some paper. Or maybe I could just let the calls go to voice mail. Our new boss should be able to handle that."

They grinned back and forth and he tried to pretend he was indignant.

"Come on now. Is that any way to treat a brand-new small business owner? Which one of you is going to be the first to pass the P.I. exams?"

"Don't be so sure of yourself, Jimbo. Bobbie and I still have some fast talking to do before we make our final decisions."

"What? Why? Bobbie? Andrea? Come on," Jim said.

Bobbie said, "She's right. And once we're done talking, it's going to be time for two of us to lay down the rules. I think you already know which two that will be."

He knew what it meant, all right.

Fond memories resurfaced of his hand in Andrea's, resting on her smooth, bare, and extremely warm thigh.

Would it happen again?

He was pretty sure it wouldn't by the time Bobbie read him the riot act.

"Just so you know, my arms are around both of you," Jim announced.

"If you're looking for sympathy for that bullet wound you so proudly show off, you're looking in the wrong places. And don't be so smug. Andrea and I are holding hands behind your back. We crossed the street that way to return to the office."

Jim sighed and wondered where it all went wrong.

About the author

Peter Duke is a Canadian author. He resides and writes in a small college town in the Province of Ontario, Canada.

Peter's gypsy spirit has taken him to some strange places in the world, but now he's content to limit his adventures to riding a motorcycle and whatever he might encounter when he's on the road. He's worked in bike shops doing odd jobs from planning and putting on rides down Mexico way, taking care of computer networking and security, and to picking up and delivering motorcycles from the L.A. basin to Las Vegas, among other things.

He's ridden over a lot of North America at one time or another from Canada to Mexico, and from Atlantic to Pacific. By far his favorite ride is up and down the length of the Baja Peninsula, where the people are friendly, the sun always shines and it's warm in the winter.

Of everything that he has experienced in his all-too-brief life, Africa is perhaps the greatest enigma. It's an amazing continent, rich in people, nature and resources, yet poor in all of those areas, too.

https://pxduke.com

peterxduke@gmail.com

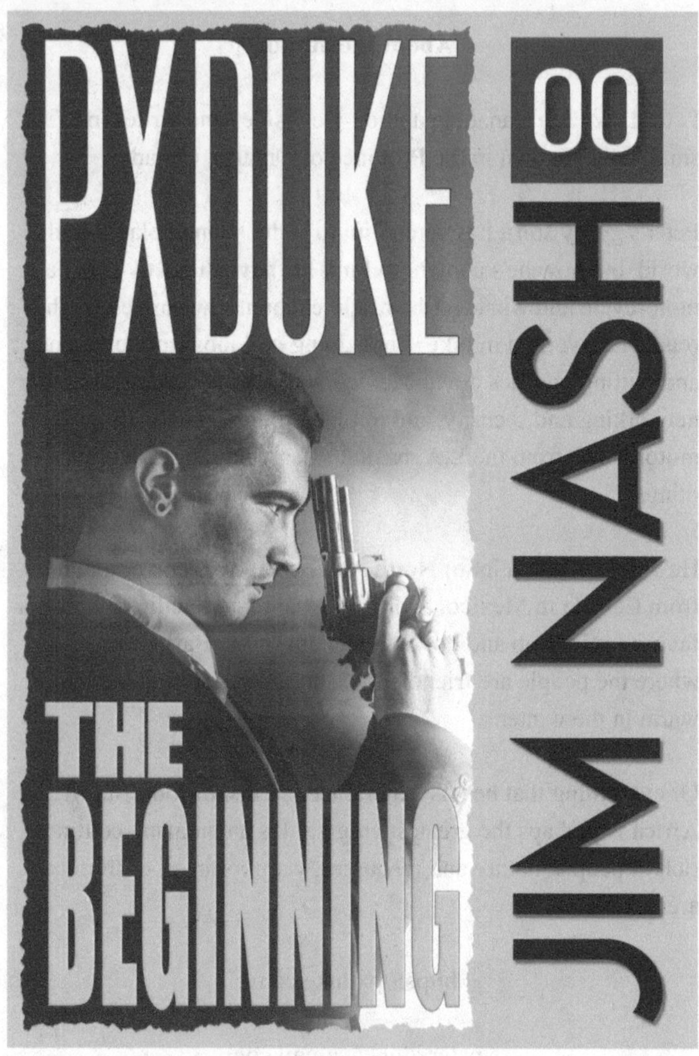
PX DUKE
00
THE BEGINNING
JIM NASH

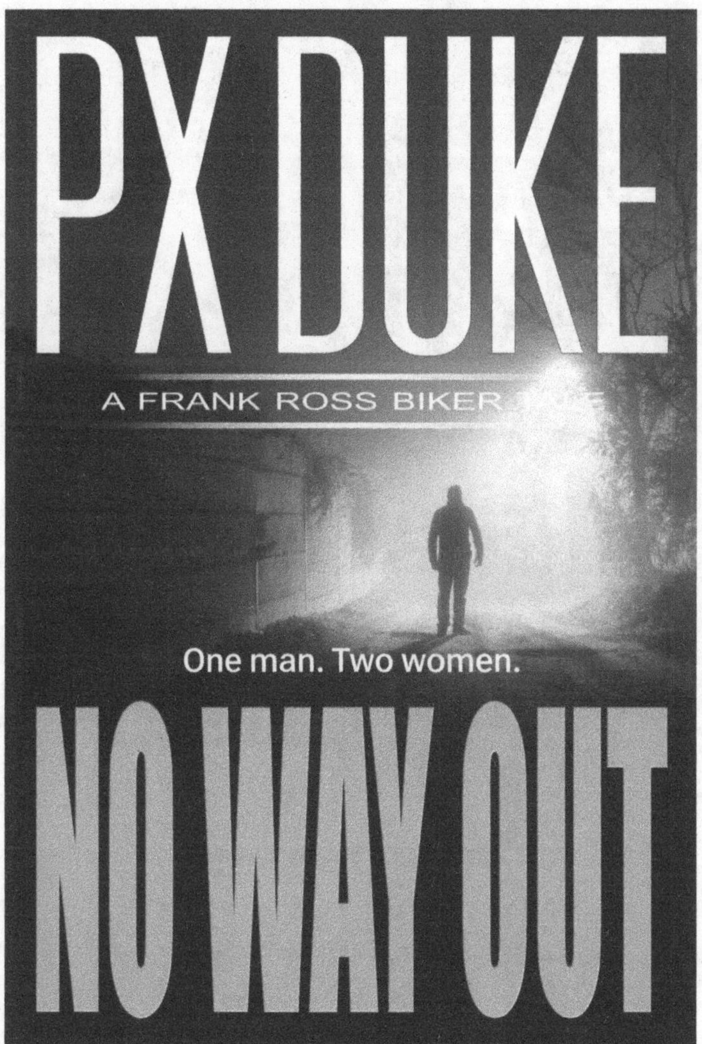

Frank Ross is out of Mexico riding north. He's just across la línea looking for shade and water. He finds it, and a lot more than he bargained for when he breaks down at a casino by the Salton Sea.

Jim Nash has to get to Washington, D.C. in a hurry. The plane he chartered is late. There's a private jet sitting on the tarmac in front of him. Buckle up with Nash & Company to find out what the rush is about when Harry Delaney gets hired to fly Jim Nash to a rendezvous neither man will forget.